Hooked

By the Author

Agnes

Bouncing

The Common Thread

Deadly Medicine

Hooked

Hooked

by

Jaime Maddox

2016

HOOKED

ISBN 13: 978-1-62639-689-0

This Trade Paperback Original Is Published By
Bold Strokes Books, Inc.
P.O. Box 249
Valley Falls, NY 12185

First Edition: September 2016

Credits
Editor: Shelley Thrasher
Production Design: Stacia Seaman
Cover Design by Sheri (graphicartist2020@hotmail.com)

Acknowledgments

Hooked is not based on a true story, but it is many people's reality. Nearly forty Americans die from prescription opiate overdoses every day, and the majority of addicts became hooked after receiving legitimate prescriptions from their doctors. Although the main character in this book, Dr. Jessica Benson, is able to overcome her addiction, the majority will struggle with this disease throughout their lifetimes. Many will die.

As a young doctor, I had nothing but harsh words for the addicts who came into the ER "seeking drugs." I thought them responsible for the lives they created, and had no sympathy or desire to help them. And as she often does, God whacked me over the head to teach me a lesson. My great-niece was born addicted. Her mom, my sister's only daughter, is one of the kindest, sweetest, most wonderful young women I know—and unbeknownst to anyone, was an addict. After surviving the trials of high school and college, she became addicted to pills at the age of thirty. It's crazy, but the reality of this terrible disease. It is an epidemic, and the only way people like my niece—and yours (or perhaps it's your sister, or your cousin, or your coworker)—will survive is with all of our help. We must be involved and vigilant, and keep pointing them in the right direction. When they fall, we have to pick them up and push them back in the right direction. Hopefully, eventually, they'll be okay.

Many thanks in the creation of this book go to the people who helped make it more authentic. Lackawanna County Assistant DA Gene Riccardo helped with the legal issues, and PA State Police Officer Rebecca Warner helped create the character she named Mac. My friend Cyd helped me through the rehab scenes, and I am grateful to her for sharing so much of her personal journey with me. My original alpha reader Margaret and two rookies, Chris and Michelle, found the flaws in my first draft and made the final story better. Finally, my niece Lisa shared much of her personal struggle with addiction to help make this a more authentic story.

Thank you to all of the staff at Bold Strokes Books for bringing this book from a manuscript to a finished product—Shelly Thrasher, Sandy Lowe, Rad, Cindy Cresap, Sheri, and the others who do such a fine job on my behalf. I appreciate it.

This has been somewhat of a crazy year for me and my family. We bought a new house, sold the old one, moved—and a week later I had emergency back surgery. I'd like to say I leaned on them, but truthfully, Carolyn, Jamison, and Max carried me. They fed me and watered me, encouraged me and entertained me. One of them, who shall remain nameless, even gave me a pedicure. That is true love, and I am truly in love right back. Thank you, guys. You're the best.

To Margaret—the smartest woman I know—
with thanks for reading me, encouraging me,
and teaching me big words.

Chapter One

Medicare Benefits

Derek Knight folded the wheelchair, hoisted it into the cargo area, closed the door, and walked purposefully to the front of the van. His dark-blue uniform was pressed; the red-and-white Pocono Area Transport Ambulance patch on his pocket matched the logo painted on the van's door. His black boots were polished and reflected the bright sun. He didn't need a jacket on this warm summer morning. Opening the driver's door, he glanced to the passenger seat, where the EMT, Pete, was reading a magazine.

"Let's get moving," Pete said. "We have a busy day."

"Everyone buckled up?" he asked cheerfully, but none of his passengers replied, a detail he ignored. "Okay, we're on our way, then."

Derek eased the van out of the drive and through the parking lot of the nursing home, then along a series of streets in Wilkes-Barre, Pennsylvania, until he reached the highway. Traffic on Interstate 81 was light, and it was a quick drive to the doctor's office five miles away. When he pulled in, Derek wasn't surprised to see the number of cars crowding the lot. It was always that way. He parked in front of the double glass doors, flipped on his flashers, and hopped out.

"What a racket the doc has going here, huh, Derek?" Pete asked as they opened the chairs and positioned them next to the van's door.

He'd been thinking the same thing as he scanned the parking lot. Dr. Ball owned the nursing home where all of these patients lived. Instead of visiting them there, every month he transported each and every resident, in the ambulance vans he owned, to his medical office. Not only could he charge for their medical care, but for the ambulance transfer as well. Good old Medicare. The doctor made a fortune but paid Derek a pittance. Derek had a hard time controlling the anger he felt toward lazy people like Pete or crooks like the doctor. He would have quit, except the fringe benefits of the job were too valuable. Much too valuable.

He helped a young man with some sort of brain disease out of the van and into the chair, then pushed him toward the doctor's front door. The man probably could have walked, but the chair helped Derek control him. With six of them to manage, he couldn't go chasing through the parking lot if the guy decided to wander off. It also gave him a seat. The doctor's waiting room was as full as his parking area. As he queued to sign in, Derek looked around. All familiar faces. That was good. New faces were good, too. There was always an opportunity for him, either way.

After he completed his task, he left the man in the chair and retreated to the parking lot, where Pete had the remainder of their charges lined up and ready to go. He helped push the other chairs, and when all six patients were inside, he went back to the van. He parked it far from the front door, turned off the engine, and began his vigil.

The strip mall that housed the doctor's office was hopping this morning, and Derek had to stay focused to keep up with the action. Cars and people moved in every direction. In addition to Dr. Ball's family practice on the corner, a lab, an ENT surgeon, a physical therapist, a group of orthopedic surgeons, a psychologist, and a dermatologist were located here. Strategically positioned in the middle of the other storefronts was a pharmacy. In the front of the parking lot, near the road, a diner drew a large crowd for breakfast.

The door to the orthopedic office opened, and Derek watched as an older man closed it behind him and turned, walking slowly down the promenade to the next door. He disappeared into the pharmacy. Derek watched the building closely, his vigilance rewarded. Fifteen minutes later, the man reappeared and began his slow journey toward the parking lot.

Derek hopped out of the van and closed the door behind him.

At a brisk pace, he met the man just as he reached a beat-up older car that probably hadn't earned the inspection sticker on the windshield. "Hey, man. How's it goin'?"

"I don't got nothin' for you. I need 'em. My back's a mess."

Derek smiled, relaxed his posture, and turned on the charm. "Oh, hey, that's okay, man. I understand. I'm not trying to take your pills from you. I only wanna buy the extra ones, ya know? If ya have extras, I'll take 'em. You make a little cash, I get some pills. Everybody wins. But if not, no biggie."

The man nodded, then sighed. "How much for twenty?"

"Ten migs?"

The man nodded and they negotiated a price, and then he clumsily crawled into his car and opened a large pill bottle. Derek waited patiently as the man counted out twenty tablets of oxycodone and poured them from his hand into a plastic bag Derek provided. When he handed them through the window, Derek thanked him and transferred the payment into the man's palm.

Looking around to ascertain the exchange had gone unnoticed, Derek slipped the bag into his pants pocket. He walked back to his van, satisfied. When he was once again seated behind the wheel, he procured two of the tablets from the bag and swallowed them with a gulp of water and began the same vigil again.

A familiar face emerged from Dr. Ball's office, and Derek watched as she made the trek to the pharmacy. A few minutes later, she emerged and he met her at her car. Like the other, it was beyond repair. "Listen," she said by way of greeting. "We need to renegotiate our price."

Derek stood taller, looking down at the diminutive form before him. Her hair was unkempt and her clothing worn, and she looked tired. He wasn't sure of her age, but he was certain she was younger than she looked. Life wasn't easy for her, but Derek was there to make it better—if she was willing to play the game. If not, someone else would.

"Jenny, Jenny. What does that mean? Haven't I always given you a fair price?"

She smiled, revealing wide gaps and rotting teeth. The sight nearly made him gag. He promised himself that he'd take all the pills at once if he ever got that bad.

"I guess it depends on your definition of fair. My kid told me the price of oxys went up, only I didn't get no raise."

Derek surveyed her, buying time, nodding. Then he surveyed the parking lot, still contemplating his response. Her intel was correct; the price of pills had gone up. It was a simple case of supply and demand. The government had set new rules for narcotic prescriptions—they could no longer be phoned or faxed to the pharmacy, and couldn't be refilled. That meant every single patient had to see their physician every month to get their meds, and with a sketchy population of people with unreliable cars, appointments were often missed. The doctors had changed their habits as well. All of the publicity about overdoses had cast a fog of fear over them, and they were prescribing fewer pills, referring more patients for injections, and trying treatment plans that minimized the narcotic component.

Thankfully, Dr. Ball hadn't grown a conscience. His office was still a pill factory. If Jenny didn't want to do business with Derek, someone else would. "Listen, Jenny. You don't take any risk. You walk out of that pharmacy and hand me a bottle, and I give you cash. I'm the one who's exposed trying to sell these. I'm the one going to jail if I'm caught."

"Yeah, and you're the one makin' all the money."

Holding up his hands to defend himself from her verbal assault, Derek nodded. "Hey, it's up to you. You can sell them to me or sell them to someone else. No big deal."

"So no raise?"

He shook his head. "I can't do it."

"Well, fuck you!" she screamed.

He turned and walked away slowly, giving her the opportunity to change her mind. He heard the car door slam before she sped away in the other direction.

"Fuck!" he said, not caring who heard him. Sure, he could deal with someone else, but Jenny had been one of his first business associates. She'd been a steady supplier since the beginning. What if his other customers began demanding raises? Some, like the first guy, were just regular folks trying to make a few bucks and were oblivious to the price their prescription medication brought on the street. Others, though, were much more savvy and might come at him with the same demands she had. If that happened, his business was in trouble. He bought pills off these people, hundreds of them a day, then passed them on to someone else. He was a middleman, and his margin was small, his profits totally dependent on volume. If his supply diminished, he'd be out of business. But if his margin went down, he'd be in just as much trouble. "Fuck, fuck fuck. What the fuck do I do now?"

He reached through the van's window and pulled out a bottle of water, leaned against the door, and sipped it as he watched the strip mall. The dermatology office was hopping, but he didn't care. Those doctors never prescribed anything good. The orthopedics office was busy, too, and that was very fertile ground. Nothing was as fruitful as Dr. Ball's office, though, and he felt more cheerful as he watched another patient leave his office and head to the pharmacy.

"Whacha got for me?" he asked a few minutes later when he met her at her car.

She pulled a box from the pharmacy bag, a small white box that easily fit in the palm of her hand. "How about thirty?" she asked and, without waiting for a response from him, began counting the foil packets within the box.

"Thirty's good." Buprenorphine wasn't his best seller, but his buyer was always happy to have some on hand. It was a powerful narcotic used to treat addiction, helpful because it was long acting and didn't get people high. Most addicts wanted the high but couldn't afford the cost. Narcotics lasted only a few hours, forcing them to dose frequently, at great expense. When addicts decided to clean up or ran out of money, they'd use buprenorphine to prevent withdrawal symptoms. A special license was required for doctors to prescribe it, and not many people had one. Dr. Ball did, though. Bup patients were a significant part of Dr. Ball's practice.

When she finished counting, the woman handed Derek a stack

of foil packets and stashed the remainder in her purse. "Some for you, and some for me," she said sweetly.

He handed her some money and walked away, and she drove off. Thankfully, Dr. Ball always seemed to prescribe enough to satisfy both of their needs.

Glancing at his watch, Derek decided to check on the patients in Dr. Ball's office. They'd been there an hour, and that left only another two hours to collect these six, return them to the nursing home, and reload the van. He wasn't worried, though. The doctor knew his schedule and always had the patients out on time. Time was very big money when you owned the ambulance company.

He walked by, looking through the plate-glass window. Pete was sitting with his back against the wall, watching television. Four of the nursing-home patients remained in the lobby. Had they already been seen and discharged, or were they still waiting for the doctor? Impossible to tell. He knew without a doubt, though, that by twelve o'clock, when he was due for his lunch break, they'd be back at the nursing home. Dr. Ball wouldn't let him down.

"Hey."

Startled, Derek turned to find a young man standing in front of the office. It was one of his regular customers, holding a pharmacy bag in his hands. How had he missed him coming out of Dr. Ball's office? Worse, what if he'd been a cop?

His heart pounding, he fought to keep his voice even. "You sellin'?" he asked.

The man smiled and nodded toward the parking lot. Derek followed, using a slower pace and a different route to his car. By the time he arrived, the man had the bag torn open and the bottles in his hand. "Vics, ninety. Xanax, ninety. Ibuprofen, ninety."

Derek reached into the side pocket of his cargo pants and retrieved three baggies. "I'll take them all. But don't you need any for your pain?"

He sniggered. "Man, I don't have pain. A few years ago I heard about this doctor. He'll give anybody anything they want. So I started comin' to him, and I sell what he gives me. Pays the rent, you know?"

Derek handed him several bills and wondered what sort of house the guy could find for such a cheap rent. He didn't ask.

"I got somethin' else for you, too."

Derek eyed him suspiciously. "What's that?"

"Information. Valuable information."

"Oh, yeah? What kind of information?"

"Before I say anything, we have to set the terms, man. Fifty-fifty split."

Derek stood tall once again, staring him down. Was everyone going to challenge him today? "Before I set the terms, I have to know what the fuck we're talking about."

He pursed his lips for a second. "Okay, okay. Here's the story. My sister, the rich bitch from up the mountain, is going on vacation. She gave my mother the key so she can go in and feed the cat. She also gave her the alarm code."

Derek stared off into the distance, thinking. This guy had given him similar information in the past, and they'd both profited from it. But it was dangerous. Derek assumed all the liability and got only half the money. He'd usually walk away with two or three grand from a job like that. Easy money for a few hours' work. Risky, though. "Fifty percent just isn't worth chancing a trip to prison."

"Oh, I'm not sure about that. She's got a nice house, my sister. A mansion. Married a guy that owns a trucking company. Lots of jewelry, expensive rugs, artwork. You name it."

"It may be valuable, my man, but I have to be able to sell it to make any money. And stolen art isn't easy to move."

"I understand they keep cash in the safe."

"Hmm," Derek answered, more interested now that cash was involved. "Give me the details."

The man filled him in, and when he'd finished, Derek patted him on the back, sealing their pact.

"See you next month," he said as he drove away.

If all went well, Derek would have an envelope stuffed with cash to give the guy when they next met. If not…well, he couldn't think about that.

CHAPTER TWO

Business as Usual

A stationary parade of cars, most with their flashers engaged, told Mac Calabrese she'd found her destination. Even though she'd spent her entire life in the mountains of Northeastern Pennsylvania, she still found the winding, unmarked roads confusing, and once in a while, she'd get lost. Thankfully, this wasn't one of those times. Her calendar was crowded because of the kidnappings in Garden and the allegations of murder that had surfaced. This traffic fatality was just another headache to deal with, putting her even more behind schedule. Her instincts told her this was going to be an awful day, and they were rarely off target.

Slowing to an appropriate speed, Mac crossed the double yellow line and passed the still vehicles, pulling to the front, where all the usual emergency responders were parked in haphazard fashion. There was another police vehicle, this one belonging to the township police. A fire engine sat in the wrong lane, its lights twirling frantically from positions high and low on every corner. A sleek medic's SUV was pulled onto someone's front lawn, and an ambulance sat beside it, its open doors testimony to the urgency of this call. Set apart from the others, the black coroner's wagon announced the news that no one ever wanted to hear.

Mac had been told there were fatalities when she was called to the scene twenty minutes earlier, and she'd spent the entire drive preparing for them. It wasn't her job to investigate crime scenes and accident sites, and she didn't like it. Someone had thought she should be called, though, so here she was.

Parking her car behind the fire engine, she hastily retrieved her badge from the bag on the passenger seat. She probably knew everyone at the scene, and more importantly, they knew her, but she liked to be ready if she encountered some rookie with an attitude doubting her credentials. It rarely happened when male state police officers arrived on a scene, but to her, it had happened too often to waste her time remembering.

A few steps from her vehicle she was greeted by Shultz, the local cop. "Nasty scene here, Mac."

"Why'd you call me?"

"They're running drugs."

"Ah," she said as they approached a white sheet covering a still but unmistakably human form lying on the right side of the road.

She stopped and turned. No one was near the body, no one to stop a photographer or nosy citizen or, worse yet, a frantic parent from penetrating the perimeter of the accident scene. As she looked back, she realized the haphazard location of the vehicles actually had successfully blocked prying eyes from getting a good look at the chaos, but someone needed to guard this body.

Raising an eyebrow, she questioned Shultz. "What kind of drugs? And can you get someone else here to help preserve this scene?"

"Backup's on the way. Looks like heroin to me, but I'm no expert. There's a duffel bag over there," he said, pointing toward the forest beside the road, "loaded with little plastic bags filled with white powder. As far as I can tell, they all have a big *H* written on them."

"Did you call narcotics?"

"On their way."

Fuck! Mac thought as she looked around. What were the mountains coming to? She was used to the pill problem, but she rarely saw heroin involved. Most people in her jurisdiction died from combinations of narcotics, benzodiazepines, and alcohol. She knew pills were becoming harder and harder to find, though, and that heroin was becoming much less expensive. She supposed it was only a matter of time until the dealers from New York and

Philly expanded their territories into hers, giving the good people of Northeastern Pennsylvania yet another choice on their menu of drugs. Another weapon to use in their slow, painful suicides.

"Any IDs on our bodies?"

As she asked, Mac squatted and pulled up the sheet. If the missing piece of this guy's skull was any clue, fatality number one had probably died from head trauma when he was thrown from the vehicle. If not for the puddle of congealed blood on the road beneath his head, he might have been mistaken for someone napping, with his arms raised above his head and his legs spread out below. He was facedown, and she was grateful to be spared the trauma of looking into his vacant eyes.

How would his mother do it, though? Did he even have a mother to claim his body, to cry over him and wonder where he'd gone wrong? Would she wonder if some part of this was her own inadequacy as a parent, or would she blame someone else for the dead-end path he'd taken?

"This one's got nothing," Shultz said, bringing her back to the present. "But the one trapped beneath the dashboard is Terrence Yield, according to his driver's license. Philadelphia address. The car's registered to a Robert Michelin, also with a Philly address. He could be the one beneath the car."

"You're fucking kidding me," Mac said, shaking her head. "How far beneath?"

"We're talking *Wizard of Oz* here, Mac. Nothing but the slippers showing when I got here. As soon as the fire boys arrived, they lifted the car up and one of the medics crawled under to check him, but of course he was flatter than a pancake."

Raising her eyes from the road, Mac surveyed the scene. Broken remains of a black SUV were scattered along the road. A few feet from her lay a headlight. A spare tire, its smiley-face cover in tatters, sat on the double yellow line. Another tire had come to rest just beyond the other. A pillow with a torn red pillowcase had landed nearby. Everywhere, she saw litter—McDonald's wrappers and bags, Dunkin' Donuts cups, Coke bottles, a banana peel. Shattered glass and pieces of metal twisted beyond recognition were mixed throughout. At the end of the trail, like a powerful magnet drawing her closer, was the crushed body of the car. It had traveled a hundred yards before finally coming to rest on its roof, in someone's front yard, the three remaining tires reaching toward the heavens, perhaps pointing the spirits of its dead passengers in the right direction.

Mac stopped again and turned in a full circle. She pointed back. "So he was traveling this way and lost control back there, based on the location of victim number one. What do you think happened? Blowout?"

"There's a little curve there, who knows? Arguing with his buddies, texting, a deer on the road and then he's suddenly off the road, hits the guardrail, bounces around, flips a few times, spews a couple of bodies and then finally stops."

"That's a colorful description, Shultz. You been studying or something?"

Mac saw the color rising in Shultz's fair cheeks and decided to stop the teasing before he fainted. He was an excellent police officer, meticulous and by the book, and she liked him. "But you're right. Unless you find a dead deer or a telltale phone, we'll probably never know what happened."

They came upon a suitcase, a cheap-looking carry-on model in surprisingly good shape. "Did you check this yet?" Mac asked.

"Yep. Opened it and closed it right back up. Money and guns. I didn't count the cash, but I found two handguns."

"Completes the picture, right?"

"It's a shame, Mac, isn't it? Three boys dead, all because they were someplace they didn't belong doing something they shouldn't have been doing."

"It's only the lucky ones that survive, Shultz." Mac had seen enough to know that. Good luck buffered people through tornados and they came through without a scratch, and bad luck lured lightning through windows and fried people in their beds.

"Yeah, but sometimes you have to make your own luck. And doing stupid shit doesn't help the cause."

They stopped at the rear of the vehicle and were greeted by Wendy Clemens, the coroner. A day earlier, Wendy had been kidnapped and nearly killed by Edward Hawk, and Mac was sure that entitled her to a day off. "What are you doing here?" she asked before her rational mind told her it was none of her business, that she shouldn't publicly question another professional like that. She shook her head and offered a smile. No doubt, Shultz already knew what had happened to Wendy in Garden. "Sorry. I'm just surprised to see you. Feeling okay?"

Wendy shrugged and offered an overzealous smile back at them both. "It's all good. Summer. Busy time. Can't slack off."

Mac gave Wendy a discreet wink. They'd casually known each other for ages—played on rival teams in the same softball league for a few years, ran into each other at the occasional party, and met in the bar after golf tournaments. And of course, they met at times like this, when their professional worlds collided. Their conversations had always been limited to a few words, though, and Mac now regretted never getting to know Wendy Clemens better. Maybe that would change in the future. Dressed in pressed chinos and a pristine white golf shirt, she looked like a total pro, someone Mac would appreciate socializing with. Just as friends, though. While she could imagine Wendy did well with the ladies, she wasn't Mac's type.

Mac cleared her throat and returned to the present. "Well, glad you're back in action. What's the plan here? How long do you need?"

"I just arrived a few minutes ago, so I'll be here awhile. An hour, perhaps. Then I'll take them to Scranton for autopsies. The schedule's open. We'll probably be able to get them done tonight."

"Excellent. Show me what you have."

Victim number two had been pulled out from under the vehicle, and Wendy lifted the corner of the sheet covering his body. Mac didn't have to worry about making eye contact with this one; the pressure on his crushed skull had enucleated his eyes. Gooey-looking pink-and-red fluids oozed from everywhere. Mac blinked and perhaps held her eyes closed a second too long, because when she opened them, Wendy had dropped the sheet. Mac didn't ask her to lift it again.

"Number three appears to have a broken neck and probably a

few other injuries that would have killed him, too." Wendy moved a few steps in the direction of the mangled car and pulled a sheet from the frame covering a missing section of the vehicle, so Mac could peer into the front passenger compartment. A young man's face peered up at her from a narrow space between the dashboard and the front seat, his neck bent severely, his chin resting in the area of his navel. His hips sat on the console. One leg was angled impossibly and wedged beneath the crushed steering wheel and the spent airbag. Mac couldn't see the other.

A voice called Shultz away, and Mac took advantage of the opportunity to talk to Wendy.

"I'm glad we're alone. I need to ask you a few more questions about Hawk."

In her role as coroner, Wendy had shown such composure, even when faced with the unbelievable horrors before her. At just the mention of Hawk's name, though, she paled and turned away, busying herself with her camera. "Sure. Just call me," she said, and Mac wondered how those photos would turn out. The big camera was shaking in Wendy's hands.

"You got it."

Mac turned and began walking the perimeter of the scene, taking it all in. She'd tell Shultz to have the traffic begin turning around. With both lanes blocked by bodies and debris, they weren't getting through here anytime soon. Reconstruction experts would look at the pattern of evidence and try to figure out what had happened, but Mac didn't figure it really mattered. In the end, it was all about drugs. She was so sick of dealing with drug- and alcohol-related deaths. It was all so senseless. The alcohol had always been around, but they'd been seeing the pills only the past few years. In neighboring communities there were violent drug deaths, too. Now it looked like she had another enemy to fight. Not just pills but heroin, too.

She didn't get it. She'd taken pills, after her knee surgery and again after a broken wrist. They did nothing for her. What did everyone else experience that incited them to pop a dozen pills at once? What was so bad about their lives that they wanted to? It made some sort of sad sense to her that the mentally ill and chronically neglected kids began using drugs in their big cities, but as far as she could tell, the people she saw using drugs here had no excuses. They were bored. They were looking for a good time. And they were dying.

It was a big problem, and it was getting bigger. What the fuck was she going to do about it?

CHAPTER THREE

Tough Love

Dr. Jessica Benson curled up on her couch, pulled the blanket up to her forehead, and sobbed. She wished she could call someone, but who? Her new best friend, Wendy, was off playing coroner, and since she'd been through the same ordeal as Jess, she'd probably fall to pieces when she was done. Her ex-partner, Ward, was working, and even though she'd promised she'd help Jess through her dark time, Jess was skeptical. She'd tossed Ward aside and broken her heart. Who could blame her if she bolted now? Her only real family was her father, and if he came over, she was likely to murder him. He'd been driving her crazy for months, but after her experience at the cabin, she was convinced he had early dementia. Her strong, loving, wonderful father was losing his mind. Just one more thing to deal with.

But who else could she call? She'd systematically pushed away her friends, eliminating the chance that any of the people who cared for her could discover her drug problem. She'd left her adopted home outside of Philadelphia to come to her birth home in the mountains and socially, culturally, and geographically isolated herself. When she'd wanted to avoid discovery, her new situation had been ideal. Now, she just felt lonely. And anxious.

She supposed she could feel a lot worse. She'd been kidnapped, drugged, and psychologically terrorized. And while Dr. Edward Hawk didn't harm her physically, she'd spent a terrifying fifteen hours as his captive, fearing for her life the entire time. The first twenty minutes had been the worst part, when Hawk injected her with succinylcholine, a drug that completely paralyzed her. She couldn't focus her eyes. She couldn't breathe, and she hadn't died only because Hawk had breathed for her. A few times during that period she'd thought she would, when Hawk abandoned her to attend to other matters. He'd come running back, though, squeezing the bag at her lips vigorously, forcing air into her lungs and oxygen into her blood, sustaining her until he could extract information from her.

After the drug wore off, he'd tied her to a chair in a supply closet, then smuggled her out of Garden Memorial Hospital in a body bag. At least she wasn't alone, though—Hawk had given the same injection to her friend, Wendy, and stuffed her in the body bag beside Jess. In the cabin at her father's hunting club, Hawk had ranted and raved as he paced the floors, threatening them with death and then promising to release them if they cooperated. Jess hadn't told him a thing, even though she thought he'd kill her. Her stupid father had talked like a radio personality, though, and his issues and his hatred for Ward became very clear as he spoke.

Her dad blamed Ward for Jess's sexuality. He blamed her for Jess living in Philadelphia. He blamed her for not allowing Jess to come home sooner and care for her dying mother. And he told Hawk that if Jess had some idea about him murdering his patients, it must have come from Ward Thrasher.

Although her father was right about one thing—Ward had been the one to warn Jess about Edward Hawk—he was wrong about everything else. Nothing was Ward's fault. Ward had rescued her from Hawk and treated her for narcotic withdrawal when she recognized Jess's symptoms, and Ward had sat by her side until she was ready to go home. Even though she'd treated Ward awfully, Ward had still taken care of her. Ward still cared. Ward was a wonderful woman, and Jess had pushed her away. Jess had lied to her and betrayed her in terrible, unforgivable ways. Suddenly she wanted Ward's forgiveness, wanted the calming presence of Ward in her life.

And because her life really and truly sucked, just as Jess

realized how much she loved her, Ward told Jess she'd fallen in love with someone else.

Jess tried to forget about Ward's new girlfriend as she dialed her cell.

"How are you feeling?" Ward asked by way of greeting.

It had been only three hours since their last conversation, but she felt like days had passed. Her life had flashed before her dozens of times as she relived her ordeal with Hawk. She was anxious and scared. And exhausted. In spite of the fact that Wendy had slept beside her and her father was in the living room wearing his sheriff's hat and gun, she hadn't slept a wink.

"Not too good. Do you think you can come over after work?"

Jess heard concern in Ward's voice. "Why? What's up?"

"Because I'm scared! Hawk tried to kill me!"

Jess heard Ward sigh. "I know, Jess. I'm sorry. I won't get out of here until eight, though, and I have to be back in for seven tomorrow morning. Can't Wendy stay with you?"

Jess felt anger rising like bile in her throat, unexpected and uncontrollable. Without trying to hide her feelings, she said, "Yes, but she went through the same thing I did, and I think she's just as scared as I am. I can't believe she went to work today."

"Maybe it's a distraction."

"Maybe. But how can you be in love with someone you just met?"

Ward was silent. "I don't know. We just clicked, that's all."

"And you really love her?"

She could almost see Ward's smile through the phone, just as she heard the joy in her voice. "I do. And she understands that I care about you, and that I need to be here for you because of what you've gone through. She's a nice person, Jess."

"You could spend the night here. On the couch. Leave for work from here."

"She's not that nice."

In spite of her misery, Jess laughed.

"Have you seen the news?" Ward asked when Jess was quiet.

"No. I'm just sort of hiding from the world. I haven't eaten, I haven't showered, and I don't even have the energy to get off the couch. But I think the reporters are still camped out in front of the house. I can hear them."

"They are. The last CNN report was live from Garden. They're here in Factoryville, too. Someone must have told them that we reported Hawk to the police, or they're just following his trail. Either way, the story's out and it's going to be crazy for a little while. Do you think you can deal with it?"

"No. I really don't."

"How much of this is Hawk, and how much is withdrawal?"

Jess tried not to snap, but she couldn't help it. This was why she'd never told Ward about her addiction—she knew Ward would overreact and blame everything from menstrual cramps to an ingrown toenail on her drug use. "I'm not withdrawing! I'm taking my Percocet every four hours, and I'm fine."

"You're sure?"

"Trust me. I know withdrawal."

"Hmm. So if it's not withdrawal, it's emotional. A stress reaction, maybe."

Jess didn't even need to think about it. She knew she was traumatized. "I think you're right."

"How would you feel about going to a hospital? Someplace that deals with post-traumatic stress disorder. And addiction, too. Kill two birds, you know? They can help you, and they'll get you away from the reporters, at least until you're feeling well enough to talk to them. Can you get the time off from work?"

Jess had already thought about work. She was an ER doctor, and she took care of people with serious medical issues. "I talked to the CEO this morning and took a leave. For a month. I can't even manage a fucking shower. How can I go to work? Lives depend on me."

"I agree. That's why I think you should try to tackle this head-on. You've been through something horrific, and who knows how it'll affect you long term?"

Jess stared at the high plastered ceiling above her, then flipped over onto her side. Rays of sunlight defied the blinds and painted streaks on the wall, across the fireplace, all the way down to the floor. It seemed she wouldn't be able to hide from the sun, and she wouldn't be able to avoid the reporters outside her house, either. Could she do any better at hiding from her emotions? "I'm scared."

Ward's voice softened. "I know. That's why you should go someplace."

"No. I mean I'm scared of going someplace. What if someone finds out I'm a doctor and I lose my license?"

"Wait. You didn't worry about losing your license for abusing prescription drugs and buying them from your patients. Why would you worry about this?"

"Fuck you," she said softly.

Ward didn't respond.

Jess swallowed the tears that sprang up again. "It all seemed rational when I was doing it. Now it seems ridiculously stupid." In truth, the addiction to prescription pain pills had crept up on Jess. They were legitimately prescribed, for a real injury, and then one day, her doctor had told her he wouldn't give her any more. Her concern at that moment had been for her pain, because she was convinced it was real. It wasn't until twelve hours passed without Percocet that she began to understand the gravity of the situation. Somehow, in treating a relatively minor injury, she'd gotten hooked on narcotics. And she was too embarrassed, and too scared, to ask anyone for help.

She'd always blazed her own trail and didn't rely on others, so she tackled her addiction alone, too. The mistakes she made were big ones, and they weighed heavily on her. Any day, the state could revoke her medical license, and life as she knew it would be over. Perhaps Ward was right about getting professional help.

But life as an impaired physician wouldn't be a picnic, either. She might still lose her license during the treatment process. Afterward, she'd be closely monitored. That wouldn't be much fun.

Yet what were her other options? She could sit around and wait for the walls to come crashing down around her, or she could be proactive and hope for leniency. She had to consider another factor as well, and Ward had very astutely pointed it out. Jess had suffered a major emotional trauma. What would the effects of that be? She'd had a drug problem before, when life was good. What could she expect after enduring the torture Hawk had put her through?

The longer she pondered her options, the more pointless it seemed to refuse help. If she didn't need it now, she would at some point. And when would she ever again get this kind of time off?

Ward cleared her throat, and Jess saved her from the burden of a reply by clearing hers as well. "I'll see if I can find a place."

She could almost hear the relief in Ward's voice. "It's a good idea, Jess."

Suddenly Jess felt panicky. What would happen? Where would she go? What about her house, and the bills, and the police investigation of Hawk? "Can you take me? I don't want anyone else to know. I mean, if your girlfriend will allow it."

Wishing she could take back the comment the moment it left her mouth, Jess closed her eyes tightly and winced. Why did she keep turning this on Ward? None of it was Ward's fault. She supposed the long hours of captivity had caused her to think about what was important in her life, and she'd realized Ward was at the top of the list. She didn't want it to be over. But the way to win Ward back wasn't with sarcasm or anger. It was by being strong and smart and good. Like Ward.

Ward groaned. "Jessssss."

"I'm sorry, Ward. I shouldn't have said that."

Ward's frustration came out in a long sigh before she answered. "I can't keep this from Abby. I'm just starting a relationship with her, and I'm not going to sneak around and tell lies while I'm helping you."

Wishing all her problems would just go away, Jess pulled the blanket up over her eyes. "Fine. You can tell her I'm going for the post-traumatic stress diagnosis, but not the addiction."

"Okay."

"Because I'm not sure I need treatment for that."

"Jess, I understand that you have this under control. You're treating yourself with prescription pain pills. But what happens if your doctor cuts you off again? Are you going to forge prescriptions like you did before? Or buy drugs illegally? It would be so much smarter to get off them, or into a treatment program. It's more stable."

Jess knew Ward was right, but she didn't want to talk about it anymore. "I'll call you when I have more information."

Jess disconnected the phone. She stared at her fingers. She'd broken two nails in her struggle with Hawk, and though she'd clipped them, they looked awful. A manicure was a good idea. Was a psych hospital a good idea, too? She'd hated her psych rotations as a medical student, thought the classes and clinical experience a waste of time. She was very much a person who'd controlled her own destiny, a small-town girl from a middle-class family who'd gone away to the big city and graduated from medical school at the top of her class. Taking no for an answer was never an option, and neither was making excuses. And that was how she saw the whole realm of psychiatry—it was a great arena for people who persistently screwed up and then blamed someone or something else for their failures.

Was that what she'd be doing if she asked for help? Whose fault was it that she was trembling too violently to get off her couch? Could she have done anything differently to avoid the violence that was delivered unto her? She knew she couldn't. She'd made bad choices with regard to her drug habit, and that was her own fault. She admitted she couldn't blame anyone but herself. She'd cried in pain, told her doctors she needed medication, and they'd given it to her. Instead of being tough and taking the pain, she'd been a wimp and took the pills. Too many pills. As a physician, she should have known better. She'd just never thought it would happen to her. Yes, her addiction was her fault. But the fear and the anxiety she was feeling now were Edward Hawk's fault. She supposed she'd been wrong all those times she'd callously blamed her psych patients for their troubles. Now, she knew better.

And she knew she needed help. Wendy was in no shape to care for her. Neither was her dad. And Ward, the one who'd always been there, had moved on. If this had happened a year earlier, Ward would have taken a leave, too, and stayed home with her, or driven her to the beach to get away. She would have held her hand, and wiped her tears, and done whatever Jess asked of her, and other helpful stuff Jess didn't even know she needed. But this was now, and Ward was gone, and who else was there? If Jess didn't get professional help, she didn't know if she'd make it through this ordeal.

Gathering her courage, she threw back the blankets and stood before she had a chance to change her mind. At the front of the house, she peeked through the blinds. It was just as Ward said. A dozen news trucks were parked on the street, their occupants standing around talking to each other and her neighbors as they waited for her to emerge from hiding.

They'd be waiting a long time.

She shuffled into the kitchen, checked the lock on the door, and surveyed the scene in back. Her house sat in the middle of the block, with homes on either side. The rear of her property was guarded by a line of hedges that offered enough privacy to prohibit anyone from spying on her backyard barbecues. It also prevented her from seeing the property beyond. She wouldn't be surprised to find more news people there, preventing an escape in that direction.

Turning back to her kitchen, she put water on for tea, then headed to the powder room. She frowned at her reflection. Her red hair was greasy and limp and hung lifeless across her shoulders. A perfectly matched pair of circles surrounded her blue eyes, and her mouth and chin were bruised where Hawk had grabbed her to hold the Ambu bag in place when she wasn't breathing. She was in the same clothes she'd changed into the night before. She supposed she should change into something fresh, but she didn't have the energy. It was all she could manage to fix her tea, and when it was ready, she took a soothing sip.

From her bag beside the kitchen table, Jess retrieved her laptop, fired it up, and sat down before it. *What the hell do I look for?* She typed *inpatient treatment post traumatic stress disorder and drug addiction* into the search engine and was rewarded with thousands of hits. Some directed her to treatment facilities, some to informative websites, others to pharmaceutical ads. Two words appeared again and again—dual diagnosis—and they helped her refine her search. She knew about the topic—the simultaneous diagnoses of mental illness and substance abuse—because of the plethora of psych patients that passed through the ER. As she read, she found she really knew very little at all.

Fuck! PTSD was a serious disorder. According to the inarguably accurate information available on the web, she could suffer a multitude of plagues due to PTSD. Depression. That seemed to have already started. Incarceration. Well, only if her past crimes came back to haunt her. She was a model citizen these days. Poverty. Quite possibly, if she didn't get her act together and go back to work. Her savings would only last so long. Relationship issues. Duh. Substance abuse. At that, she laughed out loud. Most people with this diagnosis ended up using drugs to help them cope. Since she already used them, was she more likely to lose control and slip back into a pattern of bad abuse? At the moment, her drug abuse was really well controlled. She used a consistent dose of oxycodone every day, and she felt fine. She was the most functional addict she knew.

The information she read was depressing. Overwhelming. She pushed the cover of the laptop closed, popped a Xanax into her mouth, and headed back to the couch. Her phone was there, and her father's number was on speed dial. A few seconds later, the familiar, rich timbre of his voice comforted her. Even if she was angry with him, he was still her father.

"How are you, my sweet girl?"

Jess snuggled into her blankets and closed her eyes. "I'm not doing very well, Dad. Do you think you can come over?"

Twenty minutes later, she heard his key in the lock, and she was impressed when she saw the bag of groceries cradled in his big paws. It was a fifteen-minute ride. How'd he make it so quickly and find time to shop? Lights and sirens, perhaps? He was still the sheriff, after all.

"I brought ice cream," he announced. "And all the trimmings."

"I can't eat," she said and dove under the blankets.

"Nonsense. I'll cook."

She didn't bother protesting but instead cowered under her comforter, thinking about what she'd read on the Internet. In the thirty-six hours since she'd been kidnapped, she hadn't slept a wink, and she was depressed and anxious. It sure sounded like PTSD, as Ward had suggested. And the PTSD was likely to ignite her addiction into a raging inferno. Her life was falling apart, without a doubt. In less than a year she'd left a great job, moved, buried her mother, separated from her partner, and been brutally attacked. All this while managing an addiction problem that frequently left her scrambling to find drugs. A major crisis was looming, and she had no one to help her through it. Again, Ward was right. Ignoring her drug problem, or treating herself, was a mistake. She needed to go into the hospital and get professional help.

Integrated care. That's what she needed. She'd read those words on the Internet, and it sounded right. She didn't need a psych facility that treated her PTSD but neglected her addiction, or a rehab facility that treated the addiction but ignored the PTSD. An integrated care plan would do both. If she could only find one, she'd be set.

"Here you go," her dad said, handing her a bowl spilling over with the fixings of a hot fudge sundae. Fortunately, he handed her a pile of napkins, and she wiped the bowl before digging in. Seeing the chocolate syrup and whipped cream restored her hunger, and she took several satisfying bites before she spoke.

"Thanks for this." She nodded to the bowl. "And for coming over."

He nodded and ate. "I don't suppose you'll want to leave the house with all those reporters out there."

"No."

"I spoke to the state police. They want to talk to you again. The preliminary hearing is in nine days."

She sighed, felt a frown appear on her face. The female officer had been cute, and Jess only wished she'd met her in the ER, or at a party, where they could have talked about something pleasant. Discussing Hawk was the last thing she wanted to do. Just thinking about it, Jess felt panic pushing the ice cream back up into her throat.

"I don't have to testify, do I?" Facing Hawk, even in handcuffs, was a frightening proposal.

"I don't think so. The state police just need the facts for now. And I'll be with you. I'll take care of you."

"After what happened, I think I need a little more help than you can give me." Sitting back, she looked up at him and forgot why she was angry with him. Wasn't he only, always, trying to protect her? Even with Ward, when he'd driven her away, he was trying to help her. He loved her unconditionally, worshipped her. How could she tell him her worries ran so much deeper than Hawk and what he'd done? What if the police investigated her and learned she'd obtained drugs unlawfully? What would happen to her? For so long, she'd fooled herself into thinking she had her life under control, but she'd been lying to herself. Her life was a mess.

She finally understood that, though. It was time to get it together.

He paused and looked up, met her gaze, studying her from behind the lock of hair that fell across his forehead and over his eye. The blue eyes matched her own, and she could see worry there. It seemed he understood what she *wasn't* saying, and it must have disturbed him, because her loquacious father was at a loss for words.

Jess spared him. "I don't want to talk to the police. Not right now. I mean, this is hard. Don't you feel upset that a really crazy guy tied you up and held a gun to your head? Your own gun, as a matter of fact."

Jess saw him swallow. "I was in Vietnam, honey. That was much worse than getting tied up by a little sissy man. I was upset about you. I didn't want him to hurt you."

"He hurt me, Dad. Inside," she said, tapping the side of her head for emphasis. "You can't see the wounds, but they're there. I'm nervous and scared and depressed."

"I think that's understandable."

"Ward thinks I should go away. To a hospital, to recover. I've been considering it, and she's right. I can't get through this on my own."

Bracing for his rebuttal, Jess leaned into the couch and

studied her father. He was tense on the edge of a chair and made a production of chewing his ice cream. Wondering if he'd heard her, or was confused, she looked away. It was brighter since her father opened the shades, and the room was dazzling in the sunlight. Shiny hardwood floors, carved molding around the edges of the room and the fireplace, nice art on the tables and walls. Even the television, set into a frame on the wall above the fireplace, looked classy. It was a beautiful room in a beautiful house, and she was miserable and wanted to feel better.

"What do you need from me?" he asked.

Jess placed the empty bowl on the wooden table before her and tried to find a smile. "I'll let you know."

CHAPTER FOUR

Disappearing Act

Jess leaned into her father, felt his arm surround her, protecting her from the cameras and the shouting reporters still hovering on the streets of Garden. The walk from her back door to his truck was just twenty steps but seemed to last an eternity. He waited until she was tucked safely in the front seat before depositing her suitcase in the back.

Jess pulled her hood forward over her head, adjusted her sunglasses, and slipped down on the front seat, the seat belt forgotten. The risk of dying in a crash during the quarter-mile ride to the hospital was much lower than the risk of being photographed by the media.

After managing a K turn in the confines of her driveway, a process that required several maneuvers and a string of foul words, they edged toward the street. The news crews that had respected the signs Zeke had posted and remained on the sidewalk had seemed so far away as she'd cowered in the house. Now, as they drew nearer, Jess closed her eyes but couldn't block the sounds as the reporters came to life, jockeying for position near the driveway, shouting questions at the closed windows of the truck.

Sinking lower in the seat, Jess hoped to disappear, not just to avoid the press but everything she'd been dealing with and what lay ahead as well. She felt her father's hand on her thigh, heard his words, but her senses seemed diminished by the fog surrounding her.

"We'll be there in a minute."

As she felt the truck pick up speed, she dared to raise her head. They were moving down her street, toward the hospital. The pack of reporters was behind her in the mirror, and Jess felt relief she knew would be temporary. What was awaiting her at the hospital? Surely, they'd staked out her workplace as well. Wendy was going through the same thing, with a mob in front of her funeral home, where she worked and lived on the upper floors. She'd braved them and tried to walk to Jess's house the night before, but gave up after half a block and took refuge in a neighbor's yard. The press had the good sense not to follow, but she'd still been shaken when she arrived on Jess's doorstep.

Jess felt a twinge of guilt about leaving. Would it be harder for Wendy once the reporters realized she'd skipped town? Or would they just give up and go away?

A sense of relief filled her as they arrived at the ER entrance to the hospital. Not a soul was in sight. Not a smoker in the butt hut, or an idling ambulance, or a national news reporter. Still, she waited for Zeke to back into the ambulance bay before exiting the truck. Just as he tucked the back of the truck up against the ER doors, the scene changed.

Suddenly, reporters who'd hoofed it from the house came running up to the truck. Their affiliated vans began filing into the lot. Dread replaced the relief for a moment until another vision filled her sight. Dozens of people, some dressed for work in scrubs and lab coats, others in casual attire—all of them Garden Memorial Hospital employees—began forming a cocoon around the truck.

"Stand back," someone shouted, and miraculously, the reporters responded. Unseen hands opened Jess's door, and the murmur of voices grew louder. "Doctor! Jessica! Dr. Benson! Sheriff! How do you…How did you…How does it…When did you?"

Jess wanted to cover her ears to dampen their shouts, but she suspected that image would become a front-page photo. She wouldn't give them anything more to print about her. She was saved when one of the ER nurses grabbed her elbow and eased her from the truck. His name was Mark, and he was a sexist egomaniac. Jess was sure he was helping her solely for the chance to get his face on national television, but she didn't mind. In fact, she was grateful.

"Keep your head down, Doc. I've got you."

Jess did as instructed, grateful for the hoodie as the click of camera shutters assaulted her eardrums. With Mark guiding her, she was pushed through the ER doors on a wave of friendly bodies, and after they closed behind her, Jess looked around, feeling safe for the first time in days. It was unusually quiet, but she took comfort in the space, with the rack of patient charts and the bank of monitors, the shelves of reference books and piles of forms, the computers strategically positioned around the nurses' station. Then she looked up to see Ward Thrasher, fatigue and worry on her beautiful face, and she broke down.

Uncontrollable sobs came from the depths of her, shaking her body as Ward closed the gap between them, wrapping her in her arms as she whispered words of comfort into her hair. "It's going to be okay, Jess. Shhh. It's over. He can't hurt you now."

Their bodies fit perfectly together; they were the same height, the same build, the same everything. Jess wondered for the hundredth time in recent days what she'd been thinking when she let Ward go. Could they ever be the same again? She feared the answer and instead focused on the concrete. Listening to Ward's murmurs, Jess knew she was right. It was over, she was safe.

But she couldn't help reliving the abduction, and each time it replayed in her mind, the clarity of the details became crisper. The pain of the stab wound as Hawk jabbed the needle into her flesh. The weightlessness of complete paralysis. The total terror as she understood the vulnerability of her position and that she would likely die. Hawk's far-away voice sounding so calm, as if he did this every day. And, Jess had come to learn in the days since her abduction, he did. She'd never forget the look in his eyes when she was paralyzed—the excitement, the joy he gleaned from his power. That look had faded over the hours of her captivity, when Hawk became anxious and angry and agitated. She was scared then, but never as scared as she was lying on the floor of her office staring into the blank eyes of a madman.

The office where Hawk had attacked her was only a few feet away from where she now stood, behind a set of locked metal doors. Their proximity was too much, though. She wasn't sure she could ever go into her office again, but for the moment she couldn't even debate the possibility. She needed to get away. "I have to get out of here, Ward," she said, and began walking in the opposite direction.

Jess heard Ward's footsteps behind her, then felt Ward's arm on her shoulder. "Say good-bye to your father."

Jess looked up and saw Zeke approaching, and she stepped into his arms. "I'll call you when I can," she said.

"Can I call you?" he asked, and Jess felt miserable for lying to him, but she shook her head against his chest. She wouldn't mention him on her HIPAA form, and Ward would be the only emergency contact. The less her father knew about the PTSD, the better. She wanted him to know nothing of her addiction. "I have to just rest for a while, okay? But if you really need to reach me, call Ward."

Jess could feel his sadness in the gentle way he released her, opening his arms to allow her to leave instead of stepping back or pushing her away. "I love you," she said before kissing his stubbly cheek and turning away.

"This is good. I think we can escape before your groupies realize what we're up to."

"The hospital has only a few entrances. I bet they've already staked them out."

"I hope not," Ward said as she took Jess's hand and guided her through the corridors and stairwells that led to the employee garage. The passageway was empty, as was the garage, and Jess followed Ward to her SUV. "I think you should get in the back, at least until we're out of the hospital."

Jess climbed into the cargo area beside her suitcase and rested on a bed of blankets. When she was settled, Ward took her place behind the wheel. "Here we go," Ward said loudly as she began the downward spiral to the exit.

"How's it look?"

"Shit," Ward replied. "Stay under the blankets, Jess. There's gotta be a dozen people waiting just outside the gate."

"Do you think they can see in?"

"No. And I don't think they'll recognize me. Hold on."

"Hi," Jess heard Ward say. "What's going on?"

The attendant's voice wasn't clear, but Jess could imagine the response. "Wow," Ward said a moment later. Jess felt the car begin to move, and a moment later it stopped. "Do you want to interview me?" Ward asked.

What the fuck? Jess wondered.

"I'm Dr. Thrasher," she replied, then was silent for a moment. Jess could hear murmurs, indistinguishable from beneath the blankets, where it was also growing quite warm.

"No, I don't really know Dr. Benson that well."

Jess felt the sting of that comment, because she knew it was true. She'd kept so much from Ward that she didn't feel like Ward knew her at all. No one did, really. So why was Ward here? Did she really care that much? Or was she just trying to get her face on the news? A sudden, chilling thought occurred to her. What if Ward was planning to sell her story? Ward knew everything about Hawk and much too much about Jess. And now, she was talking to the reporters while Jess cowered in the back of the car, hiding from the very limelight Ward was soliciting.

After what Jess had done to Ward, she wouldn't blame her one bit if that was her plan.

More murmurs filtered in, and then she felt the car begin to move again. "Try George's for the best burger in town," Ward said before picking up a little speed.

Jess held her breath expectantly for a few seconds, but it appeared they'd escaped the reporters. Before she could ask, Ward spoke. "All clear."

Jess pushed herself up, seeking the freedom of fresh air. She gulped it in. "What the fuck were you doing?"

"Relax. I figured I'd draw less attention if I sought it. And it worked. We're on the road leading out of town, and no one's following us."

"Why don't you pull over and get me out of here?"

Ward didn't speak, but Jess felt the car slow abruptly, heard the crunch of gravel beneath the tires. Then the door opened and closed, the hatch lifted, and fresh air and sunlight flooded the cargo area. She looked up to an extended hand reaching for her. Jess took it gratefully and allowed herself to be pulled from the car.

Throwing an arm around her shoulder, Ward pulled her closer as she steered Jess toward the front. "Let's get going before the paparazzi find us."

A moment later, they were moving again, and Jess hardly noticed the scenery changing as she thought about the journey ahead of her. Inpatient treatment at a psychiatric hospital. Wow. A month ago, she wouldn't have believed it. Hell, a week ago she wouldn't have. Yet here she was, sitting beside Ward, heading south on the turnpike toward Philly, not toward their home or the beach, but toward the Hartley Clinic. The name sounded prestigious and might have been a surgical center or a weight-loss retreat, but it wasn't. It was a nuthouse, and she was the nut.

With Ward the silence had never been uncomfortable, and it wasn't now either. They were an hour into the journey before she spoke. "Thank you."

Without taking her eyes off the traffic, Ward reached over and squeezed her shoulder. "Do you want to talk about it?"

Jess had spent the previous day making arrangements, and Ward had been working, so all they'd talked about was her need for a ride to the hospital. Luckily, the administration had been able to fill the ER schedule. Reese Ryan, Jess's college roommate, and a few doctors from neighboring hospitals were pitching in to cover the schedule. The hospital had had its fill of locum tenens doctors after Edward Hawk, and Jess was relieved to know Garden Memorial was in the good hands of people she knew and trusted while she was away. It meant she could focus on herself and her recovery.

They would admit her whenever she arrived, and she was grateful for the freedom in scheduling her day. She was putting Ward out and felt badly for it. She felt badly about everything, and suddenly the tears began again. As if she'd anticipated them, Ward had tissues at the ready and offered a handful to Jess. When her hand was empty, she placed it on Jess's knee and let it rest there.

"I'm sorry," Jess said when she could breathe enough to form the words.

Ward nodded. "I know, Jess."

"For everything."

This time Ward smiled, then turned to her and winked before fixing her eyes on the road once again. "I know. Are you hungry? Would you like to stop before we get to the hospital?"

Jess wasn't sure what she wanted. She dreaded going to the hospital, though, and she figured delaying her arrival for as long as possible was better than the alternative. "How about King of Prussia?"

"Hmm. Good choices there. What are you thinking? Calamari? Steak? Cheesecake?"

They'd eaten at the restaurants at the mall on many occasions. It was a short, scenic ride to KOP on the back roads from Wayne, and they'd taken advantage of it when they lived in Philly. "God, I never realized it, but I miss Philly."

Ward laughed. "It has its advantages. So what will it be for the last meal?"

Jess playfully tossed Ward's hand from her leg. "I'm going to the nuthouse and you're making jokes."

"It beats crying, right? You certainly have plenty of reasons to cry, Jess, but laughter feels so much better, doesn't it?"

Jess bit her lip. Ward was right, of course. Jess always tended to be too serious, too uptight. It had been one of the biggest problems in their relationship, but Jess had come to appreciate it as an asset, too. Though they were opposites in many regards, they mostly complemented each other rather than clashing.

"I'm going to spend the next half of my life learning to relax."

"I hope it doesn't take that long."

"Shut up. It's something I can work on at the hospital."

"Yes, it is. Maybe I should have asked you this earlier, but do you have everything? Insurance cards, cell phone, laptop?"

"They don't allow electronic devices. Can you believe that?"

"What? Are you sure? That sounds ridiculous."

"I'm trying to remember medical school, when we did our psych rotations. Did people have cell phones?"

"I don't think they did. There was always a line of people waiting to use the pay phones. Why, though?"

"The website says they want patients to focus on healing, to eliminate the stresses and distractions of the outside world and concentrate on recovery."

"You don't sound like you buy it."

Jess laughed. "I think the patients are calling their dealers and having drugs delivered like pizza."

Ward snickered. "The clinic has an excellent reputation."

Jess nodded. She'd read everything she could find about Hartley before placing the call to them, and she was impressed. They had programs for physicians, police and firefighters, and other professionals. The staff consisted of a variety of psychiatrists specializing in various problems and counselors of all kinds, who offered individual, small-group, and large-group sessions. They accepted most insurance as payment for services, but for the uninsured, the twenty-eight-day treatment plan cost a mere $31,000.

Jess was about to comment on that, when the meaning of Ward's statement hit her. "You looked it up?"

Ward snuck a sideways glance in Jess's direction. "Of course I did. I'm not going to trust just anyone with you."

The tears started before she knew they were coming. "You still love me, don't you?"

Ward reached across the distance between them, which suddenly seemed huge. The gentle squeeze of her hand spoke volumes. "Of course I do."

"I feel it."

"Nothing will ever erase what we had together, Jess. You'll always be a part of my life."

Silently Jess wiped her tears and her nose and eased into the seat. No matter what she'd done, she still had Ward.

"I have to ask you a favor. A very big favor."

Jess could sense Ward's fear, even though she didn't hesitate to answer. "What?"

"You're going to be my contact person and all that shit, okay. That's not a problem. But they're probably going to ask you some questions about me, to try to get a handle on my problems. Make sense?"

"Yes, of course."

"I don't want you to tell them anything."

"Okaaaay. Why?"

"You really don't know about my addiction, since I never shared it with you. And I can tell them what they need to know about the PTSD. I don't even know if I have it. They're the experts, they'll figure it out."

"Jess, the more information they have, the better they can take care of you." Ward's tone was condescending, and it hit a nerve. Jess snapped.

"I'm a doctor, Ward. I understand that. But there are things I don't want them to know, okay?"

"Like what?" Ward looked at her, her mouth open in obvious disbelief. "What could you possibly want to hide from the people who are going to save your life?"

Jess sighed. She hadn't wanted to share this with Ward, and she suddenly wished she'd hired a car to take her to the hospital. No matter what the cost from Garden to Philly, it would have been much easier than dealing with Ward. "I'm not going to tell them I'm a doctor."

"What?"

"Ward, I'm not doing it. I am *not* reporting myself to the state. I'm going to get this under control, and I'm going to do it my way. I'm going in voluntarily, for God's sake. Who does that? Only someone who's responsible, like me."

"Jessica. Listen to me. You have an ethical obligation to notify the state medical board that you have an impairment. If you do, they'll monitor you and help you through this and forgive you. If you don't report it, and someone finds out and turns you in, you'll be fucked. You'll lose your license, and who knows what else they'll do to you."

"No one's going to find out. No one knows I'm here."

"Jess, you could run into someone you know in there."

"I'll cross that bridge later."

"What about the hospital? Won't they want some sort of progress report before they allow you to return to work?"

"The hospital doesn't know I'm here. I told them I'm going away to relax and recover. I didn't tell them I'm being admitted."

"Okay, fine. What about your insurance? Someone from HR could get a call to verify your coverage, and then they'll know. What then?"

"I'm not using my insurance."

"What?"

"You heard me."

"No, I couldn't have, because I thought you said you're not using your insurance. Which would mean you're paying cash. Thirty thousand dollars in cash."

"It's a check, actually, and it's thirty-one. What's the big fucking deal? I have the money. Why can't you understand the implications here, Ward? If the state finds out what I've done, I'm screwed. My only chance to get my life back is to do it this way. Why can't you support me for once instead of having to be a fucking Girl Scout, doing everything by the book?"

Ward was silent for a moment before speaking. "It's your license, Jess. What would you like to eat?"

CHAPTER FIVE

The First Step

"Wow," Ward said two hours later as they rounded a bend in the tree-lined road and caught their first glimpse of the clinic. It was a massive structure of stone, with towering chimneys protruding from gabled sections of roof, reminiscent of colonial mansions Jess had seen throughout the Delaware Valley. She knew this one was modern; it was built twenty years earlier, not as a residence for wealthy colonists but solely as a rehab hospital. The exterior was much the same as the old psych hospital where she'd rotated during her medical school days, but she knew from her Internet search that the similarities ended there. Inside, she wouldn't find any drab white walls and gray tiled floors. The Hartley Clinic was colorful and cheerful, a bright place where the space made people feel good, or at least could help them to.

Signs directed them to a large lot, and after Ward found a spot and parked, they walked toward the portico and the hospital's entrance. Jess pulled her largest suitcase behind her, happy to be moving, grateful for the weight that caused her to breathe a little harder than normal. The effort felt good, and she felt good, so she suddenly questioned her decision to come to this place.

Couldn't she and Ward just keep driving, down to Delaware? They'd rent a beach house for the month—hell, with thirty grand they could get beachfront in Rehoboth. They'd ride their bikes and read on the beach, make love in the afternoons, and then watch sunsets over the bay.

Her legs stopped moving, and ahead of her Ward glanced back. Good, sweet Ward was reading her mind, Jess knew when the lopsided smile appeared on her face and she reached for Jess's hand. "It's going to be okay."

"I've fucked up my life so badly," she cried into Ward's shoulder.

"Badly, yes. But not sooo badly. Not beyond repair. You just need a little help. I know you think you're smarter than these people, and that you can figure out this disease on your own, but the statistics suggest otherwise."

"I'm not a statistic. Statistics are for normal people, and I'm not normal."

Ward laughed. "No, you're not."

Jess laughed, too, and lightly punched Ward's shoulder. "You know what I mean."

"Didn't you already try to wean yourself?"

Jess nodded, and her vision of Ward blurred from the tears that flooded her eyes. She had tried. And tried. And tried. She could tolerate the sweating, and the muscle pain, even the diarrhea. But the anxiety made her crazy, and in the last moments of the most recent effort she'd made at weaning herself, she truly understood why people killed themselves, because if she had no fix for that feeling, if she couldn't just pop a few oxycodone tablets in her mouth and make it all better, she would have chosen to end her own life then and there.

"I couldn't do it."

"And you don't have to, Jess. You just need treatment. That's what this is. Medical treatment, for a medical condition. It's no different than what you do every day. If one of your patients had an infection, you'd tell them to take their antibiotic. If they were diabetic, you'd tell them to take their insulin. This is no different. You have a disease, and you need to take medication to treat it."

"Is that really what you think? You don't think I'm a junkie?"

"I think you're an addict. And addiction is a disease. And you have PTSD, which is another disease. And if we stay out here any longer, you're going to have hyperthermia."

Jess looked into the bright, cloudless sky. "I wonder when I'll see daylight again."

Ward grabbed the handle of her bag and they began walking again. "Probably at your evening Stroll with the Staff."

"How about that?" Jess smiled. Every evening, regardless of weather, patients were encouraged to hike the ample grounds. Counselors and physicians led the group treks, and they all talked about a variety of topics as they took in some fresh air and Vitamin D.

"This weighs a ton. What the hell did you pack?"

The bag was stuffed with casual and exercise clothes, slippers and loafers and sneakers, toiletries, and her own bedding. "It's probably the twin comforter. I don't think it fully dried before I packed it."

Ward turned to eye Jess and her jaw dropped.

"What? You can't expect me to sleep on their blankets! Who knows who used them last? Besides, you know how sensitive my skin is."

"Jess, you are—"

Jess held up her hand. "I know, you have no words."

"Special. I was going to say special."

Jess stopped. They'd reached the portico, and just a few yards separated them from the grand front door and the unknown world of integrated care. "I want you to know that I'm not giving up on us. I know you think you're in love with Abby, but how could you be? You've known her for two weeks. I'm going to give you a little space—like a hundred and twenty miles. And a little time—like twenty-eight days."

Ward's eyes clouded and Jess saw the hesitation there. She worked quickly to remove it. "Or longer, Ward. I don't care. What's the hurry? I just want you to know I'm dedicated to getting better. My addiction drove you away, not my heart. Not my real heart."

Jess wasn't sad for the tears in Ward's eyes. She knew they meant Ward cared. Ward still loved her. There was hope.

"I want you to leave now," Jess said as Ward wiped her eyes.

"Why?"

"What's the point? I can take it from here. I'll call you when I can, and I'm counting on you for a ride home, right?"

Ward looked confused and Jess stepped closer, hugged her. "I'm good, Ward. Really." She stepped back and saw the doubt on Ward's face. "I promise I won't run away."

They both laughed, and the sound buoyed Jess. "I'll call you," she said, and before Ward could reply, a door opened and a middle-aged woman in a lime-colored pantsuit stepped through.

"Welcome," she said. "Are you checking in?"

Jess nodded. "My friend is a little nervous about leaving me, but I've assured her I'll be fine. She has a long drive ahead of her, and I'd feel better if she gets started."

The woman nodded. "Of course, that's fine. If you're okay, she can certainly be on her way."

"I guess this is it, then." Ward opened her arms, and Jess stepped into them again. Jess tried not to think about how good it felt to be there.

"I love you," Jess said, and Ward murmured the words back to her. Then Jess took the handle of her suitcase and turned, following the lime-swathed woman through the doors and into her new life.

"I'm Annette," the woman said. "I'll get you signed in, if you'll just follow me to my office."

"Jessica Benson."

"I'm an admissions counselor. That's my job title. My background is in counseling, but I do many things here. I speak to people on the phone, to make sure our services are appropriate for them. You talked to my colleague, so I'm guessing you're familiar with that process. Now that you're here, I'll ask you more detailed questions, to help determine the plan of care we need to follow with you. I'll make some recommendations to the psychiatrists—both the PTSD psychiatrist and the addiction specialist."

Jess interrupted her. "You have a psychiatrist who specializes in PTSD?"

"Let me clarify," Annette said, and she didn't seem at all condescending. She sat back in a cozy leather chair, one of four in the conversational grouping in her large office. "PTSD is not a specialty in itself. The doctor isn't board-certified in that field. But we see so many patients with PTSD that we have one doctor who treats only them, so, as you can imagine, she's gotten quite experienced at it."

"It's a woman?" Jess asked, feeling better already.

Annette smiled. "As a matter of fact, both your psychiatrists will be women. Do you feel more comfortable with women?"

"I'm a lesbian. I feel much more comfortable with women."

"Ha! You're in good hands, then. And I guess I can skip the lecture about fraternizing with the male patients."

"No worries there."

"No fraternizing with the women, either."

Jess met her eye. "You're just going to have to trust me, I guess."

Annette looked at her sideways. "Until you give me a reason not to."

Jess nodded at the not-too-subtle warning.

"Let me tell you about your day. I'm going to ask you a few questions about your history. Then I'll walk you to the detox area, where the PA will examine you and make sure you're in good health. While you're with him, your bags will be searched for contraband. Whatever is deemed inappropriate—reading material, drugs, phones—will be removed and put into a locker for you to pick up at the time of your discharge. If you're hungry, you can get something to eat then, and afterward you'll meet with the addiction specialist so you can begin treatment. In your case, since you're beginning buprenorphine, the process will be relatively benign. Most people feel normal on bup."

"I've read good things about it," Jess said. Even though she was a doctor, she knew very little about addiction and its treatment. During the past days, that had changed as she scoured the Internet for information and formulated her own treatment plan. She was here for bup, and she was sure it would help her. It had to. If she didn't stabilize her addiction, she was in real trouble.

Jess tuned back into Annette, who'd continued her speech as Jess sat daydreaming. "During the induction phase—until your dose of medication is stabilized—you won't be doing much. It's hard to predict how you'll feel, so we don't schedule anything. If you feel well, we would encourage you to begin attending some of the meetings that occur just about every hour. After your addiction is controlled, you'll begin meeting with the psychiatrist to determine your treatment plan for the PTSD. Unless the addiction specialist thinks you need to be seen sooner, of course. We try for a nice combination of structure and flexibility here, so everyone can get what they, as individuals, need to recover."

Although she was anxious, a wave of optimism came over Jess, and she felt something she hadn't felt in a long time. Hope. She was hopeful about getting her addiction under control. She wanted her life back. "It sounds like a great place."

"We have an excellent record, Jessica. People who are motivated to recover can, and we're proof of that fact."

"I'm motivated." Annette had used the word "normal" when she discussed the therapy. Jess wondered if she'd ever been normal, even when she wasn't taking drugs. She'd felt okay, maybe a little out of place at times, but she'd found a good fit in medicine. The medical field included a plethora of geeks and nerds, and she was just another one, overly smart and a little socially challenged. Without her career, she didn't know what she'd do. It was her ground, and she needed to get over this addiction, because if anyone ever found out her truth, her career could be over.

It wasn't just her career, though. If she ever wanted to win back Ward's heart, she'd have to be clean to do it. Ward would never accept her this way, and that was a big motivating factor.

"First things first. You're here for treatment for opioid addiction. Are you currently experiencing withdrawal symptoms?"

Jess shook her head. "No."

"Very well. I have a paper for you to complete, a brief medical history. Once you meet your psychiatrists—probably tomorrow, since it's so late in the day—you'll have an extensive psychiatric exam. But this will get us started. I find it helpful if I ask the questions rather than having you complete the paper yourself. Would that be okay?"

"Sure."

"And would it be okay if I type the answers into my computer as we go along?"

Jess wanted to tell her she understood the woes of electronic medical records, but she kept quiet and merely nodded.

"Do you take any medications?" she asked, and looked up, meeting Jess's eyes.

"Oxycodone. Ten migs." She nearly said "Q4," medical lingo for every four hours, but she caught herself. If she wasn't going to tell the staff at the hospital she was a doctor, she had to try hard to not act or sound like one. The task would require patience, an attribute she admittedly lacked. Allowing someone else to spend an hour extracting a history she could have accurately provided in minutes was the first test of her hospital stay. How many more awaited her?

"How often do you take the oxycodone?"

Jess swallowed her prompt reply and instead pretended to ponder the answer. "I'm supposed to take six a day. Sometimes I take four, and sometimes I take eight."

Annette nodded, and Jess expected a follow-up question regarding the source of the pills, but none came. "Anything else?" she asked instead.

For a moment Jess contemplated telling the truth about her Xanax. It could cause a fatal overdose when used with bup. She knew that wouldn't happen to her, though. She didn't take extras. If she admitting using Xanax, the doctor might not give her the bup. There was no way she could come clean about it. Her dilemma was the inevitable urine drug screen she expected within the next few hours. A small lie seemed like the best course. "I take Xanax once in a while. When I can get them."

Annette's head popped up from the computer screen, and she eyed Jess with concern. "How often do you take the Xanax?"

"Oh, once a week, maybe."

"When was the last time you took one?"

"Last night, to help me sleep." Jess smiled, what she hoped was a sad smile. "I was really nervous about today."

Annette's expression softened. "I understand. But we won't be giving you any Xanax here. It doesn't mix well with buprenorphine."

Jess tried to sound surprised. "Oh, okay. Well, I don't need it, so whatever you have to do."

"Okay. Did you bring your medication with you?"

Jess had both the oxycodone and Xanax hidden in a secret compartment in her suitcase, in case of emergencies. She wasn't about to share that information with Annette, though. "No! I didn't know I was supposed to."

Annette smiled again. "No, you don't need them. You're not allowed to take anything, even ibuprofen, unless a nurse gives it to you. Does that make sense? We want to control medication use. It might not be convenient to walk to the nursing desk for a Tums, but this practice helps curb addictive tendencies, like popping a pill."

Jess had a whole pharmacy in her suitcase. She never left home without a supply of antibiotics and other essentials. "I do take ibuprofen, for headaches. Is that okay? Can I get that from the nurse? I forgot to bring it."

"Of course. You can request anything you need, and within reason, they'll give it to you. Now, back to your history."

Annette went on to ask questions about Jess's allergies, surgeries, and family history. Unlike those of a typical family history, her questions focused on mental illness. "Any relatives ever commit suicide? Die suddenly with no explanation? Leave home and lose contact?"

How boring for Annette that Jess was an only child, that her parents had no skeletons hanging from their family trees. She shook her head. "My mom died last year from ovarian cancer. My dad is healthy."

"Oh, how awful. I'm sorry for your loss. You know ovarian cancer can run in families, right? Have you been checked?"

Of course she'd been checked. She'd had all the studies available, not just for ovarian cancer but every other disease that had shown genetic affiliation. She was a doctor, after all. "I don't really have a doctor, but I'll look into that."

"Let's talk about your social history. Do you smoke?"

Jess shook her head.

"How much alcohol do you drink each day?"

"I don't really drink much alcohol. Maybe a couple of glasses of wine a week." Jess had grown bored with the interview and studied the diplomas on the wall. Annette had her master's in counseling from Villanova. Impressive.

"What drugs do you use beside the oxycodone?"

"None. That's it."

"No heroin, cocaine, amphetamines?"

Jess met her eyes and shook her head again. "Nothing else. Just pills."

"Are you married?"

"No."

"Oh, that's right. Do you have a partner?"

Of all the questions she'd ask, why did this one cause her to flinch? Jess had managed to separate herself from the process, become analytical for the purpose of providing medical data. This was just a formality, the history-taking. Annette would gather this information, and a doctor or two would review it and probably discuss some of it with her. They'd sign off on the chart Annette created and then begin the real business of treating her.

Jess knew this and was playing along, but the question about a partner stung. Why hadn't she opened up to Ward sooner? Why had she driven her away? Now she was alone, and scared, and the one person who could help her now had found another woman.

"No," she said, and swallowed some tears.

Annette paused and studied her. "Bad breakup?" she asked.

Jess cleared her throat and accepted the tissue Annette waved in her direction. "It was a combination of things, but mostly my addiction."

Knowingly, Annette shook her head. "Addiction destroys relationships, that's for sure."

Jess shrugged.

"Okay. My notes say you don't have insurance. Does that mean you don't work?"

Jess shook her head again. Lying was becoming easier. "I left my job in Philly when my mom became sick."

"And what kind of work did you do in Philly?"

This was the question Jess had been dreading. Fabricating a profession meant much more than telling a tale; working in a field gave a person a certain amount of knowledge, and she could easily fall into that trap in the coming days. With that possibility in mind, she thought a job in health care was the best way to go, but decided it best if she were on the fringes of medicine, rather than practicing. As the ER director in Garden she'd spent many hours reviewing billing and coding, and had grown familiar enough with the process and the lingo that she could pull off a job in that field. "I worked in a hospital. I code medical charts."

"Did you attend college?"

"Yes." Jess admitted to her undergrad work at Pocono Mountains University but fabricated her major and subsequent learning experiences.

"Where do you live now?"

"With my father." She'd gone home to help take care of her mom, and she was single and unemployed. How could she afford a house?

"How is that relationship?"

"Huh?"

"Is he understanding of your addiction? Supportive of your recovery?"

Her father had no clue about her addiction. "He's very supportive."

"And he doesn't use drugs or alcohol?"

"I've never seen my father drunk. He drinks a beer on Friday night with his pizza, but that's it." Jess sighed, relieved to tell a truth after so many lies.

"That's good, that you live with him and he's behind you. The work we do here can only carry you so far when you leave. You need support outside to maintain your sobriety."

Jess nodded but felt suddenly queasy. How the hell was she going to arrange that? Other than Ward, no one knew about her addiction. And in a small town like Garden, who could she tell without everyone finding out? It just wasn't possible.

"Let's talk about payment for your treatment. Of course, we can't tell you how much your treatment will cost, because we don't know how you're going to respond to your therapy. Some patients respond quickly, but others take years to functionally recover. Insurance companies, in their wisdom, have decided that twenty-eight days is the right treatment time, so we generally suggest that as a reference point. You're here of your own free will and paying cash, so you really can leave when you see fit. We'll structure your treatment plan to get you ready to leave in twenty-eight days. Does that sound appropriate?"

Jess nodded.

"You will need to pay by the week, one week in advance. I'll need a credit card or a check today."

Jess reached for her purse and pulled out her checkbook. It was a lot of money, but what choice did she have? She couldn't use her insurance. And if she were dead from an overdose, or went to jail, money wouldn't matter at all. Why not make a donation to the Hartley Clinic? It was worth a try.

She made out the check and handed it to Annette. It was official. She was in rehab.

CHAPTER SIX

Doctor's Orders

Jess followed Annette through a series of corridors, following signs that said MEDICAL WING. The inside of the building was as impressive as the outside, with woods and tiles that warmed the interior, rather than a chilling, sterile hospital decor. They walked through a gathering room, with a vaulted ceiling, its exposed timbering giving the room a strong, masculine edge. The colors were cheerful, though—bright-yellow walls and floral fabrics covering the couches. In the center of the room, a grand fireplace reached all the way to the ceiling, and against one wall, a disproportionately small television played mutely for no one.

"This is one of the patient lounges. The other offers a Ping-Pong table and a card table, but if you want to catch up on news or your favorite show, this is the place."

"That one television? For everyone to share?"

Annette seemed to expect the remark and brushed it aside without breaking stride. "People here are focused on recovery. Too much distraction from the outside world is, well, distracting. You'll need to become self-centered. As in putting yourself at the center of your attention. Sure, you can watch a little television, but mostly you'll attend meetings, and exercise, and write, and read—articles and books about recovery, not romance novels. You'll find that, at the end of your day, you're tired. You won't even miss the television."

"What time does the day start?"

"We wake everyone at seven and expect everyone to finish

breakfast by eight thirty. That's when the first groups and meetings start. If you're an early riser, you can do morning yoga or exercise."

Annette pulled the stretchy lanyard around her neck until her ID badge triggered a set of electric doors and they opened, giving them access to the medical unit. In spite of the name, the area also had a warm feel.

A dozen people greeted Annette when they walked in. Some were clearly patients, dressed in jeans and sneakers, and others wore casual work attire. Annette introduced Jess to everyone she met, using only her first name. She was surprised that Annette could remember the names of all the patients. "Good luck," someone said. "Welcome," another greeted her. "You'll love it here," said yet another.

They rounded a corner and Annette admitted them through another secure door, into an area decidedly more clinical than the rest of the place. Every surface was some shade of gray, medical equipment and monitors crowded every surface, and two women wearing scrubs were seated at computers, their fingers flying across the keys as they undoubtedly documented in charts. Jess felt instantly depressed to think she'd be spending the next few days in this area of the building. Annette introduced the nurses before knocking on one of the two doors at the rear.

After introducing her to the PA, Annette left, carrying Jess's suitcase and all of its contraband cargo with her. She didn't have time to worry over her fate, though, as the PA began talking. He explained his role in the clinic; he was a medical practitioner and worked with the family doctor who attended to the medical needs of the clinic's patients. Since Jess had no medical concerns, he would do a cursory exam to clear her for admission, but assured her that he or the doctor was on call 24/7. "What if I need a Motrin or something?" she asked.

"I'll write an order for you to have just about anything you can think of, just in case. Mild pain meds, cough preps, anti-diarrhea meds, you name it."

"Okay, great." Jess had brought all of that, but it was good to know there was a backup plan. What if she ran out? What if they found the stash in the secret compartment of her suitcase?

The exam was by no means cursory, and Jess thought she might learn something from the PA, who checked everything from the texture of her hair to the pulses in her feet. Jess declined the pelvic exam and the rectal, and chuckled as she signed the attestation denying the possibility of pregnancy. He nailed her bulging vein on the first try and withdrew three tubes of blood for testing. He told her he was checking her blood count, chemistry profile, and for every disease known to drug addicts worldwide. After finishing, he covered her wound with a yellow, smiley-face bandage and escorted her to the door.

"Good luck," he said, and Jess felt he really meant it.

In the nurses' area, Annette was waiting for her. Shaking her head, she pointed a finger at Jess. "I found your contraband."

Fuck, Jess thought. Could she really go through with rehab without her stash of necessities? Being socially and intellectually isolated, without emergency oxys and Xanax, not to mention the tweezers for her eyebrows—she didn't think she could do it. If she called Ward now, she could be back in Garden by nightfall.

"I'm going to let it slide," Annette was saying as Jess refocused in time to see her wink. "I have a weakness for licorice myself."

Jess's heart threatened to erupt through her throat. She'd found the food—which Jess really hadn't even hidden, but apparently not the real stash. "Okay."

"Just try to keep them in your room, so no one notices." Jess nodded mutely. "And, by the way, in all my years in rehab, I've never had a patient bring their own bedding. Should I add OCD to your diagnosis?"

Jess smiled nervously, biting her lower lip. Whew! She'd forgotten about the licorice laces and never considered the comforter would be an issue. It hadn't occurred to her to use a distraction, but it appeared to have worked. Annette hadn't discovered the important stuff.

"Dr. Gompers is ready to see you," she said when Jess didn't respond. "Even though it's late in the day, she wanted to evaluate you. Are you ready?"

Jess nodded, and Annette stood and motioned toward the other room at the back of the nursing area. "Then let's get started."

As she heard their approach, a matronly woman of sixty rose from a black leather club chair and shuffled across the room to meet them. Her frumpy, gray sweater matched her hair but did nothing to flatter her. Nor did the black peasant skirt, which brought to mind visions of a whale. Jess tried not to let the doctor's appearance rattle her. The hospital had a great reputation, and Dr. Gompers was a big part of that. She was probably too preoccupied with complicated medical musings to bother with wardrobe concerns.

Once again, Annette made the introductions and wasted no time on niceties, taking her leave just as quickly as they entered. Jess was confused by the hasty departure, until Dr. Gompers began speaking. She was all business.

"Tell me why you're here," she said, after pointing Jess to the chair opposite the one she reclaimed. As she sat, she pulled a laptop into her lap, but rather than opening it, she stared at Jess. It was hard to hold her gaze, knowing she was lying, knowing the doctor specialized in treating the greatest con artists in medical history.

Addicts lied, twisted and turned facts until they could no longer separate their own histories from the ones they fabricated. The doctors and nurses and therapists who treated them were used to this and were experts at finding the holes in their patients' stories. And Jess's story looked like someone had taken a shotgun to it. She was lying about her profession and denying she had health-care insurance. Unsure if the hospital would check on her medical records and learn she was a physician, Jess hadn't told them about the wrist surgery that had seeded her addiction. The final, huge lie had to do with the PTSD. How could she tell the doctors what happened to her without someone figuring out who she was? CNN had broadcast the story of her abduction for days, and thankfully, the only pictures they'd dug up had been dated, when Jess was younger and had much longer hair. Still, if she said Edward Hawk had abducted her and paralyzed her with succinylcholine, someone would figure out she was actually *Doctor* Jessica Benson instead of a mild-mannered coder. Her house of cards would crumble, and she couldn't have that.

She'd keep it simple, she decided, and tell Ward's story instead. Ward's last night in Garden was something she could never forget.

"I have PTSD. At least I think I do—I've never seen a psychiatrist. I've been self-medicating with Xanax and oxycodone."

"And now you think you're addicted? What makes you say that?"

"I can't stop taking the oxys. I've tried. I just can't get off them."

She asked about her addiction and gave her a form called a Drug Abuse Screening Test. It asked about withdrawal, health problems related to drug use, relationship issues, criminal activity, and other questions to gauge the severity of her problem. Out of ten questions, with one point awarded for each positive response, Jess scored nine.

Next, the doctor asked about her withdrawal symptoms and gave her yet another form, this one a Clinical Opioid Withdrawal Scale, or COWS, to measure the severity of her withdrawal symptoms. Jess scored in the mild range. The doctor asked what methods she'd tried to quit, including using other drugs. She asked about prior visits at rehab. Delving deeper into Jess's drug use, she asked about the escalation of her use and about how she was able to maintain her supply of drugs.

When she'd exhausted the questions about drug abuse, she queried Jess about her PTSD. Jess told her she'd been at a bar and drugged by an unknown person. She'd reacted badly to the roofies and assaulted several people, and would have faced charges if it hadn't been proved that someone had drugged her. Unlike Ward, Jess remembered everything that happened that night.

"What brought you here? Why now, after three years?"

Finally, a question Jess could answer honestly. "Ward. My ex. I thought she'd always be here for me, even though I treated her like crap and pushed her away. Now she has another girlfriend, and

I know she won't have anything to do with me if I don't get my act together."

For the first time in their conversation, Dr. Gompers's expression changed. Jess couldn't read it. She seemed almost confused for a moment, with squinted eyes and pursed lips. That quickly, the neutral expression returned and she returned to interviewing Jess. "So Ward has moved on. But you haven't?"

Jess looked up and breathed deeply, trying to control her emotions. Why did the thought of losing Ward forever suddenly bother her so much? She hadn't cared when she fired her, or broke up with her, or encouraged her to date Abby. Why now? She kept coming back to that question, and she still wasn't sure she knew the answer. She studied the wall adjacent to Dr. Geraldine Gompers's desk. She was a graduate of the Philadelphia College of Osteopathic Medicine, just like Ward. What a coincidence. Lately, everything in her life seemed to be circling back to Ward. A good omen, she hoped.

"Ward is such a good person. Dependable. Strong. Kind. I need someone like her in my life. I pushed her away, because with her around I didn't have the freedom to use drugs. Now that I'm in rehab, it could work again. And I know this can't be serious with her new girlfriend, Abby. Ward and I have been together a long time. We met during residency, more than ten years ago. She just met Abby a few weeks ago. How could she brush me aside for someone she hardly knows?"

Again, Dr. Gompers's face moved. But it changed back so quickly Jess might have imagined it. "Wait. Ward is a doctor?"

Jess sucked in a breath as she realized her error. She should have known the lies were bound to catch up with her. But maybe she could still spin this in her direction. "Yes," she said, enthusiastically. Proudly. Shouldn't she be proud to date a doctor? "She's an ER doctor. We worked at the same hospital. That's how we met." At least that much was true.

"Does Ward, or has Ward ever prescribed narcotics for you?"

"No! She's honest and ethical…that's what made it so hard to be with her when I was…misbehaving. Until a few days ago, she didn't even know I had a drug problem. And as soon as she found out, she suggested rehab, and she even brought me here. I think that means she still cares."

"I think I'll leave your relationship with Ward up to your other psychiatrist and focus on your addiction, if you don't mind."

Grateful to have dodged a bullet, Jess nodded.

Explaining how bup worked, the doctor told Jess she needed to have moderate to severe withdrawal symptoms before starting the medication. The treatment they gave wasn't just bup, a long-acting opioid, but also an antidote to bup. The combination prevented both abuse and overdose. Taking too much caused the naloxone to kick in, sending a person into withdrawal. Timing the first dose was important, she knew. If she wasn't already in withdrawal when she started the medication, she was likely to suffer violently.

"Considering your history, I think you're a good candidate for treatment. What do you think?"

Jess nodded. "I think so, too."

"Since your COWS score is zero now, we'll play the waiting game."

She would spend her day unpacking one suitcase, attending a meeting or counseling session, and waiting to feel sick.

Rising from her chair, Dr. Gompers dismissed her and handed her over to Annette, who walked her to her room, pulling the suitcase behind her. "Your roommate's name is Bonita. She's very nice," Annette said as they walked just a few yards down the corridor. "She arrived yesterday and is doing very well. She'll be able to answer some of your questions better than I or the doctors."

Pushing open a heavy wooden door, Annette gestured for Jess to enter.

From the assortment of junk piled on the dresser nearest the bathroom, Jess assumed Bonita had claimed it and the adjacent bed. Perfect. It gave Jess the corner, away from Bonita's prying eyes. She walked that way, looked through the window to an expanse of green field and blue sky. A beautiful day to start her new journey.

"I'll leave you to unpack, but I'll catch up with you later. When you've settled in, you should go back to the desk and they'll direct you to the meeting of your choice."

"Thank you. For everything. You're very kind."

She nodded and smiled, then left Jess alone.

The room was actually quite beautiful, though small. Berber carpet lined the floors, a floral-patterned paper adorned the upper walls, and the bottoms were covered in wainscot. The ceiling was a bright white, and a fan hung from the center, its blades shaped like large leaves of a shading palm tree circling the room. The bathroom was luxuriously tiled from floor to ceiling and had a spacious shower, but no tub. It was much harder to drown yourself in the shower.

Jess stripped the bed, then neatly folded the linens and deposited them on a shelf in the closet. Next, she made the bed with her own linens, then arranged her clothing in the closets and her personal items on the shelves and dressers before sitting down.

She had nothing left to do. She'd spent fifteen minutes unpacking, and now nothing stood between her and her first group meeting other than her fear. She'd never discussed her problem with anyone. The only people who knew were a few dealers and drug addicts who'd been her suppliers when she lived in Philly. Was she ready to confess her sins to a group of strangers? Forcefully blowing out a big breath, she realized it was easier than talking to people she knew. That, she would never do.

But what if she did know someone here? The clinic had boasted of its success with treating professionals. What if one of her former colleagues was in the same predicament and had come here for help? That would just stink, because she refused to admit this part of her life to the medical board. She wouldn't spend the remainder of her career a marked woman, under constant scrutiny, like some criminal. She'd deal with this problem, and the board would never know a thing.

"I should go to a meeting," she said, but then she lay back on the bed and closed her eyes, wondering how she'd ever gotten into so much trouble.

She barely had time to consider the question when loud

footsteps and the sound of the door slamming startled her. She sat up, stared in that direction, and tried to focus her eyes through the haze of sleep still covering them.

"I am sooo, sooo sorry." A voice spoke as Jess blinked. "They told me you were coming, but I didn't know you'd be here," whoever it was said, her voice unbearably loud after the quiet Jess had been enjoying.

Finally, her eyes recovered, and the image of a woman in her thirties with short dark hair came into focus.

"It's okay," Jess said. "I was just napping, but I guess I need to get up."

"I'm Bonita Brodhead, your roomie." She bounced across the room and energetically took Jess's hand. "Welcome, and good luck!"

"Jess," she answered, deliberately omitting her surname. Why hadn't she registered under an alias?

"Nice to meet you." The woman sat on the side of her bed, facing Jess. "I hate not having a roommate. It's sort of lonely, you know? Have you been here before? I just got here yesterday, but this is my third time in rehab, so I feel like I've been here forever."

It was hard to sort out the details in Bonita's fast-flowing speech, but one thing stood out. "Third time here?" Jess was concerned. Maybe the clinic wasn't as good as they claimed.

"No, second. I came here a few years ago and got clean. I was determined to make my marriage work, for the sake of the kids. But my husband wasn't interested in getting his shit together, and he started selling my bup to get heroin, and then after a few months, I started using again, too, and, well, you know the story. Here I am again."

Once again Bonita's words flowed too quickly to allow any interjection, and when she stopped, Jess wasn't sure how to reply. It seemed sad, though, that this woman had tried to straighten out her life, and the one person who should have been supporting her had brought her down. Jess was relieved to know she'd never have to worry about that. "Wow. It must be tough when your partner is using, too."

Suddenly, Bonita bent her head and buried her face in her hands, sobbing hysterically. Jess wasn't certain what to do. They'd only just met, and she'd seemed fine, and then the waterworks began. She turned to Bonita, stepped across the gap between their beds, and sat beside her. Wasn't this supposed to be the other way around, with Bonita, the veteran, comforting Jess, the rookie? Jess rolled her eyes as she patted Bonita's leg. "Hey, you okay?"

Suddenly, Bonita looked up to face her, pools of tears flooding her big eyes. "I killed him."

"What?" Jess asked before she could filter her reply.

"My husband…Ryan…I, I, I…killed him," she sobbed.

Jess swallowed and considered the situation. Did she really want to know any more? Did she want to get caught up in someone else's drama when she could barely manage her own? Bonita's pressured speech suggested she could be manic, and that wouldn't surprise Jess at all. Bipolar patients turned to drugs to induce calm. Jess contemplated leaving the room so Bonita could deal with this on her own, but then the healer in her came out, and she patted her knee.

Bonita took the gesture as a sign to tell all, and she began talking. More slowly this time.

"He spent his paycheck on pills, and I was so mad, I used them all. When he came home from work looking to get high, he was furious and stormed out of the house. That was the last time I saw him."

She leaned into Jess's shoulder and punched herself repeatedly in the head. Jess wasn't sure what to do, so she remained motionless. Suddenly, Bonita sat up and wiped her eyes. "He couldn't find his normal dealer so he went to some other guy and bought heroin, because it's cheaper than pills. It was a strong batch and he overdosed that night. The cops found his body in his car the next morning. I checked myself in because I couldn't face our kids. How can I be with them at the viewing when I'm the one who killed their father? How can I look at him in the casket, knowing what I did?"

Fuck. That was awful. "I'm sorry about Ryan, Bonita. But it

wasn't your fault he got bad stuff. It could happen to anyone. And maybe he just used too much…it might have happened with the pills if you hadn't taken them first."

Just as suddenly as she'd begun crying, Bonita stopped. She looked at Jess, and a light filled her eyes. Her face lifted, and the change was so dramatic Jess wouldn't have recognized her in the hallway if they'd passed each other. "You're right! I didn't kill him. He would have died anyway. This is such a relief. I think I'm going to check myself out of this place so I can make it to the viewing tonight. So many people will be there that I want to see. It'll be like a reunion!"

Bonita jumped from the bed and ran to the door, opened it, and sped through it without looking back.

Shaking her head, Jess moved to her own bed and sprawled across it, resting her head on her elbow. "What the fuck am I doing here?" she asked the pillow.

Still in the same position a few minutes later, she watched as Bonita rushed back into the room and hastily swept the contents of her dresser into her suitcase. Then she dashed out the door without saying good-bye. Jess rolled over and watched the sky outside her window fade to darkness. She monitored her body and her surroundings, tracking her symptoms as minutes ticked by on her watch. Finally, she reached her limit.

"I think it's time," Jess said. The nurse studied her for a moment and nodded before ordering her to sit.

"You look like crap," she said, and Jess detected no humor in the remark. It was an accurate description of her state—aches and pains, diarrhea, sweating, sniffling, yawning, and a sense of anxiety that conjured up thoughts of a tall bridge to end it all. Her symptoms had become intolerable, as bad as they were the last time Jess had tried to quit, more than a year earlier when her Philadelphia supply had suddenly dried up.

"That's about how I feel."

The nurse handed Jess a COWS form to complete, and she did. Fuck, she was only eighteen on the scale, and she wanted to die.

The scale went to forty-three. What must forty-three feel like? She hoped she'd never find out.

After taking her vital signs—which were terribly abnormal, objective proof of the stress her body was under—the nurse handed her a white foil packet. It was just about an inch wide and slightly more in length, and paper-thin. Jess's hands were shaking as she followed the nurse's instructions and opened it. A sip of water prepped her mouth, and then she carefully placed the thin strip of medication under her tongue.

"Don't talk. Don't swallow. Just let it melt until it feels like it's all gone. The longer you wait to swallow, the better the medication will work."

Having been instructed not to talk, Jess simply nodded, trying to concentrate on something other than the acrid taste of the medication in her mouth.

Fifteen minutes later, the film had dissolved but Jess felt no better. "Another half hour and you'll know how it's working. Report back to me in forty-five minutes, and I'll give you another strip if you need it."

Too anxious to sit, Jess paced the hall, watching the clock. To her surprise, half an hour after she'd taken the medication, her symptoms had improved. Everything except the anxiety. She still wanted to crawl out of her skin, and so exactly forty minutes from her last appearance, she knocked on the glass partition at the nurses' station.

"You're early." Looking up from the computer screen, the nurse frowned.

"I figured by the time you take my blood pressure, it'll be an hour."

"Come back in ten minutes," she said, and so Jess paced again.

"It's ten minutes," Jess said when the time had passed, and the nurse glanced at the clock.

"So it is."

She didn't bother with vital signs this time, just pulled a strip out of a box that had been labeled with Jess's name. Once again she handed the packet to Jess, but this time, she instructed her to take only half.

"But why?"

"We're titrating the dose, trying to figure out how much you really need. So this time, instead of eight milligrams, you're getting four. And then if you need more, we'll give you two."

"Why are you torturing me?" Jess asked. She felt horrible and knew if she took the entire strip she'd feel much better in half an hour. The way Nurse Ratched was planning this, it could take three more hours for her to get the entire dose. But Jess realized that argument was futile, and she took the half strip as directed. Half an hour later, she was surprised that she felt much better. When an hour had passed, she reported back to the nurse.

"Two more?" she asked.

Jess hesitated. The anxiety was still there, but very mild, as if she'd had a double espresso on an empty stomach. All the other symptoms were gone. "Is it okay if I wait for a while? I think I'm okay."

For the first time since she'd met her hours earlier, the nurse smiled. "That's good, Jess. The less medication you take, the better. It costs less, and one day, it will be easier to wean down from twelve milligrams than twenty."

"Okay, I'm going with this. As long as I can get more if I need it."

The nurse swallowed a smile. "It's here in that case."

"Can I get a sandwich or something? I was too sick to eat dinner."

The nurse directed Jess to the self-serve area, where she found a premade ham-and-cheese sandwich on a hard roll, wrapped tightly in plastic wrap with packets of mustard and mayo squished inside. After adding a touch of both condiments, Jess ate her sandwich while standing at the counter.

The food tasted good. Great. She felt great. No, that wasn't it. She didn't really feel great; she just felt okay. But okay in an ordinary way. For the first time in years, she felt like herself. She felt normal.

Chapter Seven

Booming Business

Derek leaned against the van just as a sleek, black Mercedes sedan began circling the lot. The driver settled on a spot far from the other cars in the parking area. In the three years he'd been doing this, Derek had never seen the car before, but he knew who was inside. He'd noticed the occupants many times—affluent suburbanites, hooked on narcotics, coming to Dr. Ball for the cure. These people in the big cars were the VIPs, the patients the doctor took on an emergency basis, for outrageous fees. In spite of their status, they were just like all his other addicted patients—desperate. From years of watching, Derek knew some would make it and some wouldn't. They'd disappear from the office and reappear in the obituaries shortly afterward.

Three of the car's doors opened, and a middle-aged couple and a young woman appeared. The couple seemed anxious as they surveyed the parking lot, smoothing wrinkles and chewing lips. The girl, on the other hand, seemed proud. She showed no signs of withdrawal—her hair was combed, her posture erect, and she didn't seem to have the anxiety or muscle pain that came with it. She glanced around, though, more curious than nervous, and met his gaze. He smiled, and she answered with a cold stare before turning away, following her parents into the office.

Something in her attitude told him she'd be selling her bup to him soon.

His phone vibrated, and he pulled it from the clip on his belt. There was a text from Pete. "Get the fuck in here. We're done."

Derek pulled the van to the front of the building and began the slow process of loading his human cargo. First the patients, then their chairs. They were halfway back to the nursing home when Pete spoke. “We’re done for the day.”

“What?”

“Dr. Ball’s nurse said he’s canceling his afternoon patients. He’s probably going golfing.”

“Hmm. Can’t blame him. It’s a beautiful day.”

“Yeah, except I have fuckin’ bills to pay, and how am I going to do that when this jerk-off keeps cutting my hours?”

Derek understood. At least two or three times a month the doctor canceled his patients, and since he provided transport strictly for PATA, usually to the doctor’s office, he was short hours. Without the money he made selling pills, he’d be in trouble. He’d made a few grand on the robbery in Mountaintop, so he wasn’t worried, but he still needed his supply of drugs. He’d have to hurry back in his car to catch the scraps from the orthopedics office before they closed for the day.

The drive was uneventful, and fortunately Pete didn’t want to waste his money on fast food, so they were back at the garage promptly. He didn’t bother changing, just hurried back to Dr. Ball’s office hoping to do business. He breathed a sigh of relief when he pulled in. The lot was still full, as was the lot in front of the orthopedics office. Maybe the day wouldn’t be a bust after all.

His efforts were soon rewarded. A regular customer emerged from the doctor’s office and then the pharmacy, and Derek met him by his clunker. He couldn’t help stealing a glance at the big black Mercedes, still parked at the edge of the lot. What was going on with the girl?

He bought the pills, and then a few more from another customer, and decided to call it a day. He had his quota, and it was still early enough for him to enjoy the sunshine. Perhaps he’d meet his buyer early and spend some time at the park working on his tan.

He started his car just as the well-heeled family with the Mercedes emerged from the pharmacy. The parents seemed exhausted, walking slowly with their heads down. The girl appeared happy and energetic. Maybe it wasn't as he'd first thought. Perhaps she'd brought her drug-addicted parents in for the cure, rather than the reverse. He laughed at the thought. That wasn't it, he was sure. They'd strong-armed her into coming, and she was still denying her disease. She wasn't ready to quit. They were wasting their time with her, and a whole lot of money, too. That could be good news for him.

On a whim, Derek held back, watching. When the father took the wheel and guided the car out of the lot, Derek followed. They zigzagged through traffic and onto the Cross Valley Expressway. They didn't exit until they reached the affluent suburb of Dallas, and then Derek slowed down, putting distance between the vehicles, knowing how conspicuous his small American car looked compared to the expensive foreign models he saw on the roads and in the driveways. Just as he was contemplating abandoning his pursuit, the Mercedes turned left at a large stone sign marking the entrance to a housing development.

Rather than follow them, he kept driving. He knew enough. How hard would it be to find that car in a development of twenty or thirty homes? He didn't even know why he'd followed them or what he'd do if he found their house. Probably unload some of the drugs in his lunch cooler. It wouldn't have been the first time he'd marketed directly to a user, rather than through his buyer. The risk was higher, of course, but so were the profits. He'd keep an eye on this girl and perhaps help her out with some pills. After all, that was why he'd gotten into health care, to help people.

Driving back toward his apartment in Kingston, he couldn't help but notice the visual reversal of fortune that marked the landscape. The houses and cars became smaller and the weeds taller as he made his way from suburbia to the real world. His phone rang before he could lament any further.

"You up for a transfer?" the dispatcher asked him.

Derek looked at his watch. It was close to four o'clock. Between the drives back to the station to pick up the ambulance and then the patient, the voluminous stack of paperwork they'd need to complete to get paid, and the trip back, he knew he'd be committed for the next few hours. "What's the rate?"

"Regular rate, plus overtime if you're eligible."

With the canceled hours this afternoon, Derek knew he wasn't eligible for overtime for the day, or the week. But, of course, his job was all about the fringe benefits. "What's the transfer?"

"Some old guy up at Garden Memorial. Hip fracture. He's one of Dr. Ball's patients, and he needs a ride from their inpatient rehab unit to his house in Wilkes-Barre."

And there it was, he thought. Opportunity. A patient with a hip fracture was likely to go home with a prescription for pain meds, and in addition to the money he'd make for his time on the ambulance call, he'd likely pocket another hundred if he could pilfer some pills. And then, when he got the elderly guy home, who could anticipate what they'd find? Money? Jewelry? Probably no electronics, but you never knew. "Okay. I'm in."

It was an hour's drive to Garden, with Derek taking his time behind the wheel, and Ned, the paramedic, humming tunes from the passenger seat. They were paid hourly, after all. The large highways and congested towns along their borders shrank before their eyes as they climbed into the mountains. Derek knew the route; several times a month they were called to transfer patients from Garden's ER or inpatient units to the hospitals in Scranton and Wilkes-Barre.

Finally, they reached the hospital and parked in the designated area. Visiting hours had started because a steady stream of people flowed into the building, a rather impressive complex for such a small town. The ER parking lot seemed empty by comparison. Derek decided to check it out. "I'm going to grab a soda while you get started on the paperwork, okay?"

"Only if you get me one, too," Ned replied.

Derek quickly found the ER registration area, and to his delight, the waiting room was nearly empty. He turned on the charm for the young girl at the desk. "Hey, there. I'm with PATA, and we just drove up from Wilkes-Barre on a call. The ride was a killer and now my back's out. Any chance I can see the doctor in the next few minutes? We really need to get this guy home, but I don't think I'm going to get any sleep tonight if I don't get some meds."

The cute girl frowned in sympathy, then turned to her computer screen. "Only a few patients in the ER. Let me register you and I'll go talk to the doc, okay?"

Derek leaned on the counter and breathed a sigh of relief, then hobbled to a chair after she returned his insurance card. PATA's insurance plan sucked, and his ER deductible was high, so he'd need to get quite a few pills from this visit to make it worthwhile. But it could turn out to be a good source for him, and what successful businessman never took a chance?

Cute girl swiped her ID badge and disappeared behind the locked doors. Derek's eyes oscillated between them and his watch. He had twenty minutes or so before the EMT started looking for him. To his relief, the doors opened a minute later and she called him in.

"I explained it to the doctor and he'll see you right away."

Derek smiled the charming smile. "I could kiss you," he said, and she blushed in response, then directed him to his room. Seconds later, a man in a long white coat marched into the room, and Derek was afraid he was in trouble. He was an older man, probably in his sixties, and wore a shirt with a tie beneath his jacket.

"Dr. Sales. So, young man, bad back, huh?"

"Yeah. It's given me problems off and on for years. Herniated disk. They thought I'd need surgery, but the doctor sent me for some pain shots and physical therapy, and it cleared up."

"When was that?"

"About two years ago. It flared up again about a year ago, but since then it's been fine."

"What did they do for you last time?"

Derek reached for his smartphone. "I can't remember the names of all these medications. They wanted to try to reduce the inflammation with steroids, and they gave me a few other pills for pain and spasm, bed rest for a week, that kind of stuff. Let me see, here's the list." He read it aloud, then looked up again. "The doctor says it's a really high dose of the pain medicine, but he says that's what you need for this kind of pain. They only give it to you for a short time, because he says you can get hooked on those things, and I agree. I've known a few guys with drug problems, and that's the last thing I need."

"That is a high dose of oxycodone, Derek. Your doctor's right. But if you taper it like that, you should be okay from the addiction point of view. I hope it helps your pain, though. It doesn't really do anything to make you better, just sort of masks the symptoms."

"Yeah, I know. I'm just in agony now, and I thought since I was here I'd see if you can help me. By the time I get back to Wilkes-Barre my doctor's office will be closed, and the guy on call will never phone these meds in. They're strong, like you said. So it's your ER or the one in Wilkes-Barre if I want any relief tonight."

The doctor nodded understandingly, and Derek's hopes rose. If the doctor gave him the ten-day taper like he'd asked for, he'd have at least thirty tablets in his hand by the end of the day. Four hundred fifty migs of oxycodone. If he could sell them himself, he'd have a small fortune. Or perhaps he'd have a little party and get really, really blasted.

"Do you want me to send these scripts over to the hospital pharmacy?" the doctor asked after a rather thorough exam.

"That would be great. Then I won't have to wait at my pharmacy." He secretly hoped the pharmacy's system didn't link to other networks, or they'd find different prescriptions from a few other doctors, and he'd be busted. Dr. Sales might cancel the orders for his meds. Derek had been careful, though. He got a prescription only every few months, and he just used the ER about once a year. Hopefully, that pattern didn't alarm the pharmacist enough to place a warning call to the doctor.

"I'm only doing this as a professional courtesy, young man. You should really see your doctor and keep these meds on hand at home for an emergency like this. Understand?"

"I do."

The doctor went to do his paperwork, and the nurse came in

and got his history and vital signs. It was a reversal of the typical pattern, but Derek had achieved his goal. He'd be upstairs with the EMT in a few minutes. After signing his paperwork, he hobbled to the vending machine and then up the steps to meet the patient, a rather gregarious octogenarian who couldn't wait to get home.

Ned was still at his task, so Derek stored the soda bottles beneath the seat and began pushing his patient toward the elevator, limping, just in case the cameras were watching. "I'll meet you downstairs," he informed Ned, who looked up and smiled.

"Did you get my soda?" he asked.

Derek retrieved one bottle and tossed it his way. "I dare you to open it now," he said, and Ned laughed.

"You're an ass, you know that? How about swinging by the pharmacy in the basement. They have some prescriptions for him."

Bingo, Derek thought.

"I could sure use one of those sodas. Better yet, a good cup of coffee and a decent meal. This place isn't known for its food, I'll tell you that."

The patient shook his head, and Derek reached down for the other bottle, then handed it to him. "Here you go."

The man took the proffered bottle, then quickly handed it back. "Open it for me. Please."

Derek did as instructed. "What's your name?"

"Will. Wilbur's probably on your paperwork."

The elevator car arrived. "Where you from, Will?"

"South Wilkes-Barre, born and raised. How about you? What's your name?"

"Derek, and I'm from Kingston. Born and raised."

Will didn't smile at the joke. "How long's the ride gonna be? Can you put the lights on and get me home faster? There's a nice tip in it for you."

"About an hour. How'd you end up here in Garden if you're from down there?"

"Shitty luck, young man. I came up here for the Fourth of July. My niece had a family reunion, and since she's my only family, I let them haul my creaky bones up here for the party. Then one of those toddlers tripped me, and down I went. Broken hip. Left side. Had surgery, then therapy."

"Sounds like some bad luck, all right. But how are you doing now?"

"I'm getting by, thanks to that cane there."

"Do you live on one floor?"

"No, but they're planning to help me out. I just have to get through tonight, and then the visiting nurses are coming to set me up with a hospital bed. One night on the couch won't kill me."

They arrived at the pharmacy and both of them paid for their prescriptions. Derek couldn't help noticing the thick stack of bills in Will's wallet or the labels on the prescription bottles. Diazepam and hydrocodone. Bingo, again.

"So you live alone, huh?" Derek asked as they reversed their steps.

"Yeah, my wife died a while back. My niece keeps trying to talk me into an old folks home, but I don't want that. I'm happy where I'm at, with my memories of my wife and kids."

"Where are your kids?"

"One of them's in Florida. Retired there. The other's in Connecticut. Don't see either of them much. Judy, my niece, comes every week to take me shopping and cleans up a little bit, though. That's nice."

"You're lucky to have her."

"It's not about luck. She knows I've got a few bucks, and she never minds the hundred I slip her when she comes."

Derek thought back to the wallet he'd noticed in the pharmacy. Would Will notice a few missing bills? Probably not. Then he thought of the paperwork in Will's hand. Surely the wallet had been in the hospital's safe, and surely there was a receipt for it somewhere. It might be easy pickings to slip a few bills out, but too risky. Who else would they blame except him if Will decided to count his money when he got home?

They reached the van and Derek loaded Will in, finishing just as Ned arrived. "Perfect timing," he said.

Neither Ned nor Derek said much on the way to Wilkes-Barre, as Will took total advantage of his captive audience and talked the entire time. When they were just a few blocks away, Will asked a favor. "I don't have a thing in my house to eat, far as I know. Would you two mind stopping at the mini-market to pick up a few things for me? There'll be a nice tip in it for both of you."

Derek looked at Ned, who shrugged. What was a few more minutes, right? "Sure, Will. What do you need?"

He opened his wallet yet again and pulled out a hundred-dollar bill. "They'll tell you they can't cash a hundred, but you tell them you're with me and they'll do it." Then he rattled off a list of groceries that Ned checked off on the memo pad on his phone. Ned left, and Derek was alone with Will once again.

"This neighborhood sure isn't what it used to be, huh, Will?"

Will nodded in disgust. "Sure isn't. The good people have moved. Or died, ha ha ha. You'll see, Derek. When I die, some slumlord from out of town will buy up the place and convert it into apartments for college students. Party city."

Ned emerged hauling two bags of groceries in one hand and a beverage tray in the other. Three iced coffees wiggled in the flimsy cardboard, and Derek jumped out of the van to lend a hand. "I love you, man," he said with a smile.

"It's his dime," he replied, tilting his head toward their patient.

"Oh, wow!" Will said. "I haven't had a decent cup of coffee in weeks."

"The lady at the counter tipped me off that you're partial to caramel-flavored iced coffee."

"They're good girls who work in there," Will said around his straw.

Derek looked at him, slurping down the coffee, and the thought hit him like a sucker punch. His little bag from the pharmacy was in the back of the van, away from Ned's eyes, but close enough, the pills tiny enough to crush and slip into a drink, such as an iced coffee, if there was any left when they arrived at their destination. Those little pills were potent enough to knock someone out, permanently.

Derek put his drink back into the cup holder and eased the van out into traffic, then pulled into the driveway beside Will's house a block away. In the rear was a small detached garage and shrubs gone wild, giving the small yard privacy from every direction.

"Front door or back?" Ned asked.

"Front, I think. Close shot to the couch, where I'll be sleeping tonight."

"Easy enough," Derek said and looked at Ned. "Patient first, then I'll come back for the food, okay?"

"Sounds like a plan."

The automatic lift lowered Will to the ground, and Derek pushed him toward his front door. Together, Ned and Derek lifted the wheelchair up the porch steps and then through the threshold. Ned went to work settling their patient while Derek retreated to the van.

The oxys broke apart easily as he used the bottle lid and the edge of his phone as a mortar and pestle. He wasn't sure how many pills it would take. With Will on Vicodin already, he might be tolerant of the drug. But even tolerant people couldn't handle a hundred migs of oxy. Derek ground up seven tabs until they were just a pile of powder, then mixed it into his iced coffee. Grabbing the grocery bags, he closed the ambulance door and headed back into the house.

"Just sign here, sir," Ned was saying to Will. Will had taken a seat in a worn and comfy-looking recliner by his television, and the iced coffee was sitting on the coffee table a few feet away. Derek quickly switched the cups and then headed to the kitchen with the groceries. After emptying the contents of both bags onto the counter, he returned to the living room.

"Hand me my coffee, would you?" he demanded of Derek.

Derek happily complied and held his breath for a second as Will took a big swig from his drink. He didn't release his breath until Will looked up at him with a smile on his face. "Deeelicious!"

"Good. Now, how about your medication? Do you have any pain from the drive?"

He nodded. "Just a little. I'm more worn out than anything."

"Maybe you should take your pills now just to be on the safe side."

"Do you think so?"

Looking to Ned for support, Derek paused.

Ned answered for him. "It's been a long day for you, and a long few weeks. I think you should take your medication and lie down on that couch and call it a day."

"How about if I use the bathroom first?"

While Ned waited by the door, Derek volunteered to grab a pillow and blanket. "Upstairs on my bed. First door on the left."

Derek bounded up the stairs, not daring to snoop around but observing everything anyway. There were multiple items of furniture in this room and what appeared to be three additional bedrooms on the second floor. A door halfway down the hallway probably led to the attic he'd seen from the street. Who knew what he'd find when he came back later?

With the pillow and blanket in hand, he retreated to the first floor and arranged a comfy nest for Will on the old, worn couch. Then he pulled the television stand over a few feet and angled it toward the couch, and turned the end table so it was easy to reach. The iced coffee was the final addition to the arrangement.

Derek surveyed the scene. It would be a nice place to die.

"I'm going to use the facilities myself," Derek said. In the bathroom, he raised the window and unlocked the screen, then lowered the window to within an inch, allowing enough room to slip his fingers underneath when he returned later.

In the living room, Will had just reached his destination. Before he settled into the couch, he reached into his wallet and pulled out two bills. After handing one to each of them, he thanked them for their kindness. It wasn't until they were outside that Derek looked at the bill. It was a fifty.

He couldn't wait to search the house later. With Will either dead or in a deep, deep sleep, he'd have plenty of time to search for more fifty-dollar bills.

CHAPTER EIGHT

Witness Protection

Mac was on her deck when the alarm on her watch began chirping, announcing the official start of her day. It had unofficially started an hour earlier, when she'd pulled herself out of bed, ending the torture of fragmented sleep she'd endured since turning off her lamp at midnight. She'd never been a sound sleeper, but with details of a new case nagging her neurons, sleep was virtually impossible.

The details of the Hawk case were quite troubling. Sipping her coffee, she stared at the black surface of the lake, still and smooth in the distance. Above and behind her, an evergreen's broad, prickly branches hid her vision of the sinking moon and dampened the sounds of this early morning. Birds called out to one another, but they seemed respectful of the humans sleeping in campers and tents around the lake, and they kept their chatter to a minimum. Soon, the din of early risers would mark the beginning of the day, and then their children would shatter the quiet, crying and yelling in rage and delight as another day unfolded at the Endless Mountains Wilderness Resort.

The campground along the Susquehanna River had been in Mac's family for seventy years, and she'd spent her childhood here, helping run the camp from the time she was old enough to organize kickball games. Even though she had nothing to do with the operation of the business now, she still owned one of the premier spots along the lake. She'd leveraged her sweat equity for a little slice of land off in the corner of the lake, where the stream that gave it life curled through the woods. She'd built a cabin here, just three rooms, but her own personal paradise. It could be noisy at times, but eventually, all the campers went to sleep and she had this view, and this peace, and it grounded her, as it had since she was a little girl.

The grounding was helpful, a necessity. Her job gave her an inside look at the horrors of everyday life—violence done unto man by each other, by the machines they created, and, occasionally, by Mother Nature. No matter what the cause, it was awful to witness life cut violently short, and while she was determined to find justice for the people whose lives were destroyed, she didn't pretend it was free. Justice was pricy, paid for with the ulcers in her stomach and the circles under her eyes. She'd seen her colleagues die too young, from stress and the alcohol they used to manage it. It was yet another tragedy she'd witnessed firsthand.

Getting caught up in work was easy, and Mac knew she had to take time to relax. She did relax. She forced herself to. Once a week, she met with friends. In the summer, she played golf. In the winter, they watched a game on TV. She practiced martial arts and occasionally taught self-defense. She didn't date, though. She'd never found a woman who understood the commitment she'd made when she took her oath, and she'd stopped trying. Instead, she settled for an early morning view of the lake, or a good book, or a tough workout. She hoped her morning coffee with nature was neutralizing whatever evil forces were working against her.

At the moment, it seemed a very evil force was working against her, and his name was Edward Hawk. The Hawk case was promising to gray her hair. The matter had seemed relatively simple at the onset; Hawk had kidnapped three people and held them at gunpoint. It was nothing she hadn't seen before, except none of it made sense. No money was involved, and no domestic violence. The perp was a *physician,* a professional with a lot to lose. Either he'd cracked up, or he had more to lose by doing nothing than he did by committing the kidnapping. As she'd started digging into his motives, she realized Dr. Edward Hawk had a lot to lose. Although the preliminary evidence was circumstantial, it seemed the good doctor was a serial killer.

Even though the evidence was telling, and obvious to her, it was all circumstantial. Murder charges would be hard to prove. For the moment, though, it didn't matter. They had him on the kidnapping, and hopefully they could hold him in jail while they investigated the suspicious deaths linked to him. Hopefully.

The kidnapping charges had seemed like a slam-dunk, but now her case was looking more like an air ball. Dr. Jessica Benson had disappeared. She was the prosecution's key witness, and though Mac had talked to her briefly, she needed more information. The preliminary hearing was only three days away. The doctor hadn't answered her calls and had ignored email and phone messages Mac had sent. A knock at her door had also been futile, and, using her keen detecting skills, she'd determined that no one had seen the doctor for days.

She'd next approached Benson's father, the sheriff. As a victim of the kidnapping himself, he was proving to be a weak witness. The more Mac talked to him, the more convinced she became that he suffered some form of dementia. His carrying a gun concerned her, and she'd made a few calls about that, but ultimately, that wasn't her mission. Building a case was, and nothing the sheriff said helped her case. He hesitated before sentences, stopped frequently in the middle of them, and seemed to change his mind three or four times before convincing himself of his own answers. Mac suspected he was confused, but he came across as deceitful. Either way, he could be pulled apart on the witness stand like a piece of cotton candy. She could just see the defense attorney's smile as he got his client off because her witness was too confused to be of help.

The coroner had seemed a promising witness at first, but now Mac was worried about her, too. Her photographic memory enabled her to recall details that helped the case, minutiae like the mole on Hawk's left ankle and the ringtone for his phone's alarm. When Mac had first interviewed her, Wendy was shaky, but her testimony was perfect. As time passed, though, she seemed to become increasingly emotional about the ordeal, and Mac was concerned. When Mac asked her about Hawk at the accident scene, she'd paled. Now, she couldn't even speak without choking up and seemed to have a difficult time concentrating on Mac's questions. At the moment, she wasn't looking very reliable, and Mac's case wasn't looking very strong. And without a solid witness giving testimony against him, Hawk could walk.

Mac sipped her coffee and thought about Jessica Benson. They'd tracked her cell phone to the Hartley Clinic, a psych hospital outside Philly. Even if she answered one of those emails, chances were she would be in no condition to testify. When Mac had seen her, she'd looked awful, and after what she'd been through, a case of PTSD was certainly possible.

So if the doctor was unavailable, and the coroner and the sheriff unreliable, she had to find another witness. The DA didn't need much, just someone to attest that Hawk had kidnapped the three victims. Dr. Ward Thrasher might be the answer. Thrasher had rescued them all, so surely she'd be able to testify. She'd told Mac during a brief interview that she and Benson were friends, but the background check showed they'd lived at the same residence in Philadelphia for more than five years. Benson had just changed her driver's license address to Garden. Mac suspected a recent breakup, and she figured Dr. Ward was roaming around the mountains so she could stay close to Dr. Jessica.

Fortunately, the cell-phone companies had gotten around to putting a satellite overhead, and she had service. After looking up the number for the Endless Mountains Medical Center, she dialed and held her breath, hoping Thrasher was at work. Her call was transferred to the ER, and Mac was surprised when the doctor answered on the first ring.

"It seems I'm in luck this morning, Dr. Thrasher. I was hoping I'd find you at the hospital. This is Detective Calabrese from the Pennsylvania State Police. We spoke at the hospital in Garden a few days ago, and I need to ask you a few questions."

She heard a chuckle. Not the typical response she heard when calling witnesses on the phone. "Keeping doctors' hours, Detective?"

The question startled her as much as the laughter had. She must be losing her edge. Still, she decided to play along with Thrasher. After all, she needed her help. "I think cops invented the overnight shift. You doctors just jumped on the bandwagon after you saw how productive we are at three a.m."

"You could be right. I tend to get a lot done in the middle of the night. But anyway, how can I help you?"

Mac plunged forward without pause. "I have a theory. The key witness in the Edward Hawk case is missing. Dr. Benson hasn't been seen for three days. Her father won't say where she is, but I think he's protecting her. I think maybe she's had some sort of mental collapse that she doesn't want anyone to know about. After all, it wouldn't look good if a doctor came out and said she was emotionally unstable. I don't expect you to tell me if she's just taken off somewhere, or if she's in the hospital, but I ask you to tell me one thing. In your opinion, will Dr. Benson be able to testify at the preliminary hearing in three days?"

As she paused for a breath, she heard Thrasher clear her throat. "It's not likely Jess will be testifying."

Mac shook her head. Just as she thought. It was looking more and more like Benson was suffering from PTSD, and she hoped she'd come around in the year or so it would take to bring Hawk to trial. But if she didn't find a witness for the preliminary hearing, there would be no trial. "Doc, I need your help."

"Okay, sure," she said without hesitation.

Mac explained the situation.

"So you think the sheriff is losing his mind, huh?" Ward asked. "It makes sense. He hasn't seemed right for the past year. I thought it was just stress over his wife's illness and then her death. Maybe it's more, though."

"I need your testimony at the preliminary hearing, so we can establish the facts of the crime and the DA can get an indictment."

"I'll be happy to. Hawk's insane and needs to be locked up. If I can help with that, I'm in."

Mac breathed a sigh of relief. Oftentimes, people didn't want to get involved with something like this, especially when the defendant was a colleague.

"How well did you know Dr. Hawk?" she asked.

"Only by reputation, which is what started all this trouble." Mac took notes as Thrasher explained how her colleagues had complained about Hawk, eventually raising her own suspicions about his conduct. "So you work for the same company as Dr. Hawk?"

"Yes." Ward explained how rural hospital sometimes found themselves in need of physicians to staff their emergency departments, and how she and Hawk had both been filling the voids.

"Why are you doing this kind of work? I checked you out. You have an impressive resume. Why'd you leave Philly?"

She heard Thrasher clear her throat again before admitting she and Benson had been domestic partners. They'd come to Garden to care for Jess's ailing mother. "I'm sorry to hear that," Mac said. Mrs. Benson's death explained the trip back to Garden, but not the locum tenens work Thrasher had been doing. "Why'd you quit the hospital in Garden?"

Thrasher was silent. Was she thinking or not wanting to answer the question? After a moment she spoke. "Jess ended our relationship. I thought she just needed some time, so I began working for the locums company so I could stay close by and be here for her."

"How's that going?"

"It's over. Jess is dating again, and so am I. But we're still friends."

"And that's how you ended up in Garden on the night she disappeared? You were looking for her, because she's your friend?"

Mac didn't want to sound too abrasive, but it seemed like Dr. Thrasher still had feelings for her ex. That could complicate the investigation and the eventual trial, too.

"Yes, that's exactly it. I called her around four o'clock to tell her my thoughts about Hawk. Three hours later, she went missing. I was worried."

"So you went to Garden looking for her."

"Yes. My…girlfriend, Abby, came along. We checked Jess's house and her dad's place. Then we stopped at another friend's house to brainstorm. That friend, Frieda, has a nephew who's a state trooper. He was able to somehow locate the sheriff and learned that Jess was okay. It was late by then; Abby and I decided to spend the night at Frieda's, where a phone call from Hawk awakened us."

"What exactly did he say? This is important for the testimony at the trial. You'll be one of the only people who can tell what happened. Without Dr. Benson to testify, and without the coroner, Hawk could turn this around and say the sheriff kidnapped him. After all, when the witnesses arrived, Hawk was the one with the bloody nose."

"Let me start over. Hawk didn't call me. Or maybe he did. The call came from Jess's phone, and she spoke first. I remember her asking me where I was. I…it was complicated, our breakup. I didn't want her to know I'd gone to Garden to look for her. I didn't want to seem like a stalker. So when she asked me where I was, I balked. I said the first thing I thought of. I told her I was in Philly."

Dr. Ward didn't want Dr. Jessica to know she'd been looking for her. This case just keeps getting more and more interesting, Mac thought. "Then what happened?"

"Hawk got on the line, and he said—"

"This is important. How did you know it was Hawk? You only met him once."

"I just figured it was him. When Jess disappeared, I feared the worst. I'd just told her he was a murderer, and I was sure she wouldn't take my word for it. I knew she'd check out his cases or confront him. So when I heard his voice, I knew it was him. I said, 'Hawk,' and he said something about me being smart enough to figure it all out."

"So, he never said his name?"

Ward didn't hesitate but became more excited as she seemed to recall details of their conversation. "No, but I *know* it was him. Because of our conversation. He told me he was aware I'd been following him every month, and he wanted to know what I knew."

"He said that?"

"Not verbatim, no. But that's what he said."

"Okay, then what?"

"He told me if I wasn't at the cabin in two and a half hours, he'd kill Jess. And he told me he also had the sheriff, and that if he saw anyone suspicious near the cabin, he'd kill them all. And he told me I knew he would do it. I knew he'd killed already."

"So how'd you come up with this idea for a posse?"

Ward told Mac her fears about calling the police, that Hawk had nothing to lose by killing everyone, and how she knew some local guys with Quadrunners who could help her with the mountain rescue. "When you got to the cabin, what exactly did you see?"

"The sheriff had his gun pointed at Hawk. Hawk was on the floor, with blood pouring out of his nose. It was on his shirt, his pants, his hands. He was trying to hold pressure with one hand, and he held the other underneath to catch the blood. Jess and Wendy were taped to the kitchen chairs, and they both had strips of tape over their mouths."

"Did anyone else see them tied up? Or did you free them before the posse arrived?"

"Let me think. Abby was right behind me. I can give you her contact information if you don't have it. And Frieda was right there behind us. I'm sure they both saw the girls the way I did. I pulled the tape from everyone's mouth, so I don't think it was there when the guys arrived. It took them a minute to get up to the cabin. We had to cut their arms and legs free, though, so I think probably everyone saw them tied up."

"Good. That's good information, Doc. I think you'll be a powerful witness. Are you ready to testify?"

"Yes. Hawk needs to be put away. What about the murders at the hospitals? Are you looking into them?"

"Good question. I wish I had an easy answer for you. These murders, if they were murders—and I don't think we've proved that yet—occurred in at least three or four different counties. Those are just the ones we're aware of. That means multiple jurisdictions are involved. Someone from my team is looking at this, but I'll be closely involved. Have you talked to someone from the state police in Tunkhannock yet?"

"Someone was here and spoke with Abby. She's the CEO of the hospital. And they took copies of all the records we flagged. I didn't talk to anyone, though."

"You will, don't worry."

"Yeah. I didn't think I could avoid that one."

"I'm just curious, Doc. What made you look into Hawk the way you did?"

"You know what, Detective, I can't really take credit. It took a whack over the head to make me see it. When I calculated it, I realized the odds of these murders being coincidence were just impossible."

"But your evidence is all circumstantial."

"Doesn't that count? I mean, really, his patients die at a rate about five times more frequent than anyone else's. He's gotta be killing people. It's the only explanation."

Mac sighed as she leaned back and looked at the lake. Over the distant mountains, she detected a faint glow that heralded the sunrise. The birds were chattering away, and a few campers were making noises that were unmistakably human. It was all so perfect, except the circumstantial evidence made for a weak case.

"Let's focus on getting Hawk on the kidnapping charges. The murder investigations will come next."

Mac told her what time to be in court, and she closed the phone after thanking her for her time and effort. She leaned back and thought through her case again. Would it seem suspicious to the defense if the DA failed to call any of the kidnapping victims to the stand? Thrasher was an outstanding witness, but shouldn't one of the three victims testify? She supposed it didn't matter. The sheriff was crazy, the coroner was on her way to crazy, and the doctor was in exile. She didn't have any choice.

Her short hair was easy to manage, and Mac covered her fingers with some gooey stuff before arranging her thick, blond strands into a perfect bed-head coif. She smiled at her reflection. Perfect. Her blue eyes didn't appear tired, but the bags under them suggested she'd packed for an overnight trip. At least she didn't look like she'd been on a ten-day cruise. After brushing her teeth, she changed into her standard Brooks Brothers suit and headed to her office.

Guiding her Crown Vic through the unpaved roads of the camp with just her parking lights had become a rather simple effort, and a few minutes later, Mac was going full speed on the paved country road that led to the barracks and her personal office. A pile of reports greeted her, and she leafed through them, finding some things she'd been waiting for from the lab, new things that would need her attention, and phone calls to return. It amazed her how many witnesses called her late at night, or early in the morning, suddenly remembering details they'd forgotten.

Would another call to Jessica Benson help? If Jess was really sick, nothing might work. But how could Mac not try? Look what was on the line. Yes, all of the evidence against Hawk in the murder cases was circumstantial, but it still added up to serial killer. Mac couldn't let him walk. Men like him didn't tend to stop. It was a hunger, like the need for food, or air, or sex.

Mac needed to stop Hawk now. If she didn't, she wouldn't have a second chance.

That meant she needed to reach Dr. Jessica Benson.

Mac had worked with battered women in the past. Closely, in fact, as she taught self-defense to women from the shelters in local counties. They'd experienced terrible traumas, and she tried to be the one who eased their burdens. She didn't intend to make their lives harder, but sometimes, she had to do the difficult thing. If these women didn't testify, if she didn't cajole and coax and coerce, the perps who'd beaten them and raped them and robbed them would go free. And they'd do it again to someone else. It was hard to face someone who'd hurt you, a man who'd stolen your dignity and your power, and testify against him. But it had to be done. It was the only way the system could work.

Her decision made, Mac dialed Jessica's number. She wasn't surprised when it went to voice mail, just as the prior half dozen calls had. She had her speech ready when the tone sounded. "Dr. Benson, Detective Calabrese here, again. I know you've been through a terrible ordeal because of Dr. Hawk. Testifying against him is probably a scary prospect. Even the thought of seeing him again must be terrifying. But if you don't testify, Dr. Benson, Hawk could go free. And we both know if he does, he's not coming back to face any more charges. He was ready to leave the country when we caught him, and he'll be gone as soon as we give him the chance. I don't know where he'll go, but we both know what he'll do when he gets there. He's going to kill innocent people. If you can gather the strength and the courage to face him and tell your story, I guarantee you he'll go to prison for a long time. He won't be able to hurt anyone else again. The hearing is in three days. The county courthouse, one o'clock. I hope I see you there."

Mac ended the call and refilled her coffee, then went back to her desk to review the reports of other active cases in the department. It looked like the little bags found at the triple fatality in the SUV indeed contained heroin. Shultz and his colleagues had recovered seven thousand dollars in small bills and two stolen handguns from the scene. It was likely the three dead teens had already made a stop or two before their fatal crash. The accident-reconstruction team had finished their report in short order, and Mac reviewed that. High speed was the ultimate cause. The experts estimated the vehicle was going nearly seventy miles per hour on a winding road when the driver lost control. The tragedy infuriated Mac, and she signed the report and put it aside, happy to move on to other matters.

When her stomach growled hours later, she called in an order for a pizza. When it began grumbling again that evening, she looked at the clock and decided to head home for the night. She deserved at least one home-cooked meal in a day, and she planned to grill some veggies for a wrap to eat along with the fresh corn she picked up from a farm stand beside the road.

She tried to tell herself to relax, but it was useless. She'd be up before the sun again tomorrow and start all over. Hopefully, it would be a better day.

Chapter Nine

Big Steps

Leaning back in the comfortable club chair in the large meeting room that housed the group therapy session, Jess closed her eyes. Try as she might, she couldn't tune out the voice of the woman speaking about her history of sexual abuse. Or was the voice just a memory of a tale she'd heard countless times in the past week? So many women in this group had been abused as children that she felt excluded from their club, inferior in some way for choosing addiction as an adult rather than having it decided for her by the cruel influences of childhood. If they weren't abused, they were neglected, or their parents were addicts. Of the twenty women around her, fifteen of them had similar tales to tell. Sticking with Ward's story as the trigger for her downfall had helped Jess to remember the lie, but it sounded lame in comparison. She didn't want to hear any more.

She'd been at the clinic for eight days, and after just one she'd felt well enough to go home. The medication completely satisfied her drug cravings, and she was amazed to see how well it worked. After a few meetings with the psychiatrist she'd come to agree that she did indeed have PTSD, but she was convinced her case was mild. If Ward would have taken her, she would have already left, but she wanted more than just a ride home from Ward. And if she wanted more—a relationship, a home, a life—she had to go through this month and prove to Ward she'd changed.

Opening her eyes, Jess tried to focus on the conversation once again. Sarah, a new girl, was speaking. She seemed young, too thin to be healthy, and covered from neck to feet in tattoos. "So I looked at the picture on the front page of the newspaper and thought, 'Holy fuck, that's Damian.' I wasn't sure what to do, you know? I mean, it's not every day your boyfriend robs a bank, right? When I got home after work, he was high, like usual, and I told him about the picture. He just sort of flipped, running around the apartment trying to get some shit together so he could leave town. He didn't even have his bag packed when the cops started pounding on the door. There were drugs in the house and, of course, some money from the robbery, so they hauled us both to jail. The prosecutor decided I was a good candidate for drug court, so here I am. Whatever."

"Thanks, Sarah," the moderator said, and a chorus of supportive remarks from the rest of the group followed her response.

Jess regretted that she'd missed the beginning of Sarah's tale. She knew how she'd gotten to rehab, but how had Sarah ended up in an apartment with a bank-robbing drug addict? Was she another victim of abuse and neglect? More importantly, could she beat this addiction? Jess knew how hard it was, even with all the advantages she had—a good job, a good family, financial security. Not a single person she knew well used drugs. Her people were good people, good citizens. They would support her, if she chose to share her struggle with them. She wouldn't, of course. How could she, when she was hiding her addiction from the state medical board? But if anyone could make it, she could. She had every reason to get her life back, which was just what she planned to do.

What about Sarah, though, and the other women like her? How would they ever find their way? It seemed like all their friends and families were fighting the same battles. Where could they draw strength? Who could they lean on? Sure, she'd been going to the stupid AA and NA meetings, and she gained some comfort from sharing her struggle with others who understood it, but that was for an hour or two a day. Even though she didn't feel she needed the rehab, she was enjoying the process. For the first time in her adult life, she was taking care of herself instead of working, studying, reading, preparing. She was doing yoga and meditating, talking to people, and for the most part, listening. She was opening up about her own insecurities, the issues that perhaps had helped her along the road of addiction. Hearing other people's stories was comforting and affirming, but at the same time, exhausting. At the end of each meeting she didn't stick around to socialize. Instead, she bolted, back to the quiet of her room where she could breathe and refocus. Relax. Escape.

What if she didn't have an escape, because it was all around her, all the time? Jess thought of all the great people she had in her life and was flooded with guilt. Betraying them all, she'd chosen to isolate herself emotionally, and then physically, to hide her addiction. Instead of asking for help and facing the consequences, she'd chosen to hide and pretend. Most of her relationships had suffered as a result of her behavior. Many of them were beyond repair. Her father, she knew, would always be there. Wendy was salvageable. Ward was the big question.

As soon as the moderator closed the meeting, Jess slipped through the door and down the hall and into her room. After checking that the bathroom was empty, she snuck her iPad out of her suitcase, slipped it under her shirt, and headed into the bathroom. There was no lock on the door, but so far, her new roommate seemed to respect her privacy.

It hadn't taken a genius to figure out the facility's Internet password. HartleyGuest. Who the hell were the guests? Either you worked here or were a patient here, and if you were a patient, the Internet was off-limits. Shaking her head, Jess logged into her email account. She had thirty new messages since yesterday, most of them garbage. She filed them into the trash and then read the few that interested her. She was invited to play in a golf tournament, had a new coupon to use at her favorite Internet clothing store, and had endless possibilities for cheap travel. After deleting them, Jess logged in to her new account at the buprenorphine website.

If she wanted to beat her addiction, she needed to know everything about it. She'd signed up for classes to become a buprenorphine physician. She didn't intend to actually prescribe the drug, but the classes gave her a plethora of information. How it worked, how to best dose it, how to deal with the side effects. How to come off it. The drug's manufacturers recommended weaning after stabilizing patients for a year, but Jess was concerned about that. Many of the patients in the clinic had tried to wean and couldn't, and had ended up using again as their doctors gave them less medication. She wondered if it was too soon to start her own taper. She was taking twelve migs and felt good. Normal. Maybe tomorrow she'd take eleven, just to see what happened.

After reading a few articles on addiction and bup, she noted the time. Ten minutes until her meeting with Dr. Gompers. They'd met daily for the first few days, but now they were down to weekly sessions, and Jess was happy about that. The doctor was sharp, and Jess couldn't help but worry that her lies were going to be exposed.

"Hey," Jess said in greeting, trying to keep it light.

"How are you feeling?"

Jess briefly debated discussing a wean, but she knew better. The doctor had already told her she'd need to be on the medication for a year, so what was the point? If she was going to do this, it was on her own. "I feel great."

"You shouldn't be feeling withdrawal symptoms at this point, so that's good. How do you feel emotionally? How are your group sessions going?"

Now Jess felt she could be honest. "I feel guilty that I wasn't abused as a child and forced down the path of drug abuse. It's like I chose it."

"Everyone deals with the stresses in their life differently, Jess. People with good coping skills usually don't end up in my office. But there is the element of susceptibility as well."

"What do you mean?"

"Well, I'm sure you've seen this in your friends and family. Everyone has a drink now and again, but why can't some people stop until they're falling-over drunk?"

"Good point."

"So the issue I'm getting at with you here is stress management. You've relied on pills to manage your stress, as some people use alcohol. The drugs are the treatment for you. Do you understand that? They've become the problem, but they're also the treatment."

Jess thought for a moment. "I think I see."

"Bup will not stop you from feeling stressed. But now that you're in treatment, you can't pop a pill when you have a bad day at the office. And I don't advise you to start drinking. So how are you going to cope?"

Jess told her about her yoga and meditation routine. "And I think I need to reach out to people, too."

"Well, that's always helpful. That's why we recommend AA and NA meetings. And of course, you'll continue your counseling when you leave here. How's the PTSD?"

Jess shrugged. It was a difficult question to answer. On the one hand, she knew her experience was random, and like a lightning bolt, that sort of trouble should never find her again. She'd simply been in the wrong place at the wrong time. She felt vulnerable though, and even though she knew Hawk had been indicted at the hearing and was in jail until his trial, thoughts of him and what had happened to her were still enough to make her crave six Xanax at once. As her therapist had suggested, she'd begun to turn her fear to anger, and it was helping.

For the most part, though, she was good. The meetings had been somewhat helpful. Art therapy had exposed some character flaws, and psychodrama had allowed her to vent some pent-up feelings. And she was beating the crap out of everyone at Ping-Pong. She was considering a table for her formal sitting room at home. Maybe she'd finally learn to play beer pong, fifteen years after college. Like she'd told Ward, she was learning to lighten up.

"I think I'm doing well," she said at last.

"You seemed pretty poised last night."

Jess looked at her, confused, as she thought about the night before. Then it hit her. As they'd trekked around the grounds the night before, one of the patients had tripped and fallen, landing on her arm. When Jess reached her, she saw the obvious deformity and knew it was broken. They were about a mile from the clinic at the time, and though they had an ATV to retrieve her, Jess knew the arm needed to be splinted before the rocky ride back. Using someone's bulky sweatshirt and someone else's shoelaces, she'd made a passable model.

Her mouth went dry as she stared at the doctor, too scared to speak. Where was the doctor going with this?

When Jess still didn't reply, Dr. Gompers asked, "Former Girl Scout?"

Jess laughed. "Of course. I grew up in the mountains."

"Well, you handled that like a pro, and I thought perhaps you had learned the technique from your ex-partner, the ER doctor. So I googled Dr. Ward Thrasher, one of my best former students, and would you believe what I found on the Internet? She was involved in this horrible case where a doctor is suspected of murdering his patients. He kidnapped three people. One of them was a woman named Dr. Jessica Benson."

Jess swallowed as she slid down into the chair and closed her eyes. There seemed to be no point in denying who she was. She opened her eyes and met Dr. Gompers's gaze. "Busted."

"That you are. And now I'm not sure what to do. I have a duty to you, as my patient, to protect your secrets. I have a greater duty to mankind, to protect them from you. My question is, can you be trusted to practice medicine? To prescribe narcotics?"

Jess knew she should have pleaded, but she didn't have the energy. "I guess you're going to have to decide that for yourself."

"Tell me your real story."

Jess grabbed a tissue to wipe away tears that sprang from nowhere and began with her wrist injury. She told Dr. Gompers everything—how she'd written a prescription in Ward's name, purchased pills off the streets and from her patients. Then she told about going to the hospital and being attacked by Hawk.

"I want my life back, Dr. Gompers. I don't want to be an addict anymore. And I think I had things under control until this happened."

"I have a question, Jess."

"Shoot."

"How did you handle school? Premed, medical school, residency? That's a tough course, yet you made it."

Jess shrugged. "I suppose it was. But I buckled down and did it. Somehow. Then life started to happen, I guess."

"That's it, Jess! Life happens. It's what we do, and how we react when life happens, that makes the difference. You tend to melt down and take pills. That's what we have to fix about you—that tendency—so you can be successful in your recovery."

"So I need a plan B, huh?"

She nodded. "I think that plan should also involve your personal life. You already told me how Ward is too nice and lets you do whatever you want. Do you really think she's the right person for you?"

"I love her."

"I'm sure you do. But when you really think about it, if there was a plan B woman, someone else who you were attracted to, but maybe with a little more spine perhaps, would you be interested?"

Jess's pause answered the doctor's question.

"Ward has moved on, Jess. So should you. It's hard to be single, but you'll make it. Go out with your colleagues, join a golf league, do something to get out of the house and away from your isolation and your thoughts of Ward. Because if you do, perhaps you'll meet a woman who knocks your socks off."

Jess swallowed tears. Dr. Gompers's words were true. She loved Ward for many reasons, but none of them were enough to break up Ward's relationship with Abby. And none of them were enough to make Jess happy if she did.

"Perhaps you're right."

"Trust me, I am."

"So, what about me? About the little fibs I told you?"

"What I would like to do, as a professional courtesy not only to you, but to Ward as well, is mentor you. I want to talk to you every day after your release, to make sure you're doing what you're supposed to be doing. I'll see you back here monthly, to prescribe you your medication, if necessary, but mostly just to make sure you're able to function professionally."

"And you won't report me to the state medical board?"

"Not unless you give me a reason to."

CHAPTER TEN

A Long Road Home

I can't thank you enough," Jess said as she opened her freshly stocked refrigerator and grabbed a Coke. Without asking, she filled two glasses with ice and poured the drinks, then handed one to Ward.

"No trouble. I've been keeping an eye on the place for you. Just to give your dad a break. Do you want me go over the alarm system again?"

Jess shook her head. "It's not that different from the one we have in Philly." Sighing, she looked at Ward. "I just never thought I'd need one here."

"And you don't. You don't need to keep the neighbors out, Jess. Just Hawk. And the security system where he's at is like friggin' Alcatraz."

"Didn't Clint Eastwood escape from Alcatraz?"

"Bad example. Sorry," Ward said, but a smile appeared on her face before she hid it with her glass.

Jess sipped her soda as she looked around the kitchen, then at Ward. She'd never lived in this house when she wasn't an addict. Would she be able to adjust, when she had so many bad habits here? She looked around the room to the places she'd hidden her pills, hidden her secret life from her partner. And this was just the kitchen. She'd stashed her pills in many other places in the house so Ward would never find them. It had been painfully difficult, keeping her secret. Sobriety had to be easier.

"You got rid of my pills, right?"

Ward grinned. "The ones I could find."

"Right. Maybe you should do a clean sweep before you go."

Ward looked down her nose suspiciously. "Really, Jess?"

Jess thought for a moment. "No, I think they're all gone. Once you left, I didn't need to hide them. I think the bottles by the bed and in the medicine cabinets were it."

"Then they're gone. And you're okay with that?"

"I'm fine, really."

"Because I don't want you to do anything…rash."

"I feel good on the bup. I'm not worried, okay?"

Once again, Jess remembered why she hadn't shared her illness with Ward. Ward just wouldn't let go. She changed the subject. "So this whole day has been all about me. I feel great. Really, I do. I think my addiction is under control, my PTSD as well. But how are you? How's Abby?"

Ward's smile was controlled, as if she didn't want to brag about how happy she was. Jess couldn't help feeling a twinge of jealousy, but after her confrontation with Dr. Gompers, she knew she had to let Ward go. As much as they'd loved each other, Ward wasn't good for her. She'd spent the ensuing weeks at therapy thinking about that, about rebuilding her personal life in a way that didn't include Ward in an integral way.

"Everything's good. We're in the honeymoon phase now, so we think everything about each other is adorable."

"How gross," Jess said, not out of jealousy, but just because that's how she felt.

"We were that way once."

"Never. I've never been that way, ever."

"Well, maybe that explains why we're not together anymore, right? I'm a honeymooner and a little romantic, and you're more serious. They didn't cure you of the serious while you were on the inside, did they?"

Jess laughed. "Not a chance. Well, maybe a little. I'm trying, Ward. Really hard. I want to lighten up and enjoy my life. Hawk taught me that I can't count on tomorrow. I want to enjoy today."

"I'm glad you came clean with Dr. Gompers. Honesty and integrity are important to your recovery."

"I lied to so many people for so long the truth feels sticky coming out of my mouth."

Standing, she adjusted the dial on the AC in the window. While she'd been away, July had turned to August, and the little valley of Garden was starting to bake. It was hard to imagine that fall was only a month away, that Ward's time in the mountains was about to expire. Wondering about her plans, she turned and rested against the counter. "Have you decided about September?"

"I'm going back to work, and I plan to give them a few months' notice. Then I'm coming back to Endless Mountains."

Jess leaned back in her chair and studied Ward. A month earlier, the news would have crushed her. Now, she was happy. Perhaps she really had made some progress. "Good for you, Ward. You deserve to be happy."

When Ward shrugged, Jess changed the subject. "Tell me about the trial," she said. "I had seven phone calls from that cop. Seven. And a dozen emails. Why didn't you just tell her I was in the nuthouse?"

"I think she figured it out on her own. When she called and asked me to testify, she asked if I thought you were going to be available, and I told her no. She didn't sound surprised. I guess they could have asked for some sort of delay, but I gathered from listening to them talk that it might have given Hawk an opportunity to get bail, so I think they took their chances on me and Wendy and Zeke."

"And they came through, huh?"

Ward nodded. "Wendy was a basket case all week, according to Detective Calabrese, but she pulled herself together. It was seeing Hawk that inspired her in the courtroom. They say some witnesses cower before their accusers, but not her. She stood up to him, yelled at him, and gave such powerful testimony there was no way they couldn't indict him."

"And my dad testified, too? He's been a little shaky."

"Same story for him. Once he got on the stand he was a star.

I think they told him to stick to the facts, because that's what he did. He asked the judge if he could refer to his notes, and of course Hawk's attorney objected. So your dad cut right in, before the DA could say a word, and addressed the judge. He told him he was an officer of the law, and he'd made an official report, and because of the severity of the situation, he thought it should be read in court, so no one could dispute the facts. So the DA immediately motioned to have the report taken into evidence, and your father testified. It was hysterical. 'At 10:22, according to my Timex watch, I received a call from Dr. Edward Hawk asking me to meet him at the Towering Pines Sportsman's Association, in the cabin. He informed me that my daughter was there, having a lover's quarrel with the coroner.' Then he looked at the judge and whispered, 'Jessica is a lezbean. I guess the coroner is, too.' And then he continued with the testimony, telling the judge how Hawk had you and Wendy tied up at gunpoint, and how he'd told Hawk to call me because I'd put you up to investigating him. It was all written in his report, and he didn't stray from the script at all. The defense didn't even cross-examine him."

Jess swallowed a tear. Her dad had come through for her. And so had two very good friends.

"Thank you for testifying, too."

They were quiet. "And thank you for the good times we shared, Ward. It took a month of psychiatric exploration for me to understand why we're not right for each other, but it doesn't mean it was anyone's fault. What was wrong was how I handled things and how I ended it with you."

"You did what you thought was right in that situation. I would have done the same."

Jess picked a spot in the corner of the room to stare at, because she suddenly lost the courage to face Ward. "In the meetings, they tell us that one of the steps of recovery is to make amends to those we've harmed or hurt because of our addiction. So there's something I have to tell you, and I hope you'll forgive me for not letting you know sooner, but I was thinking like an addict then. Very self-centered."

Jess finally gathered her courage and looked at Ward, whose

face showed fear. Did she suspect what Jess was about to say? If she did, she should feel happy about the news. Perhaps. Jess only hoped Ward would forgive her. "The night you attacked Em and George, Ward, you were drugged. Someone slipped you Rohypnol. It was probably Em, and he was probably in cahoots with my father, but it was in your CSF. You had some sort of paradoxical reaction to it, thank the gods, because who knows what those two would have done with you if they'd gotten you out of the bar under the influence of that drug. You turned the tables on them and became violent. It's been known to happen with Rohypnol. So it wasn't your fault, the assault. You weren't drunk, just drugged. I'm sorry for not telling you sooner."

Ward's face was an unreadable mask. "When did you find out?" she asked. Jess studied her for a moment, hoping for some sign, but she simply looked stunned. Jess would have asked if she was okay, but what a stupid question it was. How could you be okay after you found out someone had drugged you and probably wanted to kill you, and as a result, your girlfriend threw you out in the cold? How could you forgive her for not telling you the truth when she learned it?

"The day I told you about Wendy. It took a long time for the CSF to come back, you know?"

Jess couldn't read Ward's emotions. She seemed flat. "What made you run the test? You said you didn't check an alcohol level or a drug screen because you thought I was drunk and using drugs, and you didn't want any proof so it couldn't be used against me."

"I know. But they held the spinal fluid in the lab, and after you told me you felt like you were drugged, I put it all together. My dad and Em's great plan to get you out of my life. I had to know, so I decided to order it. But I didn't know what to do with the results, you know? If I told you, either Em or my dad would be in serious trouble. And it wouldn't have changed things between us. The truth is, I needed to get away from you and the constant scrutiny of a relationship because I needed my space to use drugs and function. You stressed me, and I couldn't handle it, so I took advantage of the situation that night and broke up with you."

Ward nodded. “So that night was just an excuse, huh?”

Jess shrugged and snagged tissues from the box on her kitchen counter. “I was behaving like an addict, Ward. And I know that sounds like an excuse, but it really isn’t. It just is. And I’m sorry for the way I treated you, not just with the breakup. I wasn’t there for you after the injury. It was all about me.”

“I get it. I do,” she said softly. “And I think I probably enabled you, huh?”

“You’re easy to manipulate.”

Ward laughed. “I’ll work on that. Today, as a matter of fact. Abby and I are heading to the beach. I plan to be very bossy and not allow her to push me around.”

Jess smiled. “I think you have a plan.”

Their glasses were empty, and Ward stood. “Meetings every day, right?”

Jess shrugged. Her discharge plan included a commitment to thirty meetings in thirty days, just to keep her in the right place. Working thirteen-hour shifts didn’t leave much time for meetings, especially if she planned to travel to Scranton or Wilkes-Barre, where she could remain somewhat anonymous. It would be hard, but she’d try.

They hugged at the door, and Jess watched the woman she’d loved leave her for the last time. She was sure they would talk, or text, or email, but Jess had let Ward go, and, at long last, it seemed Ward was happy with that arrangement.

The kitchen was stocked with basics, thanks to Ward, so Jess went about the next order of business. Housecleaning. She hadn’t been home in a month, and a layer of dust had collected everywhere. After emptying her laundry into the washer, she wiped every surface within reach and allowed the fresh mountain air to blow away the musty odor that had taken over. Within a few hours, the house smelled better and looked better, and Jess felt better, too.

During her treatment for PTSD, the psychiatrist had suggested the diagnosis of OCD as well. If she had it, her case was mild, but she did have a tendency to obsess over trivialities and spent inordinate amounts of her time getting things just right. It was a stressful way to live—always wondering if things were good enough instead of just accepting that they were.

Satisfied. That was the word she was looking for. Was the house perfect? No. Could she be satisfied with it? She would try.

A nagging sense of obligation was irritating her, though. Detective Calabrese had left her multiple messages regarding the preliminary hearing, and even though she had her phone and iPad and could have responded, she'd elected not to. It was hard to explain, but when she went to the Hartley Clinic she just wasn't ready to talk about Edward Hawk. The passing days had healed her, though, and she thought she might finally be able to tell her tale without falling apart. She took out her phone and dialed the detective's number.

"Hello, Dr. Benson," a husky voice answered.

It hadn't occurred to Jess that the number was Calabrese's cell phone, but apparently, she was in the memory bank. Recovering from that little shock, she returned the greeting.

"It's good to know you're alive."

Jess didn't detect any emotion in her voice, and she was happy for that. She wasn't prepared to deal with anyone else's issues. She was simply being courteous.

"Yes, I'm alive. I'm just returning all your phone calls. And I'd like to thank you, as well. I appreciate your hard work. It's good to know that Hawk is out of circulation."

She heard the detective sigh. "Everything went well. The other witnesses—Dr. Thrasher, the coroner, your father—they were great. I still need a statement from you, though. And I'm hoping you'll be able to testify at the trial."

"I understand. I can meet with you whenever you'd like. I just have to work around my schedule in the ER. I return to work the day after tomorrow."

After agreeing to meet after Jess's overnight shift, they ended the call. Jess couldn't explain why, but she felt much better after talking to Mac. *It must be work*, she thought. *I'm looking forward to getting back to work.*

❖

Mac stared at the phone in her hand. So, Dr. Jessica Benson was back from exile. She'd been surprised when the doctor's name appeared on her caller ID. It had been more than a month since she'd disappeared, and almost as long since the preliminary hearing. Mac hadn't forgotten about her, but with other cases coming and going, and the Hawk murder investigation taking her time, the kidnapping case wasn't a priority.

It was funny how things had turned out with the preliminary hearing. Jessica would have seemed to be the ideal witness—she was the first one abducted and had witnessed the other two. It seemed she was Hawk's primary target, probably to learn what she knew about the investigation Ward Thrasher had started at Endless Mountains Medical Center. With no Jessica around to testify, Mac had been worried about the day in court. It had gone well, though, and the indictment was issued without any problems. Hawk's bail was denied, thanks to the testimony she'd given about his financial resources and the plane ticket he'd purchased. Unless he escaped from jail, he wasn't likely to spend a free day for many years.

A phone call interrupted her musings, and when it ended she went back to work. Her day was uneventful, filled with all the usual things a state police detective did—reviewing cases and reports, meeting with her team, interviewing witnesses. There were no traffic fatalities, and no homicides, and no testimony to give in court. When she finally crawled into bed that night, sleep eluded her once again. Thoughts of the mysterious Dr. Jessica Benson interrupted her, and Mac had to admit, they weren't at all unpleasant.

CHAPTER ELEVEN

Back in Business

Oh, fuck," Jess murmured, pulling back her face a second before the patient's stomach erupted, spewing vomit everywhere. "I need suction!" she shouted to the respiratory therapist. As she waited for the catheter, she looked at the medic hovering over the patient's chest. "Continue CPR."

Glancing at the cardiac monitor, Jess noted the pattern of waves that appeared one after the other on the screen. The CPR was flawless. The shocks and medications had been delivered. But unless she managed to pass the breathing tube into the patient's lungs and deliver oxygen to his heart and brain and kidneys, none of it mattered.

After suctioning out milky fluid and what appeared to be Fruit Loops, she tried once again to pass the endotracheal tube. From her position behind the patient's head, she opened his mouth with her right hand and slid the laryngoscope blade along the tongue and deep into the throat. Pulling upward and outward with her left hand, she turned the scope slightly back and forth, in search of the white membranous strips guarding the trachea's entrance. "Bingo," she said when the vocal cords came into view. Without taking her eyes off the cords, she guided the tube into the mouth, down the throat, and between the glistening bands. Once it was in position, she inflated the balloon that held the tube in place and stepped back, allowing the respiratory therapist to secure it and begin mechanical ventilation.

She watched the monitor, first the wavy line indicating the heart rhythm, then the one above it showing the air flow. It looked perfect, and as Jess watched, the oxygen level began to climb. After a minute she turned her attention back to the patient. "Stop CPR," she instructed the paramedic working on the chest, then looked at the monitor once again. As soon as the compressions stopped, so did the activity on the monitor. "Nothing," she said. "Okay, keep going."

Jess thought about her options. The most important step—shock—had failed. It was helpful to know why the heart had stopped, too. Sometimes correcting the underlying problem took the pressure off the heart and it would start again. And although most of the medications delivered during cardiac arrest didn't help, she gave them anyway. It was still the protocol, and psychologically speaking, it beat doing nothing.

This particular patient, who was only in his forties, had been found by his wife after she heard a crashing noise in her kitchen. A glass had shattered when he dropped it, and the medics found him lying in it. He might have hit his head when he fell to the tile, but likely, the fall had nothing to do with his current condition. Whatever had happened to him caused the fall. Heart attack? Ruptured aneurism? Kidney failure? Blood clot? Not a lot of things could cause such a quick death, without leaving any evidence behind. Trauma could, of course, but there was no history of that and certainly no signs on the body. Drugs could, too, but usually not so quickly, and the medics had treated him for that, anyway. Poisons could stop the heart, but that was an autopsy diagnosis, and not likely something she could reverse. If only they could get the heart to respond, the tracing on the EKG could clue them in to what was going on.

Young healthy men should not fall over in their kitchens and die.

But they did.

After almost an hour with no response to every trick Jess could think of, she ended the code. She asked the clerk to call the family doctor and Wendy, because she was sure this patient would need an autopsy. There was no way the family doctor would sign the death certificate and attest to the cause of death in a young, previously healthy man.

"Come with me?" she asked the medic who'd been at the man's house and the nurse who'd helped with the code. They needed to tell the man's wife.

Jess found her, along with three teenagers, in the counseling room set aside for such purposes. The fear on their faces was evident.

This was the hardest part of her job. Give her a budget meeting any day.

Half an hour later she wiped the tears from her eyes and found the doctor who'd relieved her an hour earlier. "Nothing to sign out," she said as she waved to the staff.

"Oh, Dr. Benson!" the clerk shouted. "The police detective's waiting for you in the lounge."

Fuck! Jess looked at the clock. The detective was scheduled to meet her at the change of shift. If she was on time—and something told Jess the detective was punctual—she'd been waiting an hour. Jess picked up her pace on the way to the staff lounge. It was her destination, anyway. Since her return to work, she'd been using a locker there, instead of her office.

"I'm so sorry," she said as she opened to door to find Calabrese leaning back in her chair, watching the news on the small television suspended from the ceiling.

Mac turned off the television in response. "Tough night?"

Jess closed her eyes and shook her head.

"Do you want me to give you a little time? Or would you like to reschedule? I can come back another day."

Jess thought about the four weeks the detective had already been waiting to talk to her. "No, I'll be okay." She looked around the lounge and suddenly felt trapped. Longing for escape, she looked at Calabrese and smiled. "But would it inconvenience you terribly if we move our meeting to my place? It's only a block away."

Mac nodded. "Sure. How about I pick up a couple of coffees and meet you in half an hour?"

Jess nodded. "Sounds great. Let me give you the address."

"Dr. Benson, I'm a detective. I've already got it."

For the first time in hours, Jess felt herself smiling. "I'm going to grab a quick shower when I get home. Wash the night away."

"I'll see you then."

❖

Mac procured two coffees from the local shop and selected a variety of pastries as well. It wasn't how she typically conducted an interview, but she suspected Jessica could use the comfort. Besides, she was fragile and needed to be handled carefully. And with the indictment already secure, there was less pressure. Jessica's statement was important, but Mac would try to keep it light.

Blue eyes met hers through the parted window curtains just seconds after she rang the bell, and Jessica's mouth widened into a thin smile when she saw the coffee and pastries.

"My favorite," she said, and though her smile grew wider, Mac thought she looked tired.

"Brilliant minds, I guess," Mac replied.

"Why don't we go into the living room? It'll be more comfortable."

As Mac followed her through the stately home, she couldn't help admiring the high ceilings and big windows, the wide planks that made up the floors, and the beautiful molding trimming every doorway. The house had been well maintained through the years. If she ever left her cabin by the lake, it would be for a place like this. "This is some house."

Jess's face brightened. "Yeah, it is. The sale is pending. I should own it soon."

"Congratulations."

"Where do you live?" Jess asked.

Mac laughed. It might bother some people, but not her. She was exactly where she wanted to be. "I actually live at a campground."

"Like in a motor home?"

"Yes and no. There are motor homes there, but I live in a house. Most of the year I'm surrounded by campers of one sort or another."

Jess looked intrigued. "How'd you end up there?"

"I was raised there. My grandparents owned it, and their house was on the property. I borrowed a little piece of land with a stream behind and a lake in front and built a cabin."

"You have utilities, right?"

Mac wasn't sure if Jess was serious, but she was enjoying her company, so she went along. "Nah." Running her fingers through her hair, she shook her head. "I keep my hair short so I only have to wash it every few days, and I use a strong deodorant."

Jess swallowed any further comment and then Mac began laughing. "Just kidding."

Jess chuckled. "I guess that was a stupid question. But it sounds like fun. Where is it?"

Mac told her.

"So that's a half-hour drive. You really are an early riser, huh?"

Mac shrugged. How could she tell her she spent her nights thinking about cases and had difficulty quieting her mind enough to sleep? She couldn't help wondering if Jess had similar troubles.

"How often do you work overnight?" Mac asked.

"About six days a month."

"That's hard, isn't it? Going from days to nights?"

"It's the worst. I usually sleep between shifts, but since I'm off tomorrow, I'm just going to stay awake today and make it an early night. It's already nine. If I can last another ten hours, I'll be great."

"Do you have a hard time sleeping after work?" Mac was curious about Jess, and it had to do with more than the case she was working on. Jess just seemed so confident, in spite of what she'd been through. It was as if she really didn't give a shit about anyone else's opinion. She'd disappeared after her abduction and could have damaged the case against Hawk, but it seemed she knew Mac wouldn't come looking for her. Or perhaps Jess would have come back to testify if Mac had found her. And although she thanked Mac for helping get Hawk indicted, she never apologized for disappearing.

Jess took a bite of a cinnamon roll and licked the sugary goo from her fingers. It was heavenly, and she told Mac so. Then she thought about Mac's question. Some days, she was so busy at work that she came home physically exhausted and fell into bed, unconscious in seconds. Other times, it wasn't so easy. "Sometimes. It's hard not to bring work home, especially when it doesn't go well. I tend to dwell on everything and go over it all in my mind. What if I'd done something differently?" She looked at Mac and saw understanding there. Suddenly Jess realized the detective probably dealt with some of the same difficult issues that she did. She was probably first on the scene to all kinds of accidents and homicides, and, just like Jess, she probably had to tell the survivors that their loved ones were dead.

"Does that help?"

"I think it does. I sort of work on a plan, so things might turn out differently the next time."

Mac put down her coffee and cocked her head, and Jess couldn't help noticing how attractive she was. Sitting in the oversized chair, she looked so calm and poised, yet Jess detected an energy around the detective that seemed to make the room brighter. As Jess studied her, the sun rays filtered through the spikes of her gelled hair and dusted her nose and cheeks with color. Radiant. The detective looked radiant.

"So your patient today? What would you do differently next time?"

The question was so far from where her mind had been that she needed a moment to regroup. Sighing, she studied the ceiling. "I'm not sure. I suppose I'll wait for the autopsy report. When I find out what caused his heart to stop, maybe it'll help."

"What do you think happened?"

"There's not too much on the list of things that kill people quickly. At his age, it was probably his heart. When I talked with the wife, she mentioned that his father had died at a young age, too."

"Don't they check for things like that?"

It was one of her great frustrations as a physician, and she frowned as she looked at the detective. "People who are healthy sometimes avoid the doctor until it's too late. If he'd gone for a checkup in the past decade, someone would have gotten a family history and checked his blood pressure and cholesterol, and his day would have ended a lot differently."

Watching discreetly, Jess thought the detective seemed to digest her words, looking for inconsistencies or lies, but when she raised her head and Jess met her eyes, she saw something else there. In that moment Jess realized it was no longer the detective she was talking with, but the woman. "So you get to talk to the families, too?"

Considering her job, Jess wasn't sure what the detective meant. "You mean I get to talk to the families when I'm treating the patients? Or I get to talk to the survivors, just like you do?"

"Both."

Jess was pleased that she'd caught the subtle reference. Calabrese seemed to take it all in, and Jess wouldn't be surprised if most people missed things like that when talking to her. "You must see some awful shit."

"It can be difficult, yes."

"Does it ever get to you?"

"You'd have to be dead to not let it get to you."

"How do you deal with it?" Jess asked, curious. Did the state police offer counseling? Would it make an officer appear weak if he or she signed up for it? And did this particular officer have to try harder to avoid such suspicions, because of her gender?

The detective smiled again. "I go to the range and shoot things."

Jess laughed. She could relate. It took a great deal of concentration to eye a target, to synchronize her breathing and heartbeat until everything else in the universe faded. "I like to shoot things, too. It's calming, like yoga."

"That's quite the dichotomy, Dr. Benson."

"That's quite a big word, Detective."

"Cops do go to school."

Jess laughed. "Touché."

"So how'd you learn to shoot?"

"I grew up at Towering Pines. I learned to shoot as a child." Her mind flashed to her last visit at the cabin, and she shook her head to chase the thought away. "I don't think I'll be heading out there for a while." She smiled to lighten her mood.

Mac shifted in her seat and leaned forward, her forearms resting on her knees, seeming to understand. "If you want to shoot, I'll take you."

"I haven't done it in a while."

"Maybe this is a good time to get back into it."

Jess wasn't sure how she felt about that. Would a gun have helped her in her struggle with Hawk? Probably not. More than likely, Hawk would have wrestled the gun from her and used it to shoot her.

"We'll see," she said, and smiled, holding up her coffee. "Thanks for this. What's it going to cost me?"

The detective's eyes flew up in surprise as she defended her motives with both hands raised.

Jess smiled. Her attempt at humor had been a success. "Kidding, Detective. Just kidding."

Shaking her head, she pulled a recorder out of some pocket or another, and Jess caught a flash of the gun on her right hip. "Why don't you call me Mac?"

Jess liked that idea. "Okay. Mac it is."

"All right, enough chitchat. Let's get to work. Start at the beginning, wherever you think that is," she said as she pressed the record button and spoke. "This is Detective Calabrese recording an interview with Dr. Jessica Benson at her home on Tulip Street in Garden."

Jess noticed another smile tilt the corner of Mac's mouth, and she gave the date and time as well. When her eyes met Jess's she saw gentle encouragement there, and Jess swallowed before she began to speak.

"It actually happened pretty quickly. Ward—uh, Dr. Thrasher called me to tell me her suspicions about Hawk—Dr. Edward Hawk. She mentioned that three of his patients had died of air embolisms in the past few months, at other hospitals around the Poconos and Endless Mountains. Embolisms are rather rare, so it was kind of surprising that Hawk would see three of them. Then I received an email from the coroner, Wendy Clemens, telling me that one of Hawk's patients at Garden had also died of an embolus. I just sort of felt like this couldn't be a coincidence. First of all, the odds are impossible. But I also just had a bad feeling about him. He was sort of creepy. I decided to go into the hospital to review Hawk's patient's chart and to check out other cases Hawk had. I was there only a minute when he attacked me. He knocked me to the floor in my office and stabbed me in the thigh. I had no idea what was going on after I felt the sting of the needle, only that I felt weak. Hawk told me he had used succinylcholine to paralyze me, and then I understood. Do you know what succinylcholine is?" Jess asked.

"I didn't, until this case."

"Okay, I just wanted to be sure you understand me. He told me he would let me live if I told him what I knew about Christian Cooney—that's the kid who died at Garden from the fatal embolus. Then he told me he enjoyed killing, and he would really appreciate it if I could tell him what tipped me off so he could avoid making the same mistakes in the future."

Suddenly it all came back to her, like a gust of wind cutting through a calm day. As Jess began to shake all over, the coffee in her cup spilled in her hand. She looked down but seemed helpless to stop the trembling. From out of nowhere, the detective's hands appeared, holding a pile of napkins, which they used to remove the coffee cup and then wipe Jess and the table and the floor.

"I should have gotten iced," she said, but when her eyes met Jessica's she knew she hadn't appreciated her attempt at levity.

"I knew-knew-knew I was go-go-going to d-die." Jess closed her eyes and leaned into Mac.

Mac abandoned all other thoughts and pulled Jess into her arms, back into the couch and to safety. Her few encounters with Hawk since the brutal attacks at the hospital and hunting club had shown him to be unremorseful, and at the moment Mac felt like murdering him for what he'd put this woman through. No wonder she'd skipped town instead of testifying. Mac couldn't imagine what it would have been like for her to be paralyzed beneath the hands of a cold-blooded killer. Not that she was minimizing the coroner's experience, but at least she had the benefit of knowing Jess was still alive after suffering the same ordeal.

"It's okay. He's behind bars, Jess, and he can't hurt you now. Shush," she said, over and over again, and she held Jess's head to her shoulder, pressed her body against her. "It's okay, Jess. Shush, it's okay."

They sat that way for an hour; Mac could testify to it because she watched the minutes tick by on the large mantel clock. Every few minutes Jess would take a deep sobbing breath and seem ready to emerge from her trance, only to begin again, collapsing into Mac for comfort.

She'd never done this before, and Mac felt out of her element. Hell, she could count on one hand the number of times she'd brought coffee and pastries for women she was dating. She never, ever did it for a witness. Yet something told her she needed to progress carefully with Dr. Benson, and what harm was there in offering comfort to a woman in distress? As long as no one ever found out about it, it wasn't a problem. And she was pretty sure neither of them would ever say a word.

"I think the coffee's cooled off, Detective," Jess said without moving.

"Mac. Call me Mac."

"Yes, you did say that, didn't you?"

"Should I throw some ice into it, Jess? Make it official?"

Jess nodded and released her hold on Mac. "On the door," she said as she watched the very shapely behind of the lead detective, trying to put her abductor out of her mind. Even in this condition, she had a hard time ignoring Mac's ass.

She sat back and felt cold in all the places Mac had touched her. It had been so nice to be held. Mac had made her feel safe and cared for. It was just what she'd needed, but she had to get it together. Mac was working on the Hawk case, and Jess was sure that meant she was off-limits. It was hard not to notice her, though. Everything about her was striking.

A moment later, Jess took the proffered cup of coffee from Mac and sipped. "Perfect," she said, and meant it. "That's a nice coffee shop, isn't it?" she asked, trying to redirect them.

"It sure is." Mac, too, seemed a little awkward after their time on the couch, and she sat at a distance, concentrating on a piece of fruit tart she pulled from the pastry box. Jess was grateful for the space and relieved Mac seemed to understand that the hug meant nothing, could never mean anything.

After moments of silence punctuated by shy smiles and the sounds of chewing and swallowing, Mac sat back and stared at her. "It's a life-changing experience. Being attacked. The vulnerability takes away your confidence and your strength. You feel insecure and isolated. But you're none of those things. You're a successful doctor. You have a family. You have friends. Many other women—with much less going for them—have felt what you feel, and they've gotten through it, come out even better than before."

How, though? Jess had thought her month at Hartley had strengthened her, but all it took was a few seconds with Mac, talking about Hawk, and she'd fallen apart. Just from telling a small part of her story.

"One of the best ways to feel emotionally strong is to be physically strong. A gun, for instance. But I also teach a self-defense class. And, coincidentally, a new series is starting tomorrow. You should come."

"I don't know…Mac. I have a hard time talking about it."

"So will they. This class is at the Safe House, in Scranton, so there are people there—gay boys and transgender teens, battered partners—all kinds of people who've lost trust. They not only learn to trust each other in class but also to defend themselves, so they never have to endure abuse again. You never have to go through something like this again, Jess. That knowledge doesn't change what happened to you, but it can give you strength to face tomorrow."

"Is our interview over?" She didn't think she had the strength to endure another question from Mac. All she wanted was to crawl beneath her blankets and go to sleep. In her own, safe, house. She suddenly wished for a Xanax, or three, to help settle her nerves. One of the things she'd learned at the clinic was to dissolve her stress within a stream of deep breaths, but here at home, the technique didn't seem to work.

Pulling the pillow to her chest protectively, she leaned back into the couch, willing Mac away, willing a bottle of pills to appear before her.

Mac nodded. "We'll finish another time," she said, and Jess didn't bother to walk her out.

CHAPTER TWELVE

Hot Wheels

Watching the strip-mall parking lot from his usual perch behind the van's steering wheel, Derek popped a pill and swallowed it with water from a plastic bottle. It was a typical day, a busy day, with Dr. Ball's patients coming and going, some with stops at the pharmacy, and the other doctors' patients keeping pace. Derek was happy for the flurry of activity; it meant his business would be good, too.

Grateful for the overcast sky, he rolled down the van's window and spit out a wad of gum. Chewing was a great release of nervous energy, but his gum had become flat-tasting and stiff, and it was time for a new piece. He popped one into his mouth just as a shiny, silver BMW convertible pulled into the lot. Even though it wasn't an ideal day for a convertible, with gray skies and the threat of rain, the top was down and he recognized the driver immediately. It was her. Dr. Ball's new patient.

He'd guessed her reasons for seeing the doctor when her parents had escorted her to the office, but now that she'd appeared for three consecutive days, he was sure. The doctor brought his addicted patients back frequently, to adjust medication doses and monitor side effects. He'd watched the pattern just as ancient astronomers watched the stars in the night sky, and it never changed. The addicts would come in for several days in a row, then a week later, then a month after that. Once they were stabilized, he'd see them monthly, with the exception of surprise drug screens meant to identify the bad boys and girls.

Just as he'd watched so many others, he watched the girl come and go, first with her parents in their big, expensive car, and then with just her mother. This was the first visit to the office she'd made on her own. She parked illegally in front of the building and hopped out of her car, leaving the roof open and the interior exposed to the elements. He supposed that would make it that much easier for the towing company, if anyone actually followed through with the warning printed on the sign where she parked.

She was a curiosity, the girl. Wealthy, for sure. Beautiful. Defiant. He could tell that the moment he first saw her, when she'd walked proudly behind her parents, dismissing him with a turn of her head.

The prospect of business interrupted his musings, and he met one of his regular customers at her car. They concluded their exchange quickly, and then another customer appeared from within the orthopedics office. Derek watched him disappear into the pharmacy and then reappear a few minutes later. After giving up all of his medication for a few bills, the man limped away happily. Instead of heading back to the safety of the van, Derek edged closer to the building, his senses on high alert. Of course he had a legitimate reason for being there, but he still worried the wrong person or one of security cameras scattered around the parking lot would observe one of his dealings. He'd been told the cameras weren't operating, but he didn't want to take any chances.

He paused in front of the BMW, then slowly circled it, taking in the detail. It was beautiful, sleek and trim, silver sparkling on every surface, even without the benefit of sunshine. He imagined himself behind the wheel, maneuvering the car around sharp turns on a country road or whizzing past slower traffic on the interstate. This model was meant for speed, and he suddenly thought of Dr. Ball's Porsche convertible, built for the same purpose. Why did everyone have a convertible except him? He took a deep breath to dispel his growing anger and let it out slowly. Someday, he chanted softly as he traced the outline of the pills in his pocket.

"What the fuck do you want?"

Derek looked up to see the girl staring at him. In spite of her venomous words, he detected no threat. She seemed curious, as if no one typically dared approach her and she wanted to know what sort of creature had the nerve to do so. She'd been walking toward him, but stopped and crossed her arms over her chest as she studied him from head to toe with eyes hidden behind designer sunglasses.

He smiled his killer smile, the one known to melt women's hearts. He'd been using it since he was a teenager, when he came to understand the power of his good looks. His tall, broad frame commanded attention, and his dark hair and blue eyes seemed to dazzle women of all ages. Plus, women loved a man in uniform. Somehow, though, the girl seemed immune to it all. She continued to stare.

She thinks she's tough, he thought. Derek had seen tougher. "I was just admiring your ride."

She began moving toward the driver's door. "Well, admire it from somewhere else."

He nodded but didn't move. Instead, he placed his hand on the silver surface of the car's hood. "Sure. You sellin'? Or buyin'?"

His questions stopped her again, and she quickly looked around, as if fearing a trap. "I don't know what you're talking about."

He laughed. "Oh, I think you do. Your parents dragged your ass to Dr. Ball for the cure, but you're really not interested. You'd rather get high. So, do you want to sell me your strips and buy a few pills from me, or pretend like you're seeing the doctor for acne cream?"

She looked around again, and Derek could see the façade begin to crumble. Just the mention of drugs had her on edge. She shifted her weight from one foot to the other, threw her purse farther back on her shoulder, clenched and unclenched her fingers. She was in desperate need, and he was just the man to help her.

When she looked back at him, Derek knew he'd won. "I don't have the strips. Just a prescription. I have to go to the pharmacy."

"I can meet you later."

"Can we trade? Strips for pills? I'm a little short on cash."

Derek laughed. "C'mon! You're driving a sweet little convertible like this, and you don't have any money?"

"My parents cut me off."

"Ouch," he said as he backed up a step, pulling his hands up from the car and holding them up in front of him. "That's too bad." He debated making a deal with her, but he couldn't. If he was going to do business, it had to be on his terms, especially with a girl like this, who was undoubtedly accustomed to getting her way. Establishing the rules at the beginning was essential.

He continued to back up, still looking into the big brown lenses of her glasses.

"Wait!"

"It was nice chattin' with ya," he said as he turned.

"I'll get some money, and I'll be back here in an hour," she said to his back.

Glancing at his watch, he shook his head. In an hour, he'd be at the nursing home, exchanging one load of patients for another. "Make it two," he said, and he didn't bother waiting for a reply.

He watched, pleased, as the car sped out of the parking lot and disappeared in the distance. He'd read her right and played her perfectly, and if it worked out the way he hoped, within a few days, he'd have a new girlfriend. He'd supply her with drugs, and she'd supply him with sex, and money, and a sporty little convertible.

The phone attached to his hip began vibrating, and he retrieved it, his gaze still set on the distance and the future he hoped the girl might lead him to. *I don't even know her fuckin' name*, he thought as she glanced at the screen and the text message from Pete: *Get the fuck in here.*

He pulled the van to the front of the building, into the same spot the girl had vacated, and began the process of loading his patients. A few minutes later they were back on the road. They returned their charges, consumed a greasy take-out lunch, reloaded the van, and were back at Dr. Ball's office just over an hour later.

This time, Derek had no interest in the normal routine of his business. Rather than watching the storefronts for activity, awaiting patients with full bottles of pills, he kept his eyes glued to the road where he'd last seen the BMW. He nearly missed the chance to pick up ninety pills from a regular customer, who, fortunately, sought him out near the van. Just as he handed the man his money, the BMW pulled in beside the ambulance and the girl looked at him.

Since she made no move to approach him, Derek walked to the passenger side of the car and tried the door. It opened, and he sat down and sank into the soft leather seat. With his arm resting against the wood paneling on the door he imagined reaching his hand to touch the line of dials controlling the sound system. The smell of new car filled his nostrils. Keeping a neutral expression wasn't easy.

"I'm Derek."

"Lucy."

He smiled his killer smile again, and this time he was rewarded with a change in expression, from scowl to neutral. At least he was making progress.

"Nice to meet you, Lucy. Wanna go for a ride?"

The scowl returned to her face. "I'm not a fucking taxi driver."

Derek's anger rose as tension tightened his muscles and his pounding pulse flushed his face. Who the fuck did she think she was? Just because she came from money and drove a fancy car, she wasn't better than him. In fact, she was much worse off. He used drugs, but he was completely in control of his use. He could quit at any time, if he wanted to. Lucy, on the other hand, with her suburban house and fancy sports car, was an addict. His customer. She needed him, not the other way around. He decided to remind her of that fact.

He turned slightly in the seat so he was facing her. She gripped the wheel with both hands but maintained her focus on something in front of her. "Listen, Lucy. I'm just trying to be friendly. See, I don't sell pills to just anyone. I sell them to my friends, people I know and care about. People I trust, because I have to trust someone to hand over pills. If you OD, it's on me, you know? But you don't seem like the friendly type, so let's just forget this whole thing."

Just as his hand reached the shiny chrome handle he felt her grab him. "Wait. I can be friendly, if that's what you want."

Playing coy, he shifted once again and studied her. He hadn't really had the chance to look at her closely, and now that he did, he realized his initial impression had been accurate. She was a beauty. Her coloring suggested Mediterranean heritage. She wore her long dark hair straight back, or had the wind just arranged it that way? It followed her neck invitingly, and his fingers twitched with desire to push the strands away, to weigh them with the tips of his fingers. Were they as thick as they looked? Her olive skin was flawless, and the lips that seemed painted in a scowl were full and red, even without artificial coloring. Her strong nose held up the glasses that still covered her eyes. He couldn't tell, but he'd wager on brown.

After studying her face and hearing no objection, he allowed his eyes to travel farther. Her build was slender, but her breasts were high and full, and threatened to pop through the buttons on her thin cotton shirt. He didn't let his eyes linger, but instead followed the rest of her, from her slender hips to her brightly painted red toes.

Finally, his eyes met hers again, and he smiled. "I like friendly. Let's take this baby for a ride."

"Where to?" she asked at the light, as if she'd already given in and decided to follow his command.

"Head for the interstate. Let's fly."

As she flipped the blinker, he dialed the radio to his favorite station, turned up the volume, and settled back into his seat. The powerful speaker filled the cabin with classic rock-'n'-roll, and he got lost in the music. The sun warmed his face even as the wind chilled it. When he opened his eyes, his first glance was to the speedometer. One hundred and five.

He would have suggested she go faster, but she wouldn't have heard him above the wind and the radio. He would have touched her leg for encouragement, but he wanted her attention on the road as she passed slower-moving cars that appeared suddenly before them, like obstacles on a video-game racetrack. The landscape was a blur of green, dusted here and there with other colors that passed too quickly to be accurately identified. He closed his eyes, swept away by the wind.

A few minutes later the car began to slow, and he opened his eyes to see why. Lucy had pulled off the highway at the intersection, and she cruised to a stop at the traffic light. He assumed she was turning around but was surprised when, instead, she pulled into a park-n-ride. Without speaking, she opened her door and walked around the front of the car to his door. She opened it and stared blankly at him. "Well, you want to drive, don't you?"

Derek practically jumped from the car and ran all the way around to the driver's side. After he buckled himself in, he stared for a moment. He felt like he was in the cockpit of a fighter plane, with all the fancy instrument panels and control knobs. He adjusted the seat first, and then the mirrors, and then turned to her. "Where to?" he asked.

"You're the driver," she said as she rested her head and seemed to relax into the seat.

Derek looked around. The entrance to I-81 was to his right. Ahead and behind him were industrial parks. Off to the left, he saw a big green sign and knew his destination. The Pennsylvania Turnpike. Not much traffic. Road surfaces in decent shape. Not likely to be any cops on the stretch between Pittston and Wilkes-Barre. He headed that way.

The brakes were touchy, but the car was so responsive to the subtle turn of the steering wheel that he suddenly felt an uncontrollable need to go fast. He cruised through the intersection and picked up speed as he approached the turn for the turnpike entrance. Luckily, no other cars were in sight, because he was ready to fly. Not letting up on the gas, he turned the car smoothly through the first curve and picked up speed on a small stretch of straight asphalt before another curve. He entered the turn at sixty and held tightly to the wheel as he raced through it, the little car shooting out on the other side a split second later.

"Wooey!" he screamed. Bringing his foot down hard on the gas pedal, he watched the speedometer climb quickly to a hundred and twenty miles per hour. In a few seconds, he reached a toll booth and had to crawl through it, with other cars jockeying for position in one of the three stalls. When they were behind him, he let loose once again.

Were it not for his job, and the fact that he needed to get back to work, he would have kept going all the way to Philly. Instead, he exited at Wilkes-Barre and sped down the mountain once again. He hadn't yet reached the strip mall when his phone vibrated.

"Steer for me," he instructed Lucy as he pulled his phone from his belt and checked the text. "Fuck me!" he said as he read the text telling him to get back to Dr. Ball's office.

"I'm off work in half an hour. Where do you want to meet?" he asked her.

"Can't we do this here?" she asked.

He shook his head. Even though he conducted business in the doctor's parking lot every day, this was different. She was different. He intended to get to know her. To date her. Maybe marry her. She had the kind of money he wanted and was likely to never make on his own. She was the key. And he had her wrapped around his little finger.

He reached into his shirt pocket and pulled out two tablets of oxycodone. "They're tens," he said as he placed them in her hand. Twenty milligrams of oxy should keep her happy for an hour. "How about Kirby Park in an hour? By the pond."

If she wanted drugs, she wouldn't argue with him. Still, she was silent for a moment before she nodded.

He parked next to the ambulance, hopped out of her car and into the big van, and went back to work.

"Where the fuck were you?" Pete asked.

"I met a girl. She let me drive her BMW convertible."

He burst into laughter. "Good one."

Derek didn't argue. He had nothing to prove to Pete. A bunch to prove to Lucy, though.

After hurriedly depositing his patients at the nursing home and his ambulance at the garage, he changed into his street clothes. Assessing his reflection in the mirror, he nodded approval. He looked good in a clean designer T-shirt and neatly pressed golf shorts. He jogged from the locker room to his car and lamented his ride. After seeing her car, he was ashamed. He needed to take care of that situation, fast.

At the park, it was surprisingly easy to find a parking place, and he loped toward the pond, eager to see her again. He hoped she noticed his clothes. The shirt was one of the nicest he owned, and he wanted to impress her. Hopefully, they wouldn't have to walk back to his car.

She was sunning herself in the grass when he spotted her, and he thought it fortunate that he noticed her at all. Stretched out like that, the picture of relaxation, she looked anything but an addict trying to score some drugs. If it were spring, he would have thought her a student from Wilkes University or King's College, both just across the river. In the summer, she had to be a local, and he would have thought her a student on break, relaxing after a day at her pseudo-job as a camp counselor or park-activities coordinator.

For a moment he stared, wondering if she knew how beautiful she was. Then he scolded himself for even asking the question. Of course she knew. She'd probably been told that her entire life, and he refused to be a fan throwing compliments her way, only to have them batted back to splatter in his face. He approached quietly, and rather than say the wrong thing, he said nothing, instead lay quietly in the grass beside her.

She still wore the sunglasses, and he wasn't sure if she saw him, or heard him, or sensed him, but after a few minutes, she spoke. "So, did you bring my stuff?"

"Are you always so forward?" he asked.

"I let you drive my car, and you made me wait an hour, so I figured we must be friends by now."

Derek laughed. "Tell me your story, Lucy."

"There's not much to tell."

"How old are you?"

"Nineteen."

"So you've existed on this planet for nineteen whole years, and nothing has happened? There's absolutely nothing you can tell me that's gone on in all that time?" Derek was great at math, and he silently multiplied in his head. Nineteen years times three hundred and sixty-five days. Plus four or five leap years, too. "That's six thousand nine hundred and forty days, give or take. And you haven't done anything in all that time?"

He rolled from his back to his side, facing her. Now, instead of a clear blue sky he saw her, sensually draped across the green grass, her head thrown back to face the sun, looking totally relaxed. Her oxys must have kicked in. "Not a thing."

"Okay, let's play cops and robbers. I'm the cop, and you're my suspect. You have to supply an alibi to prove your innocence."

She groaned. "What is this, third grade?"

Her sarcasm no longer singed him. In fact, he expected it. Liked it even. "Ninth. Because in third grade, we couldn't do this."

In one bend of his knee, with a little push from his arm, he was beside her, his hip to hers, his arm draped across her waist to claim her, and then, his mouth on hers. He expected a slap for his boldness, or at least a withdrawal. Instead, he got nothing. As he softly drew his lips across hers, parting them with his tongue, she was like putty, allowing him to shape the kiss by his own will. He deepened it, then backed off, sucking each lip and then darting into her mouth again, until he felt the need to take her growing irreversibly strong. He pulled back and collapsed breathlessly into the grass.

His heart pounded, and his erection did, too. He hoped she didn't notice, but she would have had to be paralyzed not to feel it against her hip as he kissed her.

"Have you eaten yet? I'm kind of hungry." He wasn't really, but he needed to do something quickly, and food seemed like an easy distraction.

"Seriously?" she asked. "I have to suffer through dinner with you just to get high? There's got to be a better way than this."

In spite of her words, she stood and looked down at him, waiting.

He held out his hand and allowed her to pull him to his feet. They began walking toward a pizza place he knew nearby. "So, where were you last night between seven and ten when the gas station was robbed?"

"Home." Turning her head, she stared for a moment then shook her head, apparently deciding to play along.

"Any witnesses?"

"Yes. My pathetic parents, who think they can straighten me out by making me watch game shows and stupid movies with them."

"Aha. The famous game-show addiction therapy. It often backfires. Anyone who survives ends up using more drugs than they did when they started."

She chuckled, and the sound of her laughter buoyed him.

"Are there any other witnesses? Siblings?"

"There is a sibling. A beautiful, proper, perfect older sister, but she's too busy preparing for the wedding of the century to spend any time watching game shows."

"When's the wedding?"

Lucy looked at the coils of silver rings wrapped around her left wrist. Apparently a watch was tangled in the stack. "Fifty-six days, fourteen hours, and eleven minutes from now."

"Seriously?" he asked.

"Close enough."

"Are you a bridesmaid?" he asked.

She shrugged.

"What does that mean?"

"If I can keep it together, my wonderful sister will allow me the honor of wearing an ugly dress so I can pretend I'm happy for her as she follows in a long line of women who marry their money."

"Hmm. So what don't you like? The dress, or the marriage, or the money?"

"All of the above."

He would have liked to give her a little lecture about how overrated money was until you didn't have enough to eat, but he refrained. He wasn't that kid anymore. He controlled his own destiny, he worked hard, and he would never be hungry again. "So why do it?"

Again, the shrug, followed by moments of silence punctuated only by the sounds of passing cars and their footsteps on the pavement. "It's just easier. If I go along with them, maybe they'll leave me alone."

"Okay," he said, as if he understood. He didn't. His concept of parents and family was worlds away from hers. He'd known that the moment he saw the parents, and their car, as they escorted her into Dr. Ball's office for that first visit.

They'd reached the restaurant, and they sat beneath the awning and looked at each other for a moment. "Your turn," she said as the waitress placed two tall, icy glasses of water before them.

"Hmm?"

"What's your alibi for last night?"

He smiled, and it felt wonderful. It wasn't forced, or rehearsed, like it usually was. It just happened. He answered as truthfully as he could. "At fifteen hundred hours, I finished work. For the next hour, I washed and buffed my car. After that, I stopped at the grocery store and picked up burgers, which I then grilled to perfection and devoured. I washed one load of laundry and ironed clothes while I watched television."

She looked as if she wanted to ask a million questions as she studied him from behind the protection of her sunglasses. In the end, she asked only one. "What did you watch on TV?"

His lips pursed as they fought a smile, he answered. "Game shows."

CHAPTER THIRTEEN

Self-Defense

Mac eagerly scanned the lot of the Safe House in downtown Scranton, hoping to see Jess's car. The community center had been built in a vacant church and had ample space and a huge parking lot, and it was entirely possible Mac had missed Jess's Jeep. She wished she could be sure Jess was coming—waiting to see her each week was a sort of torture. It had seemed to take all of Jess's energy to bring herself to the first few classes, and Mac was never sure at the end of the night whether she'd return. Sure, she thanked Mac and said she enjoyed herself, but Mac knew it was an effort for Jess to attend. That was precisely why she encouraged her to come back—she was suffering. She needed to be with people, to gain strength, to laugh a little and find a sense of community.

That must be it, she thought. *I'm just concerned about her. I need her to recover emotionally so she can testify at Hawk's trial.* Jess's testimony was the key to the kidnapping charges, the central piece of evidence that tied everything else together. With her on the stand, a conviction was almost guaranteed, and Mac could imagine Hawk going to jail for a long time. And that was great news, because the experts reviewing the suspicious deaths linked to Hawk were having a difficult time finding anything in the medical records that would convince a judge to issue an indictment. In addition to the hospitals where he'd worked in the past twenty years, they'd searched his apartment, his car, the house where he'd lived in Garden, even his parents' home in Florida. They'd found no evidence that said a mad serial killer had been there. Nothing bizarre, no trophies from victims, not a single indicator that Hawk was anything other than what he claimed to be—a hardworking big-city doctor caught up in small-town drama.

Hawk had already spoken with numerous psychiatrists, and rumor was his attorneys were going to claim he'd suffered some sort of psychotic break when he'd kidnapped the people in Garden. His lawyers planned to say he'd caved under pressure when Jess confronted him and accused him of murder, then count on his pristine record to get him a slap on the wrist for the kidnappings.

That was why Jess had to testify. Only she could confirm the kidnapping was premeditated, that Hawk had attacked her with that syringe before they even spoke a word about the murder accusations. Without Jess, Hawk's attorneys would spin it to make her look like the bad guy.

The case against Hawk wasn't the only reason she found herself loitering in the parking lot instead of going inside to her class. She really wanted to see Jess. She liked her. Perhaps a part of it had to do with the jobs they did, the burden they shared in dealing with life and death. There was more, though. Even though Jess was troubled, Mac saw a spark there, a flash of the fiery personality that matched her flaming hair. Jess said what she felt and made no apologies, and Mac found that refreshing. All too often women caved to her dominant personality, and it left her feeling drained. It was difficult for her to back down, to give over control, yet it tired her to play that role all day at work and then afterward, too. In her brief encounters with Jess, they'd shared more give-and-take than she had with some people she'd known her entire life.

It had been so long since Mac had been attracted to a woman she almost didn't recognize it for what it was. Attraction. It was totally unethical but there anyway. She truly liked Jess. If they weren't involved in this case, and Jess was emotionally stronger, Mac might have asked her out. No, she definitely would have. Any woman who could make her think about something other than work, or golf, had to be special.

That was why she was scanning the parking lot for Jess's Jeep. It was why the first glimpse of long red hair caused Mac's breath to catch in her throat. It was why the innocent, instructive touches of self-defense class caused Mac to stiffen like a rookie at her first inspection.

Thankfully, the class lasted only eight weeks. Mac ran the class four times a year, with a month off between sessions to recover and prevent burnout. In four weeks, she wouldn't have to see Jess again. Then she could whip her mind into shape and train it to think of other things. Perhaps she'd date someone. Sex with someone else might chase thoughts of Jess from her mind.

Yes, that's what she'd do. She'd start dating. And in four weeks, Jess would be out of her life. Until the trial anyway.

Resolved to forget about Jess, Mac began walking toward the former church's back entrance. She'd gone only halfway when Jess's car pulled into the lot. It was a Jeep Wrangler, designed for off-road use, and Mac had difficulty reconciling the proper physician whose every hair was in place with the woman who'd drive that car off-road through mud. Just the thought of it made her smile, though, and before she knew what she was doing, she'd paused long enough to allow Jess to hop out of the Jeep.

"What's that smile about?" Jess asked.

"Your vehicle. It seems sort of...wild for you."

"Hey, I'm offended. I've been known to be wild. Once."

They both laughed, and after a moment Jess filled in the blanks. "It's great for cruising around town. And for fishing. I can drive it down close to the streams or throw my kayak in the backseat."

"You shoot, you fish, you kayak. You really are a local, huh?"

"I wasn't for a while, but it feels good to be back. It's home. How about you? Local?

"Oh, yeah. I grew up at the campground."

Jess nodded. "Yes, you did tell me that."

Mac was a little bit offended that Jess had forgotten that piece of her personal history, but she tried to brush it off. Jess had more important things to think about. And who cared, anyway? Even if she was attracted to her, Jess was just a witness she was trying to help, nothing more. It didn't matter if she remembered Mac's name, let alone trivia about her childhood.

"I'm enjoying the class, Mac. I'm happy you suggested it."

Mac turned to her, relieved. She'd hoped Jess liked it. It seemed she did. And normally it wouldn't matter if a student liked it or not. Typically she had a half dozen students in the class, and she couldn't please them all. The self-defense suited some, but not others. Mac couldn't take it personally. Yet with Jess, it was very personal. "Really?"

Jess had to admit the self-defense class was the best thing she'd done in her month since leaving the Hartley Clinic. Getting back into the routine of work had been easy—but of course, work was always easy for her. Patients were just puzzles, some more complicated than others, but they all came with clues—signs, symptoms, lab and X-ray findings. The process of putting it all together was actually therapeutic for her, and she could totally lose herself and her own troubles as she focused on her patients. A few times a day when she wasn't at work, she'd been stressed enough to use Xanax, but she'd never caved in. She didn't have any actual physical need for narcotics—the buprenorphine was taking care of that, sitting tightly in the opioid receptors in her brain, preventing any cravings from sneaking through the cracks. The psychological need was there, though—and that's where the self-defense had come in.

Each week, she'd forced herself to get up and dress, to make the drive to Scranton to the Safe House, and to walk through the door and interact with the other human beings who saw fit to attend Mac's class. Afterward, she'd enjoyed socializing with the other students. Actually enjoyed it. For the first time since she could remember, she took an interest in others for no reason other than pure, simple pleasure. Between classes, she practiced her moves. Mac had taught her and the other students the most important principle of self-defense was avoiding dangerous situations. Jess didn't intend to argue with that fact, but she was happy to know the nose-breaking palm strike Mac had taught her.

Her knees still buckled when she thought of Hawk, but she focused on the present. This was what the psychiatrists had told her and her counselor had repeated in therapy, and she got it. She really did. She couldn't go back and change the past. When she had an opportunity, she wasn't going to forgive him, as her therapist had suggested. She planned to tell him to go fuck himself and inform him she had a syringe of succinylcholine waiting for him if he was ever released. And she intended to be smart and avoid danger, and fight to the death if she was ever in a situation where she couldn't, because she was never going to let anything like Hawk happen to her again.

She shook off the thought and returned to the present. Mac was silent beside her, and Jess felt amazingly comfortable with her. Mac's strength was not only calming, but it was also fortifying. Jess had to admit she enjoyed seeing Mac as much as she enjoyed the class. That fact was as strange as her newfound joy in engaging with people. She had to go back years to remember the last time she'd felt like this—happy, looking forward to the future, looking forward to seeing a woman. Even if Mac was taboo, Jess was happy for the feelings she elicited. It was a sign that she was alive, and healing.

"Yeah. It's fun. And it's making me feel better to know I might be able to defend myself if need be."

"That's great," Mac said as she held the door for Jess. "You seem like you're doing well."

"I am," she said, and as their eyes met, a current of electricity shot through her. Mac swallowed. Could she have felt it, too?

"Are you ready to take me on at Ping-Pong?" Mac asked, and her quick rejoinder told Jess she'd imagined Mac's reaction. Just as well. This could go nowhere.

Ping-Pong was another story, though. Jess had reached expert status at Hartley. With no television and contraband Internet, it was really the only entertainment. Group therapy didn't count. She looked at Mac and shook her head. "I don't want to make you look bad. All of these people admire you."

Mac nodded. "I see. How can I ever hold another self-defense class if I can't handle a paddle?"

"Precisely."

Mac squinted, and her eyes bore into Jess. "I'll take my chances with my reputation. You. Me. Afterward."

Jess met Mac's eyes and held them, and she couldn't control her smirk. "Game on."

They walked into the large community room and were greeted with a chorus of welcomes. One smile after another lit up the faces of the participants in the class. This wasn't therapy, and they were in no way obligated to share their stories, but it wasn't frowned upon, either. Over the course of the weeks, they'd all opened up about what had brought them to the Safe House. There were battered spouses, frightened teens, victims like her. They'd all shared, except her. Everyone there knew her story. Thanks to television news coverage, everyone in America knew her story. Instead of her classmates staring, though, or treating her any differently than they treated each other, they paid her no special attention. They laughed at her when she did something silly and laughed with her, too. They encouraged her, as she encouraged them.

"Okay, let's get started," Mac said after everyone said their hellos.

Mac taught a blended class, with a little bit of yoga, because it helped strengthen the mind, and that was a huge part of being safe. They learned physical moves for defense, which helped bolster self-confidence. Not that Mac ever wanted any of them to defend themselves. She was much more interested in her students escaping to safety than staying to fight. Finally, she taught them the psychology of both victims and perpetrators of violence.

"What's Mac's first rule of self-defense?" she asked the group as they stretched their leg muscles.

"Avoid danger," they said in unison.

Jess thought about this principle as she had a hundred times since Mac had first said it weeks earlier. At first she'd thought the advice was useless—she was still stuck in her victim's mentality. How could she have avoided Hawk? He'd targeted her, and she never saw the attack coming. But as hours melted into days, she realized how avoidable her situation really had been.

First, she'd denied the danger of Hawk. Her pride and mixed feelings about Ward had caused her to be defensive, and instead of listening to Ward's concerns, she'd been critical. Not only had that response allowed Hawk to get close to her, but it had also alienated Ward. If Ward hadn't been so persistently stubborn in looking for her, Jess would probably be dead.

After she realized the merit of Ward's accusations, Jess had put herself directly in danger by going to the hospital to investigate Hawk. What harm would there have been in presenting her concerns to the hospital authorities the next day? Absolutely none. She'd chosen to behave foolishly, though, and as a result, she gave Hawk the opportunity he needed to kill her.

Thinking about Hawk, Jess felt her stress level rising, and as she'd been doing lately, she closed her eyes and took some deep breaths to break up the tension. Eyes shut, she envisioned the smooth surface of the lake at the hunting club, added the heat of the sun on her face, and then imagined herself hearing the call of a bird swooping down close to her kayak. After a half dozen breaths, she rejoined the group. When she opened her eyes, she saw a concerned stare from Mac. A wink sent Mac's gaze scurrying to her other students and also filled Jess with a strange sense of excitement.

"Okay, everyone pick a partner," Mac said after they completed their stretching routine. "We're going to work on some punching and kicking. When do you want to punch and kick?" she asked no one in particular.

"When you can't run," they all answered.

The questions were always the same, but Jess found it was much like studying for boards. You read the same question over and over again until the answer became reflexive, until the patterns made sense. You get a flat tire on the highway. What do you do? Pull over, lock your doors, and call for help. Your car breaks down on the side of the highway. What do you do? Pull over, lock your doors, and call for help. You're in a fender-bender on a deserted road. What do you do? Pull over, lock your doors, call for help. What's the dosage of epinephrine for anaphylaxis due to a bee sting? What's the dosage of epinephrine for anaphylaxis due to a food allergy? What's the dosage of epinephrine for anaphylaxis due to anything? It was all the same. Different, but the same.

Jess looked around and realized she had no partner. There had been an even number of students the week before, but this week it appeared someone hadn't showed up. It left an imbalance in the teamwork, where one student practiced throwing punches and kicks and the other served as a target. The target also worked on defending themselves from attack.

"You can work with me," Mac said as people began appropriating padding from a cabinet. The helmets went unused in this class, but most of them chose large foam shields, arm and leg pads, or protective eyewear.

Mac donned her gear. "Let's work on nose strikes," she said, and Jess grinned. She loved this move, practiced shoving the heel of her hand into her assailant's nose again and again before the mirror in her bedroom. Each time, the blood poured from Hawk's nose, much as it had when her father had finally taken him down. This time she would hit him, though. She'd fight until death, just as Mac had taught her.

"Nice," Mac said as she ducked away from Jess's blow.

"I'm getting good at this," Jess said in chopped breaths, winded from turning her body and jabbing her arm forward as Mac had shown her.

"Jess is getting good at this," Mac repeated for the crowd, and they all cheered. "And that's the point. You want to practice a few basic moves until they're second nature. Until you're good enough at them that they can get you out of trouble, so you can—"

"Run away!" They all cheered.

"What if I want to learn more?" Jess asked, meeting Mac's eyes. Jess understood the principles of Mac's blended teaching style. Jess would never learn more than a few basic moves, but she would get good at them, and they'd keep her out of trouble. She liked the workout, though: throwing punches and kicks, stretching. "What is this you're teaching us? Karate? Kung-fu? Are you the Kung-fu cop?"

Mac laughed so hard she nearly missed blocking a punch Jess had thrown. "Yep, that's what they call me around the station."

"Seriously? What if I want to do more of this?"

Mac sensed Jess's intensity lessen, felt her ease off, and she dropped her guard. Jess's eyes held her though, and she was drawn into the deep-blue pools. They seemed the same color as the Caribbean, not just any spot, but a reef she'd snorkeled near Montego Bay. She'd been in college then, her first time in the turquoise waters of that part of the world, and she'd fallen in love with that shade. Her own eyes weren't much different, and she constantly bought shirts that matched, not just because she looked really good in them, but because she felt really good in them, too. Just seeing that color transported her a thousand miles in her mind, to a kind and gentle place where people fished to eat and braided hair in little huts by the side of the road.

Mac cleared her throat, and before she could clear her head and replace her wayward thoughts with intelligent ones, she spoke. "I could work with you. I'm not going to get you ready for competition, but I can put together a great workout, enough to make you stronger and improve your moves."

"Would it make me a better fighter?"

"Jess, take a deep breath. You've been through a great trauma, and your instinct is to want to fight back. But that's not necessarily the smartest thing. The smartest thing is to avoid danger. And the next smartest thing is to run. Only when you have no other choice, then you fight."

"Is that a no?" Jess said, her hands on her hips as she awaited Mac's reply.

It was just a little martial-arts training, Mac told herself. What could it hurt? She liked Jess, enjoyed their time together. Couldn't they be friends? The Hawk case wouldn't last forever, after all. "I couldn't train you if you're determined to attack bad guys. I wouldn't want it on my conscience if I failed or if something happened to you. But I know some people who could probably help you."

"Okay," she said and went back to kicking.

Once again Mac felt Jess had kicked her feet out from under her. Why did that keep happening? What did it even mean? Why did she care?

Mac was one of the highest-ranking women in the Pennsylvania

State Police. She'd dedicated her life to her job—to training, pushing herself by running and boxing, lifting and swimming, toning muscles most women didn't even know they had. Physically, she could do anything, handle anything that came up. Mentally, she was just as tough. Psychology had been her major in college, because she knew that was where the action was. She'd learned principles and practices of policing on the job, but her study of the mind and its pathology had been a life-long venture. The criminals she pursued never disappointed her with their abnormal psychology. They made predictable mistakes, and even their unpredictability was predictable. It sometimes took weeks, or even months, but eventually, Mac found the answers to her questions and brought criminals to trial. It was what she loved most, and it had made her life very rewarding.

Women, on the other hand, had never been her strength. They were so much less predictable than criminals. They were emotional. Instead of cold and calculating, they were warm and feeling, and they all too often demanded her to be warm and feeling as well.

And she just wasn't. Yes, she had feelings, but she'd never felt the need to express them. Her parents weren't the kind of people who doted on her and her siblings—I love yous didn't fly across the dining-room table with the rolls and butter. Her parents loved her. They'd nurtured her and taught her the important things in life—respect for herself and family and friends, the value of hard work, how to manage money. Beside her brothers she'd learned to throw a ball—and a tackle, too. Summers at the campground were filled with adventures from morning until dark settled over the place, when her father, relaxed after his long days as a cop, told them stories by the fire. They'd listen for as long as they could sit still, which wasn't usually very long. Then they were off again, chasing each other and fireflies through their idyllic little world, and they only gave up on the day when exhaustion overcame them.

Sometimes, they'd see their mother before bed. Not usually, though. Nurses didn't punch a clock in those days, and her mother stayed at the hospital until her work was done. Every morning she'd send Mac's father off with his bagged lunch, a kiss on the cheek, and a request to be careful. He'd nod stoically and head out the door ahead of the school bus.

She'd never questioned her parents' love. They showed it in dozens of ways; they just didn't talk it to death. That Mac was like them was probably her most pressing issue with women, and in the era of reality TV, it was a biggie. All everybody did anymore was talk.

This was nothing new, not a recent self-discovery. And it was okay. She liked herself, enough to not force herself into situations and relationships that weren't comfortable for her. Well, no relationships were comfortable for her. But suddenly, with Dr. Jessica Benson, she found herself thinking about something else, contemplating whether she might change, wondering if there was another woman on the planet with the personality of her mother, tough and tender enough to love a cop.

As quickly as the thought entered her mind, it passed again, and she forced herself to concentrate on Jess's technique. She had to, or she was going to find herself on her ass or drinking a mouthful of her own blood.

"Okay, that's enough," Jess said a few minutes later, after a few dozen kicks landed on target. "Can you show me again how to block those?"

"You don't take no for an answer, do you? And it wouldn't be showing you again, because I haven't shown you at all."

"That's a technicality."

Mac wanted to remind her that technicalities saved lives, in both their respective professions. Something told her the reminder wouldn't have fazed Jess at all.

CHAPTER FOURTEEN

Maintenance Program

If anyone had told Jess at their initial meeting that she'd be hugging Geraldine Gompers, she'd have thought they needed stronger medication. Yet here she was, at her second outpatient visit, and inexplicably happy to see her addiction specialist.

Because of the hundred and fifty miles separating the Hartley Clinic from Jess's home in Garden, they'd been talking on the phone twice weekly instead of meeting face-to-face. The personal meeting was necessary for a number of reasons, though. First, the DEA required that Jess submit a urine drug screen. The urine was tested for bup, to prove Jess was taking it rather than selling it on the street, and also for other drugs, to prove Jess had really been cured of her evil habits.

Somehow she'd managed to survive the first thirty-eight years of her life without ever peeing in a cup, but now the task seemed as routine as breathing. Once she'd overcome the indignity of another human being watching her *produce a specimen*, the mechanics of it weren't difficult. She rarely got any on her fingers. And she was rather proud of herself, too. Perhaps it was the next generation of Freudian psychology, but she felt really great about her negative screens.

Meeting the doctor in person was also required to obtain her prescription, and Jess had become highly motivated to stay on bup. She was functioning like a normal human being, thanks to this medication, and if she had to drive to Florida every month to get the medication, she would.

"My hands are clean," she said as she hugged Dr. Gompers, wiping them playfully on her back.

"And so is your urine, I see."

Jess laughed. Since the doctor had confronted her and demanded complete honesty, she'd felt a lightness of spirit she hadn't experienced in years. Laughing with her doctor had become routine. In spite of the fact that rules governed such matters, Jess felt they were becoming friends. Under other circumstances, she could imagine hosting the frumpy old woman for dinner or at a cocktail party of their peers. Every so often, the reality that they were peers, professional colleagues, startled Jess. Because really, their doctor-patient relationship was the crux of their association. Yes, they talked intellectually about Jess's progress, about articles she'd read about addiction and methods of weaning. In the end, though, in this office, Jess was the patient, because without the professional help Dr. Gompers could provide, she would be lost.

"How was your drive?"

"Uneventful. I came early, stopped at the house in Wayne, and packed some things I'd like to keep."

"When does it go on the market?"

"In the next few days."

"How do you feel about that?" Dr. Gompers asked as she stared Jess down over the top of her glasses.

Jess laughed. "You've got to be kidding! What a cheap question." She paused and studied the doctor, who remained silent. Did she have any other clothing besides ill-fitting black skirts and sweaters? "Actually, I feel good. I'd like the money, for one. This place put a dent in my savings, and who needs the upkeep of two houses? Psychologically speaking, I'm ready."

"Good! That's a good sign. Letting go of the past—all of it—is part of your healing. How's the self-defense going?"

"Super! I feel great about this. Empowered. And Mac agreed to work with me beyond the classes, so I can perfect my skills. I've been practicing at home, and I think I've really mastered the basics. I'm ready for more advanced techniques."

"Mac?"

"Detective Calabrese."

"I see. Any flashbacks? Depression? Drinking?"

"Once in a while, something reminds me of Hawk and I feel almost startled. Not necessarily frightened, but alarmed."

"Less often, though?"

Jess nodded.

"That's great."

"Yeah. Mac says that it's good that it happens that way, and that I learn how to work through it, because I'm going to have to face Hawk in court, and I don't want to freeze when I see him. Have a meltdown."

"That makes sense. How are you working through that anxiety? All your anxiety?"

"Oh, the usual. Two Xanax, two Percocet, and a tall glass of red wine."

Dr. Gompers gave her a stern look. "Is it my imagination, or are you cultivating a sense of humor?"

"I did tend to be a little too serious in my past life."

"Is that how you look at it? As your past life?"

Jess nodded as she sipped from her water bottle, and when she spoke again all the humor had disappeared from her voice. "My life was a few breaths from over. I don't think I can ever look at issues without classifying them as before or after Hawk. I'm trying to put a positive spin on everything, though. Past life, current life."

"Future?"

"Yes."

"What does the future hold for you?"

"Well, I've learned not to take anything for granted, that's for sure. But I want to continue to run the ER at Garden. I look forward to a lot of professional endeavors. I'm in great shape, better than I've been in years, and I'm looking forward to more of that. Exercising, playing golf, making new friends to play with. And sobriety, of course. Making smart choices about managing my stress."

"How about your personal life?"

"Well, Ward's in love, so nothing's happening there."

"But that's your choice as much as Ward's."

Jess hesitated before answering. It had been a realization, but it was her choice. She and Ward weren't good for each other. "Yes. My choice."

"That doesn't mean you'll never date again."

Jess shrugged. "It's not important."

"Perhaps not. But it's sometimes nice."

"I won't exclude the possibility at some point in the future, but…I don't know. I'd kind of like to get my addiction under control before I get involved with someone." Jess looked out the window, wondering about a life with someone who wasn't Ward. It was difficult, but she sensed she could handle it.

"What do you mean? Don't you feel like you're under control?" Jess detected concern in the doctor's voice.

"Well." Jess hesitated. What did she mean? Her addiction was under control, technically speaking. She could falter at any time, though. Slip up and fall back into the darkness. It was all about managing her stress, she thought. That, and time. Time would help strengthen her as an addict, just as it had when she'd lost her mother. Just as it was helping her let go of Ward. "I think I'd like to be in a better place, psychologically."

A rare smile graced the doctor's face. "That really does sound smart."

"I got smarter here. Part of it was just detoxifying my brain, but I've learned, too. With all the reading I've done, and the counseling sessions, and the meetings, I've learned about myself and my disease."

"One of the mantras of AA is your lack of power over addiction. You're a control freak. How do you feel about being powerless?"

Jess suddenly felt exhausted. "Well, most people are powerless in the end. But I still think I'm in control of my own destiny."

"Do you think you can control the addiction?"

Jess studied her, trying to understand the question.

"Can you use drugs in a controlled manner?" Dr. Gompers asked.

"Ah. No. That I can't control. If I take one…"

Dr. Gompers nodded and leaned forward slightly, gesturing

with her hands. The change from her normal still posture was dramatic. "I think the key is understanding your own power, what you can and can't control, and hopefully that helps you recognize dangerous situations so you can avoid them, or call for help before it's too late."

Jess looked out the window again. She'd first gazed through its glass two months earlier, when she'd arrived at Hartley for her inpatient treatment. It was now the end of September, and the view had changed. The deep greens of the woods around the clinic were fading, replaced by yellow and gold and red on many of the trees. Her view of the world was equally different. Spiritually, emotionally, and psychologically she was not the same person that she'd been back then.

"I wonder about control. Do we control more than we think, influence people perhaps? I keep wondering if I willed Hawk to keep me alive. I certainly didn't tell the bastard what he wanted to know."

"That might have been all it took, but yes, you were certainly in control of that."

"I had a patient recently. An eighty-five-year-old guy who fell and broke his hip at a Fourth of July picnic. He was from Wilkes-Barre, and of course the ambulance brought him to Garden when he fell, because it was the closest hospital. Anyway, this guy was such a riot. Flirting with the nurses, demanding my credentials before he'd allow me to treat him. He made me promise him he wouldn't die in the middle of nowhere. He begged me to transfer him for hip surgery, so he could die at home. Anyway, he made it through the surgery, and rehab, and he finally got home. He died in his sleep that night. Do you suppose he willed himself to live so he could die under his own terms?"

"It's entirely possible."

Jess laughed. "You have a really great job. Commit to nothing and get paid a fortune."

Dr. Gompers smiled. "Yes, I do. And as much as I enjoy our sessions, I suspect you're going to grow tired of the drive from Garden. I propose you find a doctor close to home for your monthly medication refills, and you can see me twice a year. Have your doctor send me reports and copies of your drug screens, so I'll be sure you're staying on track. Then I can sleep at night with a clean conscience."

Jess's eyes filled with tears. It was a strange sensation. Normally, she didn't become too emotional. "Thank you for doing this my way."

When her visit ended, Jess hugged the doctor again before making her way into the crisp fall day. Her trip home was easy, little traffic to contend with and beautiful foliage to enjoy. It was late afternoon by the time she finished unpacking her car, and she settled on her couch with her computer and a hot cup of tea. Much to her surprise, quite a few physicians in the mountains were certified to prescribe her medication. One was in Garden!

Who would have thought? While it would have made life considerably easier to see someone a mile away, Jess would never do it. She didn't plan to share her history with the community. She dialed the number for a doctor in Scranton. It was forty minutes away, but she'd make a day of it and shop, perhaps have lunch at her favorite Thai restaurant.

"Hi, I'd like to make an appointment to see Dr. Johannes," she said.

"What's wrong with you?"

"Excuse me?" Jess asked as she tried not to laugh at the woman's gruff demeanor.

"Why do you need to see the doctor?"

"Opioid dependency."

"Bup? You want to get in the program?"

"Ah, yes."

"She doesn't have any openings. I can put you on the list, though. You might be able to get in around the first of the year. What's your insurance?"

Whoa. The first of the year was more than three months away. Jess was sure she could see Dr. Gompers again if she needed, but she hoped it didn't come to that. She'd try another doctor. She disconnected the call and dialed again.

"Hi, I'd like to make an appointment with Dr. Lewiston for buprenorphine."

"We don't have any openings, hon."

"Do you have a waiting list?"

"The waiting list is full. Try over in Taylor, hon."

Half an hour later, Jess needed a Xanax. And quite possibly a few Percocet, too. She'd called nearly twenty physicians, and none had availability. With the DEA limiting the number of patients each physician could treat, the number of addicts far outnumbered the pool of providers available to prescribe medication. The patients from rehab were right—Jess was going to have a hard time finding a doctor to help her.

Wondering if Dr. Gompers might be able to assist her, Jess decided to call Hartley. They'd helped her with so much that perhaps they could do so with this, too.

In sync with the rest of her day, Dr. Gompers was out of the office. Fortunately, when she explained her situation, one of the nurses offered a solution. While they talked, the nurse faxed a list of licensed physicians to Jess's home number. The list was disappointingly short, but it was a place to start.

On the third try, Jess's luck seemed to change. "We don't accept insurance," the woman told her.

That was fine by her. Jess didn't plan to ever divulge her secret to her health insurance company. That was the first step to informing the world about her addiction.

"And our only openings are in the IOR program."

"What's IOR?"

"Intense outpatient rehab."

"What's the difference between intense and regular?" She'd gotten quite the education at Hartley, but this was a term she hadn't heard before.

"This is a program for people at high risk. The doctor sees you more frequently, monitors you more carefully, and sometimes prescribes higher doses of bup or even other drugs."

Jess thought for a second. Could that be bad? It might be inconvenient to see the doctor more frequently, but it certainly wouldn't hurt her. And it might even help. Determined to stay on track, she found herself nodding at the phone.

"Yes, okay. IOR sounds good."

"Okay. He can see you tomorrow morning. It's a thousand, in cash."

"Dollars?" Jess was startled. Most of the clinics charged between two and four hundred dollars. A thousand was unheard of.

"Well, that's for the month, dear. And, of course, for all your medications."

"Every month?"

"No." The woman laughed. "Just the first month. After that, it's five."

"Hundred?"

"Yep. Five hundred. So should I book you? I've got a waiting room of people here who want to talk to me. I gotta get off the phone."

Jess thought of the dozens of calls she'd made. Her best chance was at an office in Scranton, where the waiting list was only about two months. Between the cost of gas and the cost of her time, in the end, it was probably less expensive to pay the thousand dollars than to drive back to Hartley. If it was only for a few months, Jess could afford the expense.

Still, this habit was proving to be expensive. She'd spent thirty thousand dollars on her inpatient stay, and her medication would cost her about five hundred a month. Add another five for the doctor, and it was almost more affordable to buy pills on the street. Almost. She shook the thought out of her head. Money wasn't an issue here. Her life was.

Jess couldn't believe how good she felt since beginning treatment with bup. Gone was the anxiety about her supply, worrying about her doctor cutting her off, wondering what she'd do for pills if that happened. The fear of discovery had dissolved. Instead of sneaking her meds every few hours, now she took two tablets in the morning and was set for the day. Bup's long half-life allowed that convenient, once-daily dosing. There was no withdrawal, no sweating or shaking because she'd pushed herself to go an extra hour without her drugs. She couldn't say anything bad about bup or the way it had changed her life. Even if it cost her fifteen hundred dollars a month, it was worth it.

"Okay," she said at last. "I'll take the appointment."

"Fine. Dr. Ball can see you at ten tomorrow morning."

CHAPTER FIFTEEN

Dark Knight

Humming a tune, Derek poured tea over the ice in two tall glasses. He couldn't help feeling happy. Business was better than ever, and his cash flow was steady. Using a tip Lucy had unknowingly supplied, he had robbed her aunt's house while she was out of town and now had a few extra bucks in his savings account. Lucy was crazy about him, and he was beginning to like her almost as much as he liked her money. For once in his life, everything was going great.

"I'm really sorry about your kidneys," he said as he fluffed the pillow behind Tim's head and handed him his tea.

"Oh, Derek, thank you!" Tim said in his typical dramatic manner, his arm brushing along his forehead before falling back onto the pillow. "I don't know what I would have done without you all these years."

"Oh, you would have managed. I mean, a lot of eager teenagers want to walk dogs at six a.m. and wash antique cars by hand. In the hot sun."

"A man can't be rushed from his sleep at an early hour, Derek. It's unhealthy. And don't forget the skills you've learned. How many kids your age can practically run an entire apartment complex single-handedly? Probably not too many." He answered his own rhetorical question before continuing. "And I know why you did it all, Derek. I know why you're so good to me. It was all for Rita, Derek, wasn't it? If you hadn't helped me out the way you have through the years, I wouldn't have been able to keep her here on such cheap rent."

With a shrug, Derek took the cup back and placed it on the table. He remembered the times his mom couldn't afford the rent, yet Tim had never thrown them out. All he'd asked from Derek was snow removal in the winter and lawn care in the summer. And walking his dog, morning, noon, and night. Then some garden work, and plumbing and electrical. Derek couldn't count the shocks he'd suffered trying to rig the old fuse boxes in the complex. Tim hadn't done badly with Derek's free labor, but still, he'd been kind.

"If I didn't have a handicapped cousin, Derek, I'd leave it all to you."

"That's really nice of you," Derek said, and just the thought made him happy. It was good to know Tim cared about him, because he certainly cared for Tim. He would have been an easy target if Derek was so inclined, but he wasn't. It was about structure, and stability, and companionship. Tim provided all of that.

It was never about money with Tim. If he left the apartment complex to his cousin, that was fine. Hopefully, there wouldn't be a rent spike. As long as he continued to help out around the place and keep an eye on things, he could probably negotiate a fair rent with the new owners. But hopefully, that wasn't something he'd have to worry about any time soon.

Another worry was on his mind, and as he sipped his tea, he wondered how to introduce it. He needed a new car, and he needed it now. With his vision failing, Tim no longer needed his. Derek had been taking care of that car, detailing it inside and out, since he was old enough to ride a bike. He had the money, and he'd checked the value of the car on the Internet. He just needed to work up the nerve to ask Tim to sell it to him.

"Do you want to do the bills, now, before I go out?" he asked Tim.

"Sure, sure."

"And you're going to let me take the car, right?" Derek sucked in a breath. It's now or never, he thought. "Would you consider selling me the Benz?"

Suddenly anxious, Derek pulled out the stack of mail and began sorting through it.

Tim patted Derek's thigh affectionately and laughed. "I've been waiting for you to work up the nerve to ask me that. No. I won't sell it." He paused and looked at Derek with vacant eyes. Then one corner of his mouth turned up into a half-smile. "But I'll give it to you. You've been good to me, Derek, and I want you to have it. You're the only one who loves that car as much as I do."

"You don't have to give it to me, Tim. I can afford to buy it."

"Been saving, have you?"

Derek nodded.

"I'm proud of you. That's why I'm giving it to you."

Derek could have kissed him, or at least hugged him, but they didn't have that sort of relationship. Instead, he squeezed Tim's hand. "Thank you, Tim."

"You're most welcome."

"I'll have you sign these checks, and then I'll balance your checkbook for you, okay?"

"How many checks?"

"For all the bills, it'll be seventeen checks. Just over eight thousand dollars."

"And the deposit?"

"The usual. Just over twenty."

"Okay, where do I sign?"

Derek placed Tim's hand on the business check ledger, and he began signing. His vision was poor but good enough for this task. While Tim worked his pen, Derek threw open the blinds and let in a squint-inducing light, then wiped down the dusty surfaces that appeared in the gilded rays. When he'd finished, he began stuffing checks into envelopes. Running a large apartment complex entailed paying many bills.

"You'll feed me before you leave, won't you?" Tim asked.

Full of adrenaline now, Derek made a bold suggestion. "How about if I let you rest, and then we'll go to the notary and sign over the car?"

Tim seemed to be thinking. "Can we go to the pancake house?" he asked after a moment.

An hour and a half later, Tim's belly was full and Derek's step was light. They'd signed the papers. The car of his dreams was now officially his.

"Watch it!" his mother screamed when he rushed into her apartment and threw open the bedroom blinds.

"It's after five, Mom. Time to get up. I have something to show you."

Yanking the covers over her, she refused to listen.

"C'mon," he said as he handed her a breath mint. It did nothing to combat the odor of stale alcohol on her breath or in the room, but it was something. In a little while she'd pull herself together, and for an hour or so before he went out to meet Lucy, they'd pretend they were like a normal family, watching game shows together. Before his vision went, Tim used to join them. Now it was just Derek and his mom. They'd watch until his mother grew bored and decided to head out to the local pub.

"What?" she asked, peeking out from under the covers.

"Tim gave me the car!"

Squinting, she shook her head. "You're a lucky fucker, do you know that? No one ever gave me anything in my whole life. Everything I have, I worked for."

Feeling a little sad, Derek couldn't help looking around the room. Seventies wallpaper blanketed the room, a dilapidated bedroom set sat in the center, the bed covers were old and faded. The things she'd worked for were right here, in four rooms. She had no property, no car, no savings. In forty-five years of life, she'd accomplished nothing. It made him sad but also determined. His life was going to turn out differently.

"I'm going to get one of those vanity plates," he said. Grabbing a piece of paper, he wrote some letters on it and handed it to her.

She squinted at the writing before breaking into laughter. "Cool. *Derek Knight*, right?"

Derek looked at the paper. DrKnit. Dark Knight. "Yep, that's right," he said.

CHAPTER SIXTEEN

Healer

Chirping birds greeted Jess as she opened her back door and walked the few steps off her porch to the detached garage that housed her car. A bright, cloudless sky overhead told her it was going to be a magnificent fall day. After debating for a moment, she began the process of taking the roof off her Jeep. It was a long drive to Wilkes-Barre, but she was betting on the forecast. She'd stay dry, and the sweater over her shoulders would keep her warm enough. The sun and wind would do her good.

The reporters had left Garden when the next big story came along, and while Jess cringed about yet another oil spill, she was grateful for the relief. Multiple people had assured her she'd be safe from reporters, for a while, at least. She had Hawk's trial to look forward to, and that was sure to be a zoo. She wasn't taking any chances, though. Since the picture aired around the world showed Dr. Jessica Benson with long, flowing, dark-red hair, she'd lightened it a few shades and started pulling it up. Today, she wore a French braid. With her sunglasses on, she was sure no one would recognize her.

Navigating the smaller roads on her way to Wilkes-Barre proved a challenge. The neighboring town was having a garlic festival, and a parade of cars sat in bumper-to-bumper traffic as a tractor-trailer attempted to back into a spot where other vendors had parked in a converted farm field. Who would have known? Once she cleared the traffic, she quickly reached the highway, and before she knew it, the exit for Dr. Michael Ball's office was on the right. The drive had taken more than an hour, and Jess was disheartened to think she'd have to make this trip regularly. The elevation of Garden, at sixteen hundred feet, was more than a thousand feet higher than Wilkes-Barre. That meant much more snow, and she dreaded making that drive during a storm. The same cold front that dumped heavy rain on Dr. Ball's parking lot would leave a foot and a half of snow in Garden.

Don't get down, she told herself. *You've come this far. What does a drive matter?* Besides, when something opened in Scranton, she'd make an appointment there. It was twenty minutes closer, and they were cheaper. Frowning, she thought of the thousand dollars she'd be paying Dr. Ball to treat her today. Ouch! She supposed it was money well spent, but still, she wasn't wealthy. Her savings had a limit. She hoped the IOR plan included a massage and a pedicure. She could really use both, and with the money she'd spent recently on her addiction, she hesitated to blow another two hundred bucks at the spa.

The parking lot was packed, and Jess opted to park away from the other cars. Surveying the place as she walked, she concluded that the strip mall was an impressive piece of property, with nice landscaping in front and around the large marquee. The fronts were made of stone and glass. Most of the offices were medical, and Jess liked that. She imagined a nice network of colleagues referring to each other and communicating well about patient care. It made sense.

Dr. Ball's door was a grand glass structure, plainly painted, with no indication that he treated addicts. DR. MICHAEL BALL, FAMILY MEDICINE, it said, and listed the phone number below. Inside, it was much the same. Jess felt as if she'd entered a medical spa instead of an office. There was marble tile everywhere, and brightly painted walls gave the office a cheerful appearance. Tasteful drapes adorned the windows, and pleated shades were open to allow in the sun. Plants sprouted from every open space, and they were fed a stream of sunlight from skylights in the ceiling. Framed replicas of famous paintings adorned the walls. A dozen people waited comfortably on opulent leather couches and chairs, some watching the giant television, others reading magazines.

The waiting room was impressive. Hopefully, the medical care was as exceptional.

Looking around the room, she checked for other addicts. She saw a mother with a child. A father with two. An elderly couple. Several elderly people in wheelchairs, sitting next to an ambulance attendant. A few younger patients sat reading and watching television. No one looked too bad off, she thought. *If they're bup patients, Dr. Ball's doing a good job in treating them.*

The registration process was fairly easy, since Jess was paying cash. No insurance precertification was necessary. They simply scanned her driver's license, had her fill out a few forms, and took her money. Judging by the waiting room, Jess figured she'd be in the office for a while. She pulled out her Kindle and picked up where she'd stopped reading her book.

An hour later, a nurse poked her nose through the door that separated the lobby from the treatment area and called Jess's name. The clinical area was just as well done, with the same marble and coordinating colors, plants, and skylights. Following the nurse to her room, she looked around for any sign of other bup patients. All of the dozen doors were closed, though, and the staff members she could see were hard at work at computer screens or scurrying about.

Once inside room seven, the nurse directed Jess to a scale where she measured her height and weight before taking her other vital signs. Then Jess sat on a leather love seat and studied the room. There was a pedestal sink with more marble, a tall armoire instead of cabinets, and more paintings on the walls. A large television was playing mutely on one wall.

"Hmm?" Jess asked.

"Have you used buprenorphine before?" the nurse asked, seeming not at all perturbed by Jess's lapse of attention.

Jess sat back and told her story. Half an hour later, when it was all recorded into the electronic chart, the nurse excused herself, and Jess turned her attention to the television. After she'd watched a few minutes of golf lessons, the door opened and a man walked in. He was tall and well built, with wavy black hair streaked with silver. Jess figured he was her own age, maybe a year or two older. His spotless white lab coat was neatly pressed, as were the pants that draped from beneath it. His black loafers were freshly shined.

Not surprisingly, his voice boomed. “I’m Dr. Ball. I read the nurse’s note so I know a little about you, Jessica, but please tell me in your own words why you’re here.”

“I need a doctor to prescribe my medicine.”

He shook his head, seemingly disappointed. “Sobriety is about more than medication.”

His smug demeanor made Jess want to smack him, and it was difficult to hold back a sarcastic retort. “I understand. I’m seeing a counselor and attending meetings as well.” Occasional meetings, she had to admit. And since she’d convinced her counselor of her great progress, her therapy was only monthly.

His smile was much too wide to be genuine, and his perfectly straight teeth were brighter than the sunrise across the Atlantic. “Yes, that’s all very good, but my patients have such great success because of their involvement with my personalized programs. You not only get your medication here, but your therapy and group sessions as well. That way I can monitor your progress very closely, make adjustments if necessary, and ensure your compliance.”

This program sounded like a pain in the ass, but Jess suddenly understood the higher-than-average fees. And if his success rates were high, who was she to question him? She was a newly minted recovering addict, proud owner of a one-month chip from her meetings. Even though she’d been at Hartley for a month and had been studying online, she still knew next to nothing about addiction. She would learn the real lessons with time.

“So how often will I visit the office?” she asked.

“Daily until you’re stabilized. Then weekly, to ensure you’re trustworthy and not selling your medication. And then monthly. Your meetings here will be weekly, but you can come more frequently if you’d like. We have nice groups. They meet every day, morning and evening, and are well attended. Our psychologists will determine how often they need to see you—weekly, biweekly, monthly.

Whatever is necessary to get you on the road to recovery and keep you there."

Jess began to sweat and fought the urge to bite a nail or chew her lip. This is impossible, she thought. Who could do this, she wondered. Then, as Dr. Ball listened to her chest, she tried the strategy she'd learned in the past weeks. Accept it. Deal with it. *It's only for a few months*, she thought, still wondering how she'd fit all these trips to Wilkes-Barre in around her busy ER schedule. Well, she supposed that was one of the perks of being the department director. The schedule was hers to manipulate.

Dr. Ball hardly noticed her silence as he continued. "I see you're taking twelve milligrams of buprenorphine and three milligrams of naloxone combined."

Looking up, he waited for her response. "Yes."

"And how long have you been taking that dose? Three months?"

Jess nodded. Two. Close enough.

"Well, that dose is too low. All of these so-called specialists try to stabilize you with a low dose, and really, what sense does that make? An addict's brain is all about getting more, trying to satisfy that addiction. Open receptors in your brain cause you anxiety and cause you to misstep and fall off the path of recovery. You need to be taking twenty-four migs."

Jess was shocked. Dr. Gompers was happy with her dose. Everything she'd read had indicated she should take the lowest possible dose of medication to stabilize her addiction. She'd titrated the dose at Hartley, and she felt good on twelve. On eight, she'd still been shaky, but twelve was a good dose for her. Why take more? Sure, she had empty opioid receptors in her brain, but they weren't annoying her. Her occasional stress did cause her tremendous anxiety, but so far, she'd been able to deal with it.

She supposed *so far* was the key observation. What would happen when she fell apart, when she wasn't able to cope? Would she start abusing again?

As before, the doctor didn't seem to notice her hesitation as he rambled on. "There's a meeting in two hours. I'd like you to attend. In the meantime, you can get your prescription filled and come back. We'll give you your medication here, make sure you're taking it right, and then I'll see you tomorrow."

Handing her a script, he smiled. "You're going to do great here, Jessica."

Jess forced a smile in return as she accepted the prescription. It was for just three strips of bup. Truthfully, she didn't need to get the prescription filled. The bottle from Dr. Gompers was in her medicine cabinet at home, and she'd already taken her dose for the day. Her twelve-milligram dose. Should she take another twelve, as the doctor suggested?

"Just go right over to the pharmacy," the clerk instructed her. "And when you come back, you can go straight back to your room."

Jess walked slowly toward the pharmacy, wondering what to do. Would Dr. Gompers be available to discuss this? Probably not. Sure, she'd return Jess's call, but it would be too late by then. She'd been hesitant to bother Ward lately, but she always seemed happy when Jess called.

It was interesting, really, to talk to Ward and see how she was growing as a person. She'd been weak in her relationship with Jess, but with Abby, she seemed to find a true equal. The balance of power was more neutral, and Ward seemed more confident, even in her dealings with Jess. After handing the prescription to the pharmacist, Jess went outside and dialed the number for the ER in Philly.

"How'd you know I was working?" Ward asked after Jess greeted her.

"I took a chance. How's it going?" Jess asked. "Packing up?"

"I hate it. But it fills my time when I'm not working, and every time I go to Abby's, I take some stuff with me."

"She doesn't mind your taking over her house?"

Ward laughed. "She's trying really hard. We bought some new furniture and a painting. Trying to make it ours instead of hers, you know? It's so perfect, though, that I really don't want to change anything."

"Do you have your own room to escape to?"

Jess heard Ward take a deep breath. "Jess, it's so fucking small we trip on each other. I don't know what we're going to do about that."

"How about an addition? Remember we talked about putting on a sunroom? If you hire the right architect, they'll design something that blends right in with the existing structure."

"You think so?"

"I do. Those guys can do wonders."

"That's good news. Because I really want this to work out."

"I hope it does, Ward. You deserve someone who appreciates you. I'm sorry I wasn't her, but I'd feel redeemed if this pans out with Abby."

"We were good for a while, Jess."

"Yes, we were. Now enough of this mushy stuff. I need some medical advice. Don't think like you're treating me. Think like you're treating a patient." Jess went on to explain Dr. Ball's plan to double her medication dose.

"Wow, Jess, that seems really stupid. Everything I've read about this says it's just as addictive as heroin, so it will be very difficult to wean. If your goal is to get off this stuff eventually, why give yourself a bigger hurdle to jump? And why take a higher dose than you need? It doesn't make sense to me. Unless you feel shaky or something."

"I actually feel better than I've felt in years. I don't really think I need more, but he's sort of pushing it on me. He says the people he treats are very successful and don't relapse."

"Jess, I don't know what to say. Do you feel like you're in danger of relapsing? Do you have a plan if you do get to that point?"

Jess had shared her adventures in rehab with Ward on the ride home from Hartley. Ward wasn't surprised that Dr. Gompers had figured it all out. "Dr. Gompers gave me her cell. I can call her if I'm in crisis. She's going to turn me in if I screw up, so I'm very motivated to stay on the straight-and-narrow path."

"So don't take the extra medication. I mean, take the prescription, but don't use it. And then if you need it, it's there. But it doesn't sound like you need it. Wait. You won't abuse it, will you?"

"I don't think so. I think I'm good."

"How about if I keep it for you? Just give you a few days' worth at a time."

"What's your plan? UPS?"

Ward chuckled. "You know I'll be in the mountains, so…I can meet you."

"What about Abby?"

"Abby would like to have you over for dinner. Meet you properly and all. She'd understand. What do you think?"

"About you being my keeper, or having dinner with my replacement?"

Ward must have sensed Jess was teasing, because she answered with a rejoinder. "Both."

Jess went right back at her, and for a moment, she thought of the good times with Ward—only for a moment, though, before she thought of Mac. "Maybe. Can I bring a date?"

"Sure! Do you have a date?"

"I'm working on it."

"Really?"

Jess smiled at the image of Mac that lingered. It was a ridiculous thought, she and Mac, but a pleasant one. She was fodder for fantasy, and while Jess hadn't actually thought about sex in a long time, maybe she was on her way back. Not that she'd share that with her ex, though. "I'll talk to you soon, Doc. Thanks for the free advice."

Jess collected her prescription and headed back to Dr. Ball's office for further instructions. This time she had no wait. She was taken back to the same room, and immediately after Jess closed the door, the nurse opened it. "I know you've done this before, but I want to be sure you're doing it right."

Jess debated arguing with her about the dose, but she didn't want to rock the boat. She peeled back the foil packet and removed the strip.

"Okay, one more," she said.

Jess had to speak up. "I already took twelve this morning. I need only half of that one."

The nurse nodded and watched as Jess placed half a strip under her tongue.

"Perfect! Now don't swallow, and don't drink anything. I'll be back to check on you in a few minutes."

As soon as she left, Jess pulled the melting strips from under her tongue and flushed her mouth with water. She was sure some had absorbed, but hopefully not enough to impair her on the drive home. She felt fine to function on the twelve-milligram dose, but how would she feel with double that?

A few minutes later the nurse found Jess engrossed in a novel. It took her just about a minute to go through the COWS score, which was zero, as it had been for the past two months. When they finished, the nurse offered Jess a remote. "The chair reclines, and you'll find blankets in the armoire," she said.

After she took her leave, Jess opened the doors to the cabinet. For a medical office, it had few of the expected supplies. One shelf held cotton balls and swabs, while the others were stacked with pillows, blankets, reading material, and CDs. A small CD player was tucked into a corner, and a college-dorm-size refrigerator sat on the bottom shelf, next to a basket of snacks. Jess opened the fridge, pulled out a Snapple, then grabbed a pack of Oreos before reclining on the chair.

"Oh, no!" the nurse said when she came back in. "You're not supposed to eat or drink anything for twenty minutes." She looked at her watch. "It's only been fifteen."

"I think I'll be okay," Jess said. "My COWS score is still zero."

The nurse went off to find the doctor, and Jess picked up the remote to channel surf while she waited. It took him nearly half an hour to respond to the crisis.

"How do you feel?"

"Perfect."

"Aha! I knew twenty-four milligrams was the right dose for you. Now if you'll gather your things, you can meet some of my other patients in the therapy room."

Jess collected her food and her purse and followed him down a hallway and through another door. A dozen men and women stood talking. Around them, three rows of cushioned stadium seats formed a semicircle.

At his entrance, eyes turned to the clock and then back to Dr. Ball. "I don't mean to interrupt your meeting, but I want to introduce your newest member. Jessica, this is our Narcotics Anonymous group. Listen to these people. They have a lot to share and can really help someone just starting out. Now I'll leave you in very capable hands. I'll see you tomorrow morning at nine."

He must only know one script, Jess thought, the one for new bup patients. She was well on her way, and judging by the cost of this experience, both in time and money, she planned to sober up quickly and get off the bup. Should she explain it all to them, or just go with Dr. Ball's version? *No*, she told herself. *No more lies.*

They had coffee, of course, but instead of a burnt pot and paper cups, it was served in tasteful floral mugs and brewed in a Keurig. A plate of pastries sat close by as well. *I'll get fat if I spend too much time here*, she thought. Another reason to get totally clean.

Jess sat next to a woman her age and introduced herself. "Kayla," the woman said. "I'll teach you all the ropes."

"Really?"

"Oh, yeah."

"How long have you been doing this?"

"With Dr. Ball? Two years. Before that, another two years."

"Would you mind if I ask your dose?"

Kayla laughed and suddenly looked younger. Her brown hair, cut short, fell in sassy waves that danced with the movement of her shoulders. Matching eyes seemed to smile on their own when she looked at Jess.

"He wants you on twenty-four, right?"

"Yes! I've been stable on twelve for a few months, but he insisted I'd feel better on twenty-four."

"He does that with everyone. I was on sixteen when I started here, and he tried to bump me up, but I wouldn't take it."

"What did you do?"

"Well, I just saved the extras, you know? Then, after a few months, I had like a hundred extras, so I sold them."

Jess couldn't believe a woman she'd known for only thirty seconds was confessing to a felony, but then again, she should have known better than to be surprised by anything that was said during an NA meeting. It was all anonymous, and participants were encouraged to be honest.

"Yeah, there's a guy out front you can sell them to. The ambulance driver."

Jess didn't want to hear anymore. "I'll keep that in mind."

"Only don't sell this month's dose. They do random drug screens and med counts, and they'll check the serial numbers on the package to make sure they're yours."

Jess's jaw dropped. She couldn't believe a doctor that seemed to push these meds then worried about his patients selling them.

Kayla must have read her mind. "The DEA requires random counts. Drug screens, too."

"I see. But why push the twenty-four-milligram dose?"

"I think he owns the pharmacy. He can't have more than a hundred patients, so he can't sell more by getting more patients. He can only push more on us."

Jess felt more and more confused. Why do all this—the beautiful office, the CDs and blankets in the exam room, the cookies and Keurig, the NA meetings and private counseling sessions—if he didn't really care about his patients' recovery?

Were bup doctors graded the way surgeons were, by the number of post-op complications? Did bup doctors get red marks against their names if their patients relapsed? If Jess did the math, Dr. Ball's hundred patients were bringing in fifty thousand dollars monthly to his practice. That was a lot to lose. Perhaps if they were overmedicated and less likely to fail, he looked better in the eyes of the DEA and wouldn't be shut down for his patients' failures.

"What kind of markup do you think pharmacies make?" Jess asked. "Twenty-five percent? At two bucks apiece, that extra strip is making him two hundred dollars a day."

It seemed like peanuts compared to the money he made on office visits, but a pharmacy that prescribed three hundred bup strips a day was certainly profitable.

Jess shook her head. "Can't you go to another pharmacy?"

"They frown on it. Dr. Ball says he knows this pharmacy is a good one, and they'll always have a supply on hand."

"Three hundred a day," Jess observed.

"He's making a fortune."

Jess couldn't argue.

The meeting was called to order and everyone recited the pledge, which Jess had committed to memory, and she was invited to speak, since she was the newcomer. She gave the story she'd been telling since Hartley about being attacked and having PTSD, then turning to drugs to cope. Everyone sympathized, congratulated her on her decision to get sober, and welcomed her to Dr. Ball's program. No matter what her feelings about Dr. Ball, this meeting was the best one she'd ever been to. The people were bright and articulate, no one used foul language, and they all shared insightful opinions when appropriate. *I guess that's what I should expect from people who pay a small fortune for their therapy*, she thought.

"The next meeting here is tonight at seven. And of course, there'll be a seven a.m. meeting tomorrow, and a noon meeting as well."

The group stood and gravitated toward the coffee, but Jess opted for a water to replace the tea she'd finished. Every member of the group approached her, introduced themselves, congratulated her, and offered phone numbers if she wanted to reach out after hours.

"I think I'll come tomorrow morning," Jess said. The meeting and socializing would lead right into her doctor's visit, and it might be quicker that way. She hadn't planned to attend another meeting—only one a week was required—but she'd enjoyed it. Maybe Dr. Ball was right. These people could help her.

With a bounce in her step, and with an older man named Barry beside her, Jess made her way out of the office, through a door hidden in plain view at the front of the building. As she talked with Barry about his recipe for pumpkin bisque, she smiled at the handsome ambulance driver who met her gaze from behind a wheelchair.

CHAPTER SEVENTEEN

Blown Cover

Derek watched the front door of Dr. Ball's office, just as he had a million times before. This time, though, he was dressed in jeans and sneakers, and sitting in his Mercedes. He wasn't buying or selling today, just watching.

When the woman with the flaming ponytail had appeared at the doctor's office on two consecutive days, Derek knew why she was there. Yet another addict looking for the cure. Something bothered him about her, though, and that's why he'd called in sick on this bright fall day. He planned to follow her and learn her secrets. Maybe it would pay off, and maybe not, but his instincts told him something was going on with her, and he always trusted them.

Her Jeep was already parked in the lot when he'd arrived at eight, and he realized she'd come for the early NA meeting. He began watching both doors, then, but she wasn't in the small group that exited the building a few minutes after his arrival. It was after ten when he finally saw her, looking energetic and happy. He must have her on some good drugs, Derek thought.

Waiting until a few cars separated them, Derek pulled the Mercedes into traffic behind her and followed her through a few lights until her destination was obvious. He fell back as she entered the on-ramp for Interstate 81 and followed from a distance. The white Jeep was easy to keep in sight, and he stayed behind her along the route as she merged onto Interstate 380 near Scranton, then Interstate 84 heading into the Poconos and New England. When she turned off at the Garden Exit, it hit him.

The ER doctor from Garden had been kidnapped by the psychopathic doctor. She'd been on the news, and he couldn't help noticing how attractive she was. Holy shit! he thought. What was her name? He drove past the exit, no longer needing to follow her. He had the information he needed, but how would he use it? The doctor was an addict. Was this because of what happened? He doubted it. That wasn't enough time to get hooked and then clean. Maybe the kidnapping had pushed her over the edge, though, and she'd had a major crisis and ended up in rehab. Now she needed outpatient treatment, and like so many others who could afford it, she'd gone to Dr. Ball.

Lucy had told him about the doctor's fees for treating drug addicts. His patients had to have money. Tons of it. Or was he treating the redhead for free, a professional courtesy extended to his colleague? Knowing what he did about Dr. Ball, he doubted it. Dr. Ball was interested in making money, not giving it away.

Derek pulled off at the next exit and into the rest stop. Suddenly, he was hungry.

"How ya doin'?" a middle-aged woman in a waitress's uniform greeted him.

"I'm famished," he said.

"Where ya from?" she asked as she handed him the menu. "French toast's the special today, with real maple syrup, made just up the road. Three slices of bacon and hash browns come with it."

"Sold," he said as she poured his coffee. "Kingston," he said. "Down near Wilkes-Barre."

She nodded in understanding. "What brings you up this way?"

Derek hadn't thought about it, but like so many other good liars, he could always come up with something in a pinch. "I had to drop off a friend. He met a girl from New York, and he's visiting with her for a few days."

"If he has a girl in New York, he'd better get a car." She laughed at her own joke, and Derek did, too.

"Isn't this the place where that crazy doctor was killing people?" he asked.

The waitress stood more erect, and her expression turned

serious as she shook her head. "One of the victims was from right over that way," she said with a nod. "I hope they fry him crispier than your bacon."

Appetizing, Derek thought. "Where's the hospital? Are the reporters still here?"

"The hospital's just a few miles away if you go on the back roads, like I do. Some of them reporters stopped here, asked me a few questions about the victim, Dr. Benson, the one that was kidnapped. She was born and raised here. Her father's the sheriff."

Benson. That was her. Jessica Benson, kidnapping victim and drug addict. Derek's mind raced with possibilities.

He was only an emergency medical technician, and the state required him to complete a disclaimer about drug and alcohol abuse. He had no doubt the physician standards were the same, or higher. So what had Dr. Benson stated on her application for a license? Surely she hadn't admitted to her addiction, or she wouldn't have a license to prescribe narcotics. She had to have lied. And now he knew her secret.

The breakfast was fabulous, and he purchased a small bottle of the local maple syrup and drove home thinking about how he could get the most out of Dr. Benson. Blackmail? It was possible. He imagined she was loaded, since she could afford Dr. Ball's fees. Maybe he'd just use her for drugs. He could take Lucy and a few other friends to the ER, and they could walk away with hundreds of tablets of oxycodone. Those were his immediate thoughts, but if he kept ruminating, more would come.

He wasn't sure what he'd do, but he was in no hurry. Even if Dr. Benson weaned herself off bup, he still knew her secret, and one way or another, he'd use that information.

Chapter Eighteen

Fall Ball

This was a great idea. Thanks for making me do it," Jess said.

Wendy sat behind the wheel of her SUV, weaving her way across the Poconos on old country roads, heading toward Blue Ridge Trail golf course. She was Jess's partner in a charity tournament, and Jess was glad for the opportunity to sit back and relax while Wendy navigated. The skies were clear and the temperature warm enough that she could grip her clubs without wearing ski gloves. Her mood was as sunny as the sky, which was good. Some days, she had to force herself out of bed and off to work, repeating mantra after motivational mantra for encouragement. Other days were good, but this one, so far, had been great.

Wendy interrupted her thoughts. "I know you hate to golf in the cold, but it'll be fun."

"I've been practicing. It's a good stress release." One of the guys at NA had told her he did woodworking to relieve his. Someone else cooked. The self-defense was good, but Jess needed something else to help her manage. Hitting golf balls was physical but also required her complete concentration. The mental exercise was, in this case, more important than the physical. "How are you, my friend?"

"I'm good, Jess. I have my moments, you know? I feel the shock all over again, when that needle hit my thigh. I was confused, until he started talking, and I just felt ice go through my veins when I realized what had happened. Total fear. I relive that moment again and again. Once we got to the cabin, I had hope. I just kept thinking of a way out. My mind saved me, I think. But those few seconds, before I knew what was happening, I was petrified. My therapist has helped, and seeing Hawk in court helped, too. I really let him have it, and he's going to jail for a long, long time."

"Have you heard anything about the murders? Why haven't they pressed charges?"

As the coroner, Wendy had more dealings with the police than she ever did. "Oh, I don't think they'll press charges for a while. There's no deadline on murder charges, so they'll take their time and make sure they have him. There's no smoking gun, just a lot of circumstantial evidence. Just about every body was exhumed and autopsied, and I'd assume they ran tox panels on the remains. I'd bet they're looking for traces of sux and insulin and potassium and everything else they could think of. But even if they find something, no one can prove it was Hawk."

"He told us he murdered those people. Doesn't that count?"

"I'm sure it does, but his attorney will probably say we're lying or something, just to get back at him for the kidnapping."

"There has to be something else, Wendy. Something that proves he murdered those people."

"Like what?"

"I don't know. But he came after us with succinylcholine. Where did he get it? Should I check if any's missing from the pharmacy?"

"Hmm. Let's go even further. If you're Hawk, waiting for an opportunity to murder someone, you have to be ready, right? I mean, you can't go digging through the Pixus when someone's crashing, right? So where's his stash?"

"The police searched his car and apartment. I don't know. I suppose it's easy to hide a small syringe or two."

"This is good, Jess. Talking. Thinking about how to nail him."

"I guess. What if he escapes? What if he comes after us again?"

"If he escapes, he'll be out of the country in no time. His parents are gazillionaires. He'll avoid jail but live his life as a fugitive."

"I don't think I'll ever feel safe unless he's dead. Unless I see his lifeless body and check his pulse and know he can't hurt me anymore. Isn't that strange? I've always been against capital punishment, and I don't know if I want him to die for his crimes, but I know I'm not safe with him alive."

"Isn't that what your self-defense is for? If you see him, flatten him."

"Don't make fun of me. This class is great, and it's done wonders for me. You should come." She was certainly better prepared to defend herself than she was before Hawk attacked her. Her skills would certainly have protected her had she known then what she knew now. She'd never have put herself in that dangerous position. Avoid danger: Mac's first rule. An ounce of prevention is worth a pound of cure: her mother's rule. All the important women in her life sure made up good rules. Thinking of her horrible experience still made her tense, though. Time to change the subject.

"How's your golf game?" she asked Wendy a moment later.

"It sucks. I'm not here to win. I'm here to check out the women."

Chuckling, Jess flipped the hair from her eyes. "Well, you'll have lots of eye candy to feast on. A hundred and forty women, all of them golfers. What more could you ask for?"

"I think I'm ready to settle down."

Jess thought about Wendy's declaration. She'd been settled down for a long time, but she hadn't ever really been settled. Now that her drug use was under control, though, she was beginning to think more clearly. More normally, perhaps. She hadn't been a good partner to Ward. They'd shared a house and expenses, but even when they did things together, Jess was there in body only. Her mind was consumed with drugs. When was her withdrawal going to start? How long could she push herself until she needed another pill? Where would she hide them when they went away for the weekend? What if customs found them as she was attempting to enter a foreign country, and how would she live without them if they were confiscated? It had all been so stressful that, ultimately, she just withdrew. Stayed home and avoided those situations. Pushed Ward away.

Now that she was sober, she wondered what a relationship would be like. She could actually be present for it and might enjoy it. And it seemed, whenever the topics of women, or attraction, or relationships came to mind, thoughts of Mac Calabrese followed closely behind.

Jess wondered about Mac. Was she single? If she wasn't, she had a very understanding partner. With the time Mac spent at work, and at the gym, and then teaching self-defense, she had little left to give. Then Jess chided herself. Mac was off-limits, and her thoughts were getting her nowhere.

Wendy was pathologically early and so was able to find a premier parking place near the bag drop. After donning their shoes and sweaters, they found a golf cart with their names. Since Wendy had registered, their twosome was listed under her last name. Clemens/Benson. They were scheduled to start as the B group on the third hole. "Ready to hit the range?" she asked. "Or do you want to use the restroom first?"

"The range, I think. We'll beat the crowd."

❖

"I love it that you live on the golf course," Mac said to her good friend Gayle. "I'd like to be able to drive my own cart around like I own the place." They were pulling out of Gayle's driveway and then headed along the street toward the golf course.

At that, Gayle hit the gas on the little BMW golf cart, and Mac laughed. They'd played a practice round the night before, followed by drinks and dinner on Gayle's deck, and Mac had spent the night in the guest bedroom, although she suspected Gayle would invite her into the master bedroom if Mac ever indicated an interest. She had none. Gayle was a good friend, though, and a great golf partner, and they'd played many tournaments together over the years, often capping off their rounds just as they had the night before. Now their clubs were still on the cart, and Gayle headed directly to the practice area. "Don't use up all the good shots on the range, Mac. I'd really like to win this year."

"Don't you worry about me. You're the one who partied all night. How can you even stand this morning?"

"Years of practice, my girl."

Mac smiled and returned her attention to the road. The driving range was just ahead, and only a few women occupied the dozen stalls. One of them had red hair pulled into a ponytail and looked remarkably like Jess. Jess was off-limits! Why did she think of Jess so often?

Grabbing her entire bag from the cart, she shouldered it and headed toward the far end of the range. The girl who looked like Jess had a great ass, and Mac couldn't help admiring it and the long legs draped in perfectly tailored, coffee-colored slacks. She even wore brown golf shoes. Her swing looked good and produced a high, arcing ball that landed near the flag a hundred yards down the range. "Nice shot," she said, because it was.

The woman turned, and the look of shock on her face told Mac she was just as surprised to see her as Mac was. The raised eyebrows came down, and a smile replaced the large O her mouth had formed. Jess looked absolutely beautiful. She rested on her club as she greeted Mac. "I didn't know you golf."

"I didn't know *you* golf."

"What does this say about your detecting skills?" she asked, her lips puckered suspiciously.

"They're a little off around you," she said, before she could stop herself. A blush crept up her cheeks, and her neurons were working full speed to come up with an escape plan when Jess spared her.

Turning her head slightly, she had a small smile at the corners of her mouth, and her blue eyes sparkled. "Yeah. I get a little off when you're around, too."

They looked at each other for a moment, and a connection seemed to form, as they both stood by the acknowledgment they'd made, that something really did exist between them. It wasn't the heat that Mac usually felt around women she was attracted to; it was more of a comforting warmth. Like coming in from the cold.

"I like this course," Jess said after a moment.

"Oh, do you play here often?"

She shook her head. "I've only been back home for a year, so I haven't played anywhere often. But I've played it a few times over the years. How about you?"

"I play here all the time, in a league. And my friend Gayle lives on the course, so I can hang out when I'm not working."

"I didn't realize you take time off. It seems like you're always on a case."

"Yeah. I am. It's a tough job. Tough on relationships." They'd acknowledged the attraction, and Mac had to throw that out there. A relationship with a cop wasn't easy. If that was what Jess was thinking.

"Well, you have to take advantage of the time you get off then, right? You are off?"

"Yes. Barring a catastrophe beyond imagination, I'm off for the entire weekend, in fact."

Jess seemed to ponder that statement for a moment. "Maybe we can have dinner tomorrow."

She couldn't get involved with Jess. Jess was a witness in a kidnapping, potentially a murder investigation! But dinner wouldn't hurt, would it? They'd just eat. She had to eat somewhere. And they could talk. Talking was supposed to be good. She could talk about self-defense. And, apparently, golf. "I'd like that. But we can't discuss business. I'd like to talk about us." Mac felt herself blush. "I mean about ourselves. You and me. As individuals." She laughed at the mess she'd made of her reply. "I'd like to get to know you better."

Jess studied her. "That sounds like a line."

Remarkably, it wasn't. For the first time in her life she'd met someone who intrigued her, instead of just piquing her interest. "It's not, really."

Jess swallowed her laughter. "Go hit some balls and I'll catch up with you later."

Jess put another ball on the tee and whacked it down the range, but she'd lost her concentration. Mac had the same…feeling…she had. What it meant, Jess had no idea, but she thought she wanted to find out.

After a few more shots, she walked over to Wendy. "I'm going to the putting green. I'll see you there."

"Was that Detective Calabrese?"

"Yep."

"Small world. I'll pick you up at the practice greens."

Jess chipped and putted a few balls, but her mind wasn't on golf. The mental exercises she'd been using to stay calm were failing her. But it wasn't bad, she realized. She wasn't thinking of pills to calm her nerves, but of Mac. Her spiky blond hair. Her expressive blue eyes. The tight mouth, so serious at times, opening up in a wide smile. And the muscles Jess had seen and felt during self-defense classes. Mmmm. This kind of distraction wasn't bad at all.

Breakfast had been at seven, just before Wendy picked her up, but she grabbed one of the free energy bars offered at the registration area and slipped it into her purse, just in case. She saw a few familiar faces in the crowd and spoke with several ladies she knew, some old acquaintances and others she'd met over the past months, thanks to Wendy. One was an ER doctor from Scranton, who reacquainted her with yet another ER doctor whom she'd known since residency. And Dr. Reese Ryan, her college roommate, had been trying to contact Jess since the incident with Hawk. Jess just hadn't felt like talking. She apologized for not returning the calls and thanked Reese for her concern.

"I'm just glad to see you're doing okay," she said, then changed the subject to safer topics like golf and gossip about old colleagues. By the time Wendy pulled up, Reese had Jess laughing so hard she thought she'd pee her pants. Jess promised to call, and this time she'd keep her word. Reese was a good person, funny and sharp, and a good friend. Jess needed some of those in her life.

Wendy pulled the cart into the queue with dozens of other carts, and after they listened to the rules of the tournament, they were off. Following the carts in front of them, Wendy easily found the third tee. She pulled off to the side to allow others to pass. "Who are we playing with?" she asked.

"No idea. I think we're paired alphabetically."

Since Wendy had registered, they were alphabetically a C. Just like Calabrese. Jess looked up just as another golf cart pulled over and Mac hopped out. "Are you guys three-B?" she asked hopefully.

"That's us," Wendy said.

Mac had walked toward their cart, toward the passenger side, where Jess rested her arm on the cart's sturdy frame. Jess dropped her voice to a whisper. "Do you think the fates are trying to tell us something?"

Mac looked serious. "I think if you can golf with someone, and they don't make you want to pound your clubs into the ground, you have a chance to be good friends."

"You're right. Friends. And I've played with a few people I wanted to strangle before the round was through."

"Please don't confess homicidal fantasies to me. These days we have to take all threats seriously. I'll have to report you."

Jess straightened up as she caught the stern expression. "I'm sorry, Mac. I didn't mean…"

Mac laughed and patted her arm. "Just kidding. I'd like to strangle some golfers, too."

Jess swatted her in return. "That wasn't funny."

Mac wiggled her eyebrows, then turned and introduced her playing partner. Gayle offered them all a shot of Irish crème for their coffee and told them the coffee was optional. She opted for the coffee-free version and realized it was going to be an interesting round of golf. She was unsure if she'd be able to hit a shot knowing Mac was watching.

The A group took the tee box and hit while Jess and her foursome stayed back, respectfully quiet as they watched the others. When the tee cleared, Mac looked at Jess and winked. "How about a wager, Doc?"

Jess stood behind her oversized driver and pretended to study Mac. "You look like a ringer to me, Mac. And if you take advantage of me, who could I report you to? You're the law."

"I think your father could put me in my place."

Jess thought about it for a second. "You're right. Are you thinking you against me, or my team versus your team?"

"As much as I'd like to challenge you, it might be impolite to exclude Wendy and Gayle."

"Another time then. For the one-on-one."

"It's a date."

Jess nearly gasped, and as their eyes met, she saw a blush creeping up Mac's face, a shade that surely matched her own. She smiled and turned away, but not before the heat warmed her all the way through.

"Wendy. Are you up for a wager? A buck a hole?"

"Ah, Mac!" Gayle said as she waved her hand, threatening Mac with the lit cigarette that protruded through her fingers like a weapon. "You just jinxed us!"

In the end, Jess and Wendy were no match for Gayle and Mac. They managed to win three holes, one because Gayle and Mac screwed up, and two because they actually played well. In the noisy clubhouse after the golf, they mingled for a few minutes before taking their places at tables decorated with golf trinkets and balloons. Many of the women held wine and beer, but she noticed Mac stuck to water. She didn't even try to hide it; she just sipped it straight from the bottle.

"I'm having a few friends over to the house. Why don't you join us?" Gayle asked after the awards were presented.

Jess looked from Gayle to Mac, who suddenly became interested in her salad. No encouragement there. She was about to decline the offer when Wendy responded for them, without bothering to even look Jess's way. "We'd love to."

It was only three o'clock, she had nowhere to be until the following morning, and it was another chance to mingle, to fulfill the promise she'd made to herself to have fun. To talk to Mac.

"Left out of the parking lot, first right, third house on the left."

"Left, right, left. Got it."

"You'll see cars," Mac said as she sipped her water.

Jess nodded as she bit into her salad. "What's gotten into you?" she discreetly asked Wendy when she saw Mac and Gayle engaged.

"Chrissy. I talked to her at the bar and she mentioned Gayle's after-party. I was kind of hoping for an invite. You don't mind, do you?"

Jess didn't face Wendy, but instead looked up and noticed Mac watching her. "No, I don't mind at all."

❖

"It's a little cold for the pool, but it is heated, so if you'd like, hop in. And the hot tub's open, too," Gayle said as she led them from her kitchen to her deck. "Clothing is optional."

An outdoor kitchen awaited them, as did twenty women, most of whom Jess recognized from the golf tournament. Without being obvious, she looked around, hoping to spot Mac, but saw no sign of her.

Being more social in light of her recent infamy was difficult, but for the most part, people were respectful and didn't ask questions about Hawk. The more tasteful ones mentioned it, just to get it out in the open, and quickly moved on. That was the case with the first woman who Jess spoke with, someone she'd played softball against in high school twenty years earlier. They'd seen each other occasionally over the years, and Jess had always liked her. "Hi, Karen," she said.

"I'd ask how you are, but I can only imagine. I'm glad that fucker's in jail, and I hope they fry his ass. The course was in great shape today, wasn't it? Heather came within two inches of a hole in one on number ten. Her ball mark was right next to the cup."

"Did she at least make birdie?"

"Nope!"

They talked about the tournament, which was a fund-raiser for a local charity, and about their hostess, who seemed to be more popular than the alcohol that flowed freely from a tap and several bottles along the bar. Karen's partner, Heather, was perched on a stool and pouring generously. Since Wendy was enjoying herself so much, Jess stuck to water.

"How long have you guys been together?"

"Twenty years, I think. A long time."

"Thinking of marriage?"

"She's planning it. We have a good friend, an accountant, who tells us to do it right before we die, to save on inheritance taxes. Otherwise it costs us money."

Since marriage had never been an option for her, Jess had never spent much time fantasizing about it. She and Ward had exchanged rings on a tropical island once, but it wasn't legal, and she hadn't given it much thought. Their commitment wasn't about a ring. Now that the Supreme Court had whipped everyone into shape, Jess had started thinking about it more. How wonderful to enjoy the same basic human rights as everyone else. Karen was right, though. If one partner got bumped into a higher tax bracket because of the marriage, it could be costly.

Another acquaintance joined the conversation, and before long everyone was talking about marriage. Four couples were recently engaged, two had already gotten married, and others were contemplating the commitment. Jess wondered if anyone at the party was single.

Gayle brought bowls of snacks around, and Jess used the break in the conversation to sneak away.

"I thought I'd never get you alone," Mac said from behind her as she exited the bathroom.

"If I'd known you were trying, I'd have escaped sooner."

Mac took her hand and pulled her in the opposite direction of the noise, onto a round alcove on the corner of the porch complete with two rocking chairs. "Can I get you a drink?"

"No, thanks. I've been nursing a bottle of water."

"Designated driver?"

"I guess Wendy deserves to have a little fun."

"Don't you?"

"Who says I'm not?"

"So you can have fun without drinking? That's a rare and unusual talent among the women I know."

"So you don't drink?"

Mac laughed. "Hell, yes. But if I drink when I'm golfing, I play like crap. And if I drink now, I'll be stuck here all night. So I have to pick my moments."

"Sounds pretty smart."

Pushing gently with her toes, Jess sent her rocker into motion and settled into it, enjoying the moment. The noise from the party on the other side of the house seemed to fade as she studied the trees surrounding Gayle's house. She could see every color of the autumn rainbow in the foliage, but now their arms were giving up the leaves they'd carried all spring and summer, resulting in piles of color on the ground.

Mac seemed to notice her observation. "It's pretty, isn't it?"

Jess nodded. Since her abduction, she'd been trying to take more time for the little things that made life so good. Talking to people. Cooking. Exercising. And enjoying nature.

She'd spent most of her childhood outdoors, riding and playing in the streets of Garden, then at the hunting club, where she and her friends swam in the lake and boated and hiked. She'd left that life when she went to the big city to study medicine, and she hadn't realized how much she missed it until she came back. Periodic, three-day visits weren't enough to reimmerse herself in mountain life, and her longer trips, vacations, were always to Europe or the islands of the Caribbean. It had been a year since she'd returned to Garden, and it was finally starting to feel like home again, in a way Philadelphia never could.

Jess swiveled in her rocker and smiled at Mac. "I never realized how much I love it here, until I came home again. Something was missing, but I never could figure out what it was. Now I know. I need to be outside, getting my daily vitamin D."

"Makes sense to me," Mac said as she replaced the cap on her water and set her own chair rocking. "How long were you gone?"

Jess told her the story of her journey to Philly for med school and residency, how she'd fallen in love with Ward and decided to stay in Philly. "It seemed like coming home wasn't an option back then."

"You're right. The culture has certainly changed in the past few years. I bet you wouldn't hesitate to move home now."

Jess nodded. "You're right. Sometimes I feel like kicking myself, because I missed so much time with my parents, hiding in Philly where I could be out. Now my mom is dead, and I think my dad is starting to get a little dementia, so I don't have much time left with him either."

Mac smiled understandingly. "You can't dwell, Jess. Your parents raised you to go out into the world and be independent. I don't know them, but I don't think they would have wanted you to stay in Garden and work as a waitress at George's Pub. They wanted you to go out and explore the world and find your place in it. For a while, that place was Philly. I'm sure the things you learned in Philly made you a great doctor, and now you've brought those skills back here to help your friends and neighbors. Now this is the next phase of your journey."

Mac's words brought tears to her eyes, and she turned away before Mac spotted them, studying the foliage again, thinking back, remembering her mom. Packing food for Jess to take back to Philly. Washing and folding her laundry at the kitchen table when Jess came for her monthly visits during med school and residency. She could hear her mother's voice, asking when she was coming home, and her own voice, making excuses because her addiction sucked up all her energy and she didn't have any left for the trip. Finally, as her mother was dying, the wonderful talks they had. Her mother told her to have a child, because she needed to get grounded. A child would fulfill her, she said. And then, those words every child wanted their parents to say. I'm proud of you.

At least I had a few months with her, Jess thought. *I smartened up in time to help my mother through the last part of her life, and I'll help my dad through this. And I let Ward go, so she could find happiness. Maybe I can find some, too.* Seeming to sense Jess's thoughts, Mac interrupted them.

"I didn't mean to make you sad. Should I tell you a joke?"

"Hmm. I guess it's worth a try."

"Knock knock."

Jess laughed. "Really, Mac? A knock-knock joke?"

"See, it worked. You're laughing already."

"Tell me the punch line, Mac."

"I don't need to. You're already laughing. My work here is done."

"That's mean."

"Okay. Knock knock."

Jess looked at her skeptically. "Who's there?"

"Boo."

"Boo who?"

"Please don't cry."

Jess laughed again. "Okay, I promise. No more crying."

"So, do you really want to have dinner with me? Because I'm free tomorrow night, and I'd love to spend more time with you."

Turning, Jess met Mac's gaze. The bright eyes held her, warmed her. Comforted her. "I'd like that, too."

"What time? Where?"

❖

Even though Jess had been expecting Mac, the ringing doorbell nearly caused her to jump out of her chair. As she rose, she smoothed the wrinkles from her pants and checked herself in the ornate carved mirror in the grand hall. Hair down and in place. Lipstick still intact. Silk shirt draping elegantly, long chain accenting everything perfectly.

Mac's warm smile of greeting was replaced by an appreciative one as she checked Jess out. "You look great."

Dressed in a form-fitting Brooks Brothers suit, as always, Mac looked stunning as well. Tonight, though, instead of the white or light-blue shirt beneath, Mac had worn teal. It turned her eyes, and Jess immediately thought of the Caribbean. She couldn't stop herself from touching the color. "You, too," she said softly. Their eyes met for a moment before Jess forced herself to look away.

They headed to Lake Wallenpaupack, a short drive from Garden, to a new restaurant Mac had heard about. Jess hadn't spent much time out in the year she'd been home, so she was happy to eat anywhere other than her own kitchen. It was an easy drive on the back roads, and not surprisingly, Mac had insisted on taking the wheel of her state-issued Crown Victoria.

"So you keep your police car with you all the time?"

"I never know when I'll get called."

"Sounds like a tough job, Mac. How do you do it?"

Mac was quiet for a moment as she seemed to contemplate the answer. "It's just what I do. It's what I've always done, so it seems normal to me. Isn't that kind of what it's like for you as a doctor, never knowing when you'll get a call from a patient?"

"For some doctors, yes. As an ER doctor, I'm not technically on call. I get assigned shifts to work for the month and that's my responsibility. If I have a conflict, I have to work it out, because I own those days. As the ER director, though, it's a whole different story. I'm on call twenty-four seven. If a doc has an emergency and can't find a replacement, I'm it. If there's a bus crash, I'm the one they call. If a doctor hurts a nurse's feelings and we need an intervention, I'm there."

"Do you get called often?"

"Often enough that it's stressful. But I'd rather be in charge of the problems than not, you know?"

"Yes, I know exactly what you mean. I can make things happen the right way, and that's important. When I'm leading an investigation, I know it's being done properly and that the evidence will be processed and protected, because I'm in charge of the locker, and I know what I need to do to make the prosecutor's job easier."

If the number of cars in the parking lot was an indicator, dinner was going to be good. Mac finally found a spot as someone else left, and she pulled in and jumped out to help Jess with the door. As they walked, Jess felt a gentle hand on her back, guiding her toward the podium where a hostess smiled warmly in greeting.

"Your table will be ready in a few minutes. Would you like to wait here or have a seat at the bar?"

"Would you like a drink?" Jess asked. "Maybe a nice glass of red wine to chase the chill? I mean, I know you don't drink a lot, so don't feel obligated." Jess shut her mouth and shook her head, grateful when Mac rescued her. "It has gotten cold. A cab would be nice."

The day before, Mac had worn shorts for the golf tournament, and this evening, she'd pulled out her heavy jacket. September was still laying claim to the calendar, yet it felt like winter.

"Do you spend much time at the lake?" Jess asked as she looked around the bar.

Mac hadn't been to this particular restaurant before, but she liked the look. The bar appeared new, and bright. This was a place to laugh and have fun, not to drown your sorrows and fade into oblivion. She did socialize at the lake, though. "Only if I'm invited out, I guess. I have my own lake and, truthfully, not a lot of time. I prefer a quieter setting to wind down."

"Do you boat on your lake?"

"Non-motorized boats only."

"Kayaks?"

"Oh, yes. Lots of kayaks and canoes, fishing boats, floats. There's a dock to jump from, with a slide, and another floating dock about a hundred yards from shore. All the big kids swim out there to get away from their siblings."

"Do you join in the fun, or just watch?"

"Sometimes I go out early, before they're all awake. But sometimes I join the fun. They play baseball off the dock. The pitcher and the batter are on the dock, and the batter hits the ball and then has to swim to first base. It's a lot of fun on a hot day."

"You pitch, right?"

Mac looked guilty. "What makes you say that?"

"You like to be in control, Mac."

"Don't you?"

"Well, like I said about my job, it's better to make the decisions than bitch about them. But I've learned in the last few months that you can't always be in control of everything. I'm working hard to relax."

Just then, they were called to their table, and Mac couldn't help admiring Jess as she walked before her. Her hair was down, and the waves fell softly to her shoulders. A shirt a few shades darker than her hair draped to her waist, and navy-blue linen pants hugged her hips and ass perfectly. The pants were tucked into blue leather boots adorned with a dozen buckles and snaps and zippers.

They sat opposite each other, on the deck. It had been enclosed in a plastic tent, and a heater nearby ensured their warmth. The panel facing the lake remained open, and Mac had a view of the boats stealing the last hours of autumn.

"How are you doing with relaxing?" Mac asked.

Jess had spent the past twenty-four hours thinking about nothing but Mac. There was an attraction between them, and Jess wasn't sure where it was going, but she had to talk to Mac about some things before they could be involved. Her PTSD and her trip to Hartley, for one. Her addiction was the biggie. She suspected Mac knew about the first issue, and she decided to start there.

"I'm sure you suspected I had a little…crisis…after Hawk. I went to a psychiatric clinic for four weeks to get some therapy. I read that an experience like the one I had could cause serious long-term problems, and I didn't want that, you know? I was too afraid to leave my house after the attack, couldn't even get out of bed. So I decided to get away and talk to people who could help me deal with what happened and put it behind me, sort of. Get through it, anyway."

Jess looked to Mac for encouragement, some sign that she was interested and that Jess should continue.

"I kind of figured as much when you weren't around for the preliminary hearing."

"Sorry about that. I was in no condition to face Hawk."

"And now? Could you face him?"

"Now, I'm looking forward to it. I want to make sure he's in jail forever. And with the murder cases, I hope he's executed." Jess dipped a wedge of bread into oil and bit into it, savoring the taste of herbs and garlic and the thought of Hawk dying. It would make her feel better, not to see him dead, but to know he'd never escape from prison, or accidentally get parole and hurt someone again. Hurt her again.

"I hope it works out that way," Mac said, and Jess detected some hesitancy in Mac's voice.

"I know you can't really talk to me about this, but how's it going? I mean, I think the kidnapping is easy. I testify that he drugged me and kidnapped me and that's that. But what about the murders? Those victims can't testify. Is there enough evidence? Wendy seems to think it's all circumstantial and he might be about to wiggle out of the charges."

"It would be nice to have something concrete on him. We can say that five of Hawk's patients died of insulin overdoses, and that's an improbable coincidence, but unless we have a bottle of insulin with Hawk's fingerprints on it, it's hard to prove he gave the injections."

"Oh, my God!" Jess said and sat forward, her mind reeling. Hawk had injected her in her office and then left to attend to matters in the ER. She had no idea what he'd done with the syringe of succinylcholine he'd used to paralyze her. But later, when he'd attacked Wendy, he'd put her into the body bag with Jess and then deposited the syringe of sux into the sharps container in the back of the hearse. It had been two months earlier, but might it still be there? How often did Wendy change it?

"Mac, the syringe of sux he used to paralyze Wendy. It's in her hearse. In the sharps container."

Mac leaned forward and patted Jess's hand. "I like your thinking, Doc. That's excellent. We already went through the sharps container from the hearse and every one at Garden Memorial. We found the syringes of sux, but unfortunately, no prints. He must have worn gloves or wiped them, because they were clean."

Defeated, Jess sat back. "Oh, well."

"Don't feel dejected, Jess. Keep thinking. When one door closes, find a window. That's the only way to solve a case."

"I guess it's kind of like medicine, your job. When one medication or therapy doesn't work, try another. Sometimes the clock is ticking, because the patient is very sick, and you get it right. Sometimes…not."

Mac sipped her wine and looked over Jess's shoulder to the lights on the lake. "I hate to think about the ones that got away."

Jess leaned forward. "Let's not let Hawk get away."

They hadn't even glanced at the menus but hastily selected

soup and entrees when their server appeared to take their order. When their server left, Mac placed her hand over Jess's.

"He'll go away, Jess."

"For how long?"

Mac shrugged. "I'm sure the DA will add aggravated kidnapping charges, which will tack on a few years to his sentence. But he's only thirty-eight years old. He'll get smarter in prison, more evil. When he gets out he'll be late forties, early fifties, and totally fucking lethal."

"So we can't let him get out, Mac. How do we do that?"

"Make the murder charges stick."

"How?"

"We need something that ties him to the murders. Like the aforementioned syringe of insulin with his fingerprints all over it. When they exhumed the body, they found high levels of insulin in a patient who died a few months ago. If they could find the same type of insulin in a vial with Hawk's fingerprints on it, that would be a really good clue."

"He had to keep his stuff somewhere, so why can't you find it?"

Steaming bowls of pumpkin soup were placed before them, the Gruyère shavings on top beginning to melt into the liquid. Both Jess and Mac brought spoonfuls to their mouths and blew on them before tasting. "Mmm," Jess said.

"Very good," Mac agreed.

"So how long do you think he'll get for the kidnapping?"

Mac had thought about the case and couldn't say she was entirely comfortable with it. Since none of the victims had been harmed—technically—Hawk's lawyers had tried to have the charges reduced to misdemeanor from felony. Because he'd drugged his victims, though, they'd kept the more serious charges. For now, anyway. She'd talked to the DA and could tell he was a little nervous. Hawk's parents had hired a dream team of lawyers, and he was worried about what kind of nonsense they'd try. One thing was certain—Hawk would have the best defense money could buy, and his lawyers would exploit any loophole in the law, any flaw in the case, and use it to help their client. Mac didn't think it would happen, but it was possible Hawk could walk away with no jail time at all.

Of course, if that happened, the DA would immediately file murder charges, and Hawk would go directly back to jail, without passing go or collecting his two hundred dollars. But unless the evidence was solid enough to hold him, his million-dollar lawyers would then get him off on bail, or worse yet—have the charges dismissed. And if that happened, if he was set free, Mac was absolutely sure Hawk would bolt, and he'd start murdering people in Buenos Aires or Cape Town, or wherever he fled.

She had her work cut out for her, and the woman sitting across the table from her made her determined to find the evidence she needed to make sure Hawk got his date with the executioner.

Chapter Nineteen

Evidence

Jess sometimes thought the eleven rooms in her house were too much, but since she'd been working out with Mac in what had once been the library, she was glad for the space. It beat the testosterone and noise at the gym hands down.

All the time together had a drawback, though. Jess had given up on fighting her attraction to Mac. Now she was just fighting the urge to act on it. They hadn't even really hugged yet. After dinner at the lake a couple of months earlier, Mac had given her a polite hug when she walked Jess to the door. Since then, when they went their separate ways, their farewells were similar. Friendly. Courteous. Safe. And, Jess knew, that was how they had to stay, because if she pulled Mac too close, her mouth would go from Mac's cheek, to her ear, and her neck…

Jess stopped and gazed in the mirror. She looked great. Her body was toned, and thanks to the workouts with Mac in addition to her own routine, she'd never been in better shape. She'd grown strong, both mentally and physically. If only she was strong enough to stay away from Mac until after Hawk's trial.

She descended the stairs and found Mac stretched out on the floor of the library. They'd discovered a used wrestling mat in the newspaper, and it was a perfect fit. Jess had bought a treadmill and placed it beside her elliptical, and Mac had started running there on the days Mother Nature made it unsuitable to exercise outdoors. Like today, the day before Thanksgiving. She'd finished at the office at seven and had come to Jess's and run on the treadmill. Jess had worked until seven as well but hadn't gotten out of the ER until almost eight, so she'd arrived just as Mac was finishing her third mile. She'd said hello before running up the steps to change.

Mac caught her breath at the sight of Jess in clinging workout pants and top. Very little was left to the imagination, and Mac needed no such temptation. What had happened to her? She'd always been so calm and cool, and now here she was, all heated up over the one woman she definitely couldn't take to bed. She looked away as Jess began to stretch. If she watched, her resolve might just crumble and she'd do something regrettable.

After a few minutes, Mac finished on the treadmill and they began their self-defense routine. As they went through stretches and poses, kicks and punches, Mac was pleased to see how far Jess had come. She took the classes more seriously than anyone Mac had ever coached. She'd worked with many victims, and they were all motivated, but few of them saw it through. Jess, though, was a dynamo.

When they finished, Jess offered Mac a drink. They took their water to the couch in Jess's living room and collapsed onto the sofa.

"How are the dinner plans coming?"

"It's my first turkey, but I think it'll be fine. I'll be cooking at my dad's, and I helped my mom with Thanksgiving dinner for about thirty years. I'll figure it all out. And you?"

"I'll go to my parents' early and just follow orders. Mash! Slice! Pour. I'm great at that stuff. I'm not a bad cook, either, but there isn't enough room for all of us in one kitchen. After dinner, I'll play with all the nieces and nephews. I always try to take this weekend off so I can spend time with them. They come from Ohio, Maryland, and Harrisburg for the holiday, and it's the one time of year we're all together."

"How about some wine, Mac? I kind of feel like wine."

"Do you have any cheese?"

"I'll see what I can dig up. Come help me."

Mac uncorked a pinot noir while Jess sliced a wedge of cheese and spread crackers on a plate, then followed her back to the living room. Jess pressed a button and the gas fireplace came to life, instantly warming the room.

Mac sat forward and sipped from the large balloon glass. "What's that?" she asked, nodding toward the pile on the table.

Jess reached out and ran her fingers gently across the cover before meeting Mac's gaze. "Photo albums. My dad gave them to me. It seems my mom chronicled my entire life in albums. Photos, artwork, newspaper articles. It covers everything from my birth announcement to the piece in the *Garden Press* when I was hired as ER director."

Mac was impressed. "Wow. That's some gift."

"Yeah, it is. I haven't really gone through them. It's a little emotional, you know?" Jess swallowed hard. She'd had the books for two days and had done little more than glance at the covers. Her father had found them on the top shelf of the pantry.

"C'mon. Let me have a peek. I'd like to see you with pigtails and no teeth."

Jess thought she was ready, and so they sat beside each other, looking at random albums. The first Mac chose was third grade, and she did indeed find the picture she was looking for. Jess as the centerfielder on the high-school and college softball teams was another highlight.

"Ah, medical school," Jess said when Mac chose the third album. The cheese was gone, and they were into their second glasses of wine as she opened the book. It started with her letter of acceptance, which took up an entire page. Beside it was a picture of Jess in her parents' kitchen, holding the letter, the smile on her face lighting up the room.

It was fun to go through the pages with Mac, reliving that wonderful time of her life. They studied pictures of her classrooms, her in full protective garb outside the anatomy lab, behind a microscope. A picture of Jess with the first baby she delivered was also enlarged to fill the page, as did the shot of her over a pig's foot as she learned to suture.

"What's this?" Mac asked as she turned the page and saw a picture of Jess donning a white lab coat.

"Oh, that's the white-coat ceremony."

"What's that about?"

"When you're a medical student, you wear a short coat. It's sort of like a scarlet letter because it marks you. Everyone in the hospital knows you're the lowest life form. But when you graduate from medical school, when you're a full-fledged doctor, you get to wear the long coat. So they have a ceremony where the attending physicians—our teachers—'coat' us."

"Do you wear one? Whenever I go to the doctor, she's in street clothes. She could be the secretary for all I know."

Jess laughed. "I do because I wear scrubs to work, and so does the janitor, and I don't want the staff to confuse us."

Now Mac laughed. "You'd be the cutest janitor at Garden Memorial," she said as she gently poked Jess in the ribs.

Jess felt herself blushing and concentrated on the page before her, although she couldn't deny the thrill Mac's compliment gave her.

"Actually, I like wearing my coat. First of all, it's warm, so there's that. But it has huge pockets, for my stethoscope, pens, whatever I need."

Suddenly, Jess's mouth went dry and she turned to Mac. Her eyes opened wide as a thought came to her. "Oh, God, Mac. Hawk. He always wore a lab coat. Did you find it? We might discover something in his pockets."

Mac stared at Jess and seemed to be thinking, and then she reached out to her. "I don't think we did, Jess. Is there some place in the hospital where he might have left it?"

"Hawk used the physicians' lounge all the time. He showered there. I wonder if he had a locker there?"

"We searched in the break room but couldn't find anything. Is that what you're talking about? The room where I met you that morning after your night shift."

"No, this is in the back of the hospital, next to the elevators."

"Is it too late to check?"

"Not if you're on the medical staff, and I am."

Jess looked down at herself. She was dressed for a workout, not for the office, and she'd had a glass of wine, but she didn't care. This was too important to wait. She stood. "Let's go."

They took her car, and she parked it in the vacant spot near the ER designated for physicians. Jess didn't feel guilty at all. She was a physician, and as far as she was concerned, this was an emergency.

Walking briskly, they quickly reached the physicians' lounge. The large room was papered and decorated exquisitely, with tasteful prints and dried flowers, and club chairs arranged in a conversational grouping around a large table. Mac followed Jess through a doorway where large wooden lockers lined both sides of the wide hall, leading to the men's restroom. The lockers were eighteen inches wide and stretched eight feet from the floor.

"How many doctors are on staff?" Mac asked as she looked for some identifying feature on the doors. She found numbers, discreetly engraved across the top. In all, there were sixty lockers in the room.

"I don't know. But not everyone has one. I don't. I only come in here once in a while. It's easy enough to change clothes and shower at home since I live a block away. But I bet Ernie can tell us. He's the night janitor for the main floor."

Jess walked calmly to the phone on a desk tucked discreetly into a corner and put it to her ear. She pressed one button. "Hi, Renee, Dr. Benson here. Can you page Ernie to the physicians' lounge, please?"

A second later she heard the page overhead, and she leaned against the chair, thinking. Could this little adventure lead to something? Might Hawk have had a locker, and if so, would they find something inside that could incriminate him?"

"Hi, Doc. What's going on? How are you?"

Jess smiled at Ernie. He was a neighbor of her parents, and she'd known him practically her entire life. He'd been one of the first to congratulate her when she was named ER director, and he made her job easier by taking care of all the little problems that popped up in her department.

She explained her concern. "The police asked me, Doc. Dr. Hawk never had a locker in here. I saw him hanging around all the time, but I think he was just showering and watching television, eating takeout. He told me he didn't like to throw his food in the can at the apartment, because of the smell."

"Who do all these lockers belong to?" Mac asked.

"Hold on. I have a list."

Ernie pulled out a ring of dozens of keys and inserted one into the last locker door. Inside he found a clipboard and pulled it out. After scanning it, he handed it to Mac.

"So these lockers with no name next to them, they're empty?"

"Yes."

Mac walked along the row, starting at number one, which was assigned to a doctor named Quick. She pulled on the handle, but it didn't open. Following the same process, she went through eight lockers. The ninth had no name beside it. When she lifted the handle, it opened.

"So what happens here? When you assign a locker, you insert the locking mechanism?"

"Exactly. And I keep a copy of the key in case they lose it."

"So all of these unassigned lockers should be open, correct?"

"That's right."

"Let's try them."

They went through thirty lockers on one wall and were on their way back on the opposite side when Jess pulled on a locker that didn't open.

"It's unassigned," Ernie said, looking at his clipboard. "It should open."

He examined the locker more closely. "That's strange. There's a lock in there."

Jess's heart pounded, and she worked hard to slow her breathing as Ernie tried each key in his box of locks. None of them opened the locker.

"What do we do now?" Jess asked.

"Drill it out."

Jess met Mac's eyes and saw no hesitation there. "Do we need a warrant or anything, Mac?"

"The original warrant is still good. It covers the entire hospital."

While Ernie went for his drill, Jess and Mac were quiet. Jess studied Mac, amazed that she showed absolutely no emotion. They were so close to opening the mysterious locker, one that could give them evidence about Hawk, and she looked so calm, leaning against the wall, her long frame looking sleek in the sweat suit she'd worn for their workout.

Ernie didn't make them wait long; his drill took only a minute to destroy the lock inside its wooden cage. When it was free, Ernie tried the handle and the door flew open.

Jess walked toward it, and Ernie backed off, seeming to understand her need to search the space. Inside, a silver briefcase, the kind a secret government agent might carry, sat sideways on the floor. On the top shelf, a toiletry kit took up most of the space. Hanging from a large coat hanger was a crisp, clean, white lab coat.

With a trembling hand and burning eyes, she pulled it toward her, turning it so the name embroidered on the chest was visible to her.

Closing her eyes for a moment, she gathered her strength. When she opened them, the front of the coat faced her, and she looked down to the spot above the left breast pocket.

Twelve letters were embroidered in red thread: EDWARD HAWK, M.D.

"It's his," she heard Mac say, but it seemed as if she were in a dream, her voice far away.

Stepping back, Jess braced herself against the bank of lockers and allowed Mac to retrieve the toiletry bag and the silver briefcase. When Mac carried them to the table, she followed, forcing one foot in front of the other, and collapsed into a chair, still holding Hawk's coat. Then she realized what she held, and she dropped it to the floor. "I can't touch that thing! It belonged to him!"

Mac nodded, and Jess looked to her, trying desperately to focus her eyes. Midway into her first deep breath, an effort to regain her calm, Mac reached out and took her hand. "You okay?"

Jess nodded mutely, and Mac moved closer, wrapping an arm around her shoulder as she pressed her lips to Jess's hair. "He can't hurt you anymore, Jess. But we might find something in here to hurt him."

Mac was right. Jess picked up Hawk's lab coat and peeked into the breast pocket. Carefully, she removed three pens. From his left lower pocket, she pulled a stethoscope. From the right, she pulled a small glass vial, then held it up.

Her hand began to shake as she looked at Mac, not seeing her, but him. "It's the sux."

Mac knelt before her until she stopped shaking, then Jess nodded toward the bags on the table. "Open them."

"Do you want to step back?"

Jess shook her head. She'd come this far, and it had been her idea in the first place. "No, I can do it."

The toiletry bag held no surprises, and then Mac turned her attention to the briefcase. It had a three-number spinning combination lock. "If you get me a pick I can probably open it that way," she said to Ernie.

"Why don't you just drill it? How hard could it be? It's just a little briefcase."

"We could, but I don't know what's inside, and I'd rather preserve it if I can."

Mac called her team, mostly to come and take photographs of the area, and while they waited, she began playing with the lock.

"Remember the game Mastermind? Where you guess the number?"

Jess nodded, suddenly excited. "It has only three digits. How hard can it be?"

Mac started with zero, zero, zero, and not surprisingly, the lock didn't give. It took Mac fourteen minutes to key in all the numbers leading up to seven, eight, nine, but when she did, the lock snapped open.

"Got it," she whispered. She reached for Jess's hand and squeezed, then turned back to the case.

Placing the case on the flat surface of the table, she carefully examined the outside, then slowly lifted the lid. When it was open, Jess could hear her sigh of relief.

"What's in it?" Jess asked, leaning closer to see.

"Not much. A couple of pens. His employment contract. But

these briefcases sometimes have secret compartments. I'll bet this one does."

Jess watched as Mac ran her hands along the inside of the suitcase's bottom, then the lid. Her hands suddenly stopped moving and she looked at Jess. "I think I found something."

Mac turned her arm back and forth, then lifted it, and a gray-colored plastic plate slipped free, exposing another compartment within the top of the briefcase.

As Jess watched, Mac pulled out a small stack of papers from behind a net in the secret space.

"What is it?"

"Death certificates. Four of them are blank." Mac looked up and Jess saw a strange look on her face. "Two of them are signed by Hawk, and they're dated, and they have names on them. One of them is Christian Cooney." She handed the papers to Jess. "The manner of death is homicide."

CHAPTER TWENTY

Turkey, with Gravy

Derek rang the doorbell beside Lucy's front door and waited, flowers in hand and a smile on his face. Lucy's invitation had been a surprise, and he still wasn't sure of her motives. Sure, he'd wanted this invitation since they first met, but had she asked him to Thanksgiving dinner to make him happy, or to prove to her parents that she was doing well, or to satisfy their curiosity about the man with whom she was spending so much of her free time?

Answering the door was the tall man whom Derek had noticed that first day, the driver of the big Mercedes, Lucy's father. She'd told him he was an accountant for a pharmaceutical company, and he acted the part of a successful professional. His sweater was thick and looked expensive, as did his cashmere pants and leather loafers. He greeted Derek with a booming voice and nearly crushed Derek's fingers with his firm handshake.

"Hi, I'm Hal. You must be Derek. Happy Thanksgiving. Come in, come in," he said, nearly pulling Derek off his feet. "No need for flowers, but come this way, and we'll find them some water."

Derek followed him down a hallway, through a sitting room, and into the kitchen. Lucy's mother worked beside two other women, putting the finishing touches on their dinner.

"Sofia, an admirer brought you some flowers."

Sofia looked up, and her eyes brightened when she saw the bouquet Derek had procured from Weis Markets just a few miles from the house. It was a last-minute idea, but from her expression, Derek knew it had been a good one.

After drying her hands, she accepted Derek's gift and hugged him. "We're so happy to have you here, Derek. Lucy speaks so highly of you and seems so happy since you've been dating."

Derek was genuinely touched at the warm welcome and couldn't help smiling. "It's nice to finally meet you."

After a promise that dinner would be ready soon, Sofia chased them from the kitchen and into a two-story great room with a wall of glass facing the woods beyond. In the center of that wall, a fireplace was hard at work warming the room. A young woman and a man were already there, sitting on an oversized couch. He introduced them as Lucy's sister and brother-in-law.

"Can I offer you a drink?" he asked Derek.

Derek had been busy since receiving his invitation, studying the Internet, learning about wine. He'd read that white was the best to serve with turkey, but what was he supposed to drink before the turkey? Shit, shit, shit. The last thing he wanted was to look stupid to Lucy's dad.

"I was hoping to have a glass of wine with dinner, so I think I'll pass for now."

"Well, I'll have this finished before dinner, so I'll go ahead, if you don't mind."

Throwing a few cubes into a tall glass, her dad didn't wait for Derek's reply as he poured a hefty shot of vodka over the ice. He lifted the glass in Derek's direction before putting it to his mouth. After tasting it, he sat down. "So, Lucy tells us you're a paramedic and hoping to go to pharmacy school. How interesting! I work for a pharmaceutical company, you know."

Derek swallowed hard. What the fuck was she thinking, throwing out lies like that? He'd taken a few classes in the paramedic program at the community college, but he didn't really like school enough to stick it out. Then, he'd found his little niche and didn't need any further education now. "Yes, she mentioned that."

"Well, we all have to start somewhere, and no matter where that place is, the important thing is that you keep working toward your goals. That's the key to success, Derek, constantly working toward your goals."

"Stop lecturing, Dad. He's here to relax."

Lucy walked over to the chair where he was sitting, eased herself onto the armrest, and kissed his forehead. "Hi."

Derek beamed, although he did wonder how he'd pull off the charade. Then it hit him. He already was a pharmacist. Lucy was a brat.

Maybe it wasn't a bad idea, though, pharmacy school. He could use some of his money for it, and then he'd have access to all the pills he wanted. He'd own his own candy store.

They chatted about football, one of Derek's least-favorite subjects, then travel, something he knew nothing about. Fortunately Lucy's sister and her husband had no difficulty keeping up the conversation. Finally Sofia called them to dinner. "Hal, will you please call Mike? Maybe he forgot the time."

Just then, the doorbell rang and Hal went to answer it. Lucy led them to the dining room, where a table was set for twelve. Three women and two men were already seated. Lucy introduced them as her grandmother, aunts, and uncles, then pulled out a chair and pushed Derek into it.

Trying to appear sophisticated was hard enough, and he felt totally out of place in the sport coat and tie. He appreciated Lucy's playfulness and winked at her in solidarity. To his surprise, she leaned over and kissed him, right on the lips. It wasn't a sweet, soft kiss, though. It was a loud, sloppy kiss, intended not to give pleasure but to gain attention. It seemed to work, and several people around the table cleared their throats, Lucy's mother trying hard to hide the anger in her eyes with the fake smile on her face.

Saved from further embarrassment, Derek was relieved to hear the booming voice from the doorway. "Am I too late for pie?" someone asked.

He looked up to see Dr. Michael Ball, both arms extended and offering wine. Derek nearly fainted. What the hell?

"One of the wine magazines is raving about this, Sofia. It goes great with turkey."

He walked around the table to hug Lucy's mother, and this time her smile appeared genuine. Just as quickly he scanned the table, nodding politely as his eyes made the rounds. He stopped when he reached Derek.

"I think you know everyone, except Derek."

Dr. Ball nodded and introduced himself. "Mike Ball, Derek. Nice to meet you."

Clearing his throat, Derek smiled. "I actually already know you, Dr. Ball. I work for you."

Ball laughed as he gracefully sat in a chair beside Lucy's dad. "Well, then, why aren't you working today?"

Everyone laughed, except Lucy, but they were saved from further banter as the food arrived. The two women Derek had seen in the kitchen went about the business of placing plates of salad before everyone and then politely retreated. Derek ate quietly but listened to the conversation around him. It seemed Dr. Ball was a neighbor, and his wife and children were at her mother's house in New Jersey for the holiday. He was on call and hadn't been able to accompany them. He didn't seem upset about the separation.

Lucy's brother-in-law was in his third year of law school, and they were living in an apartment, which was dreadful. They were already searching for houses close to their parents'. Her grandmother promised a nice donation for a down payment, when they managed to find their dream house, and the aunts and uncles offered advice about where to search for a "starter house."

What would they think if they knew he'd grown up in an apartment, with a thousand square feet of space, with no father and a mother who spent her days sleeping off the night before? Closing his eyes, he shook off the thought. He wasn't that kid anymore. He had a job, and he was making money. He would make something of himself, make himself worthy of people like this.

Between bites of food and sips of wine, Dr. Ball caught his eye. "Is that your Benz?"

Derek nodded.

"That's some car. A real classic."

Finally, something he could talk about. "Thank you. I really love it."

"How long have you had it?"

The pseudo-lie was easy as he slipped into another role, where he wasn't the poor kid. Besides, Tim was the closest thing to a father he'd ever had. "My dad bought it new, and I was the washer and waxer all these years, so he recently signed it over to me."

"I'd like to see the inside of that. Maybe I'll let you drive me home later."

"You walked, Michael?" Sofia asked.

He winked. "I can't risk a DUI."

Everyone laughed, but Derek didn't get the joke.

"I'd be happy to give you a lift, sir."

The servers reappeared and removed their plates, replacing them with bowls of squash soup, followed by large trays of traditional Thanksgiving delights. After dinner and dessert, they left the dining room and split up, with most of the women heading in one direction and the men returning to the great room to watch football. Derek was thankful Lucy stayed with him, and they managed to sit and talk even while everyone else shouted at the television screen.

An hour or so later, Dr. Ball stood. "I'm ready for that ride, Derek," he said.

Derek found his jacket and his keys, while Dr. Ball said his farewells. They met at the front door and he led the doctor down the stone pathway from the house to the driveway. Since he'd arrived last, the car was in back. "Nice," Dr. Ball said as he walked around the car, admiring the exterior. He opened the passenger door and sat, then inspected the interior.

"Where to?" Derek asked.

"Just one house over. The way you came in."

The development was so large Derek couldn't see the house Dr. Ball mentioned, or any of the others. When he'd been stalking Lucy he drove through, but all he could catch were glimpses of color through the lines of trees in front of them. Dr. Ball's house didn't appear to him until he was a hundred yards into the driveway, and Derek couldn't help commenting. "Wow. Some house." It was even bigger than Lucy's, two expansive stories with six garages. Three were attached, three set apart, in a building designed to look like a carriage house.

"Pull over there," he said, pointing toward the detached garage. Derek parked where instructed and got out of the car, watching as Dr. Ball opened the door with a code punched into an electrical panel beside one of the doors. As the door rose, a classic Corvette appeared before him. It was painted red and wrapped in some sort of bubble wrap, but its shape was unmistakable.

"This is my baby, a 1976 Corvette," he said, then chuckled. "One of them, anyway." He walked a dozen feet to the next garage stall, where another car was shrouded in plastic. "This is my summer car. It's a 2015 Porsche. I like how it handles on the country roads. Over there is an Aston Martin. The James Bond car."

"Wow. You have some collection here."

Dr. Ball didn't answer but instead began walking back toward the house. "I have to do something with my money," he said, and pressed the code for the other garage.

From somewhere deep inside Derek a seed of discontent sprouted, and it grew with each step he took, filling his belly, forcing the breath from his lungs. Before he could think about it, he reached for the knife he always carried in his pocket, and it was open and against Dr. Ball's throat before he knew what he was doing.

"Where's the money now?"

The doctor stood perfectly still, and even though he was two inches taller and many pounds heavier than Derek, he seemed frightened.

"Let's not get carried away, Derek. Put the knife down and walk away." His words were staccato, whispered.

"I want the safe, Doctor. Where is it?"

"Derek, I don't have a safe! All my money comes in insurance checks. It's all deposited in the bank."

"Yeah? What about the cash you collect from your *special* patients?" His voice grew deeper, angrier. "What about the two thousand a week I pay you to do business in the parking lot? Do you deposit the cash, Doc? Do you report that to the IRS?"

"We have a nice deal going, Derek. Why ruin it?"

"I'm not ruining anything, Doc. We can still do business. I'm just taking a little bonus."

"Okay, okay. I have a safe. It has some money in it. It's all yours. Just take that knife away from my throat."

"Walk," Derek commanded him, and he did, slowly, leading Derek just a short distance to a large butler's pantry.

"In there," he said, pointing with his right hand.

"Open it," Derek commanded as he grasped Ball's left hand and pulled it up behind him, causing the doctor to flex forward.

Ball walked slowly toward a bifold door three-quarters of the way along the left wall of the closet. It collapsed to the right when the doctor pulled, exposing a black vault door. It reached the ceiling from the floor, and the combination dial was just about eye level. Dr. Ball was forced to bend to see the small numbers on the dial, alarming Derek. "Easy. This knife is sharp."

"I got it. I just have to bend a little to see the lock, okay?"

"Move slowly."

The doctor shifted, but Derek held his left arm tightly, wedging it farther up between his shoulder blades. The silence in the house was so deep he could hear the dial spinning, in between the spurts of breath the doctor sucked in. Then a loud click echoed across the pots and pans and canned goods, and the door opened beneath the doctor's hand.

Moving slowly, he stepped back, offering Derek a glimpse of the treasures inside. There were three shelves. The top held boxes that were the right size for jewelry and were labeled as such. Emerald necklace. Diamond teardrop earrings. Diamond tennis bracelet. The shelf below was also filled with boxes. "What's in there?"

"Collector pieces of art. Drawings, paintings, statues."

Fuck. He didn't want jewelry or art. It was too hard to move, and he'd come here for cash. There had to be cash somewhere. "What's on the bottom?" he asked.

"Look for yourself," he said.

To do that, Derek would have to bend forward, around the doctor, compromising his position. "What the fuck's there?" he asked again, as he pulled the doctor's arm tighter.

Suddenly, the doctor leaned back and jammed his heel into Derek's shin. The pain consumed him and he jerked back, the doctor's arm wrenched from his grasp. As the knife slipped from his neck, Derek's opportunity went with it.

With a rage that had brewed for twenty years, he overcame his pain and lunged forward, plunging the knife into the doctor's neck. Taken by surprise, he turned, twisting the knife in his throat, and Derek heard a gush of air, a gurgling, as his trachea was lacerated through and through. Surprisingly, there was little blood, but the doctor dropped to his knees anyway, holding his neck, trying to piece back together with his hand the severed tissue that was bleeding, not just blood, but air, and life.

Stepping back, Derek pulled a roll of paper towels from a shelf and wiped his knife, then his hands. The wounds he'd inflicted were fatal, but he paid no attention to the doctor. Instead, he leaned forward and pulled out one of the bags from the closet floor. It was a shopping bag, with handles, the kind intended to promote recycling, filled with money. He found eight bags in the safe and carried them all to the edge of the closet before checking on the doctor.

The pool of blood beneath his head had grown to about a foot in diameter. Much of it seemed to be soaking into his thick, woolen sweater, which made Derek's trek around the body much easier. His eyes were open but unfocused, and he was still but trying to breathe through the hole in his neck.

Death was imminent, and Derek didn't look back as he walked out the door. He hadn't touched anything except the money, so he wasn't worried about fingerprints. As for other evidence, like hair, or fibers, he had to keep his fingers crossed that he'd left no DNA. It took two trips to haul the money to his trunk, and he washed up with the baby wipes he kept in the car. He had a few stains on his shirt that could pass for gravy, but after a little attention with water from the bottle in his car, they nearly disappeared. He stuffed the paper towels and the baby wipes into one of the bags of money, closed the trunk, and hopped back into the car. He intentionally left Dr. Ball's garage open. The murderer had to get in the house somehow, right?

It took only a minute to drive the few hundred yards to Lucy's house. When he looked at the clock, he was startled to see he'd been gone only fifteen minutes. It seemed like hours had passed since Dr.

Ball had run his fingers across the smooth surface of the Mercedes's hood.

Lucy was standing in the driveway, smoking a cigarette. She didn't seem suspicious at all, and he kissed her, both to calm his nerves and to give an appearance of normalcy. He always kissed her when he saw her.

"Did you get to see the car show?" she asked.

"Yeah. He talked for a minute, but I wanted to get back. I didn't want to leave you in the middle of the real-estate hunt."

After blowing a ring of smoke, she smirked. "It's worse, now. They're looking at the sale papers, planning their Black Friday attack on the malls."

"Will you go with them?"

She shrugged. "I try not to rock the boat too much, you know? I'm doing well in my classes, hanging out with my sister a little bit."

Derek knew she'd gone to Philadelphia with her mother the weekend before, and she'd seemed to enjoy herself. They'd texted a few times, and though she'd complained a bit, her overall mood seemed to be good.

"Wanna swing?" she asked.

Derek hesitated for a moment. He was sure the police would question him when the body was found, and it was crucial that he had an alibi. Should he go into the house so the others could see him or just rely on Lucy? He debated as they walked, then made his decision. The bench-style swing, hung from a large shade tree, could be seen from the great room where the football played on TV. As they walked by, Derek innocently knocked on the window and waved to everyone inside.

"They're pretty obnoxious, aren't they?" she asked.

"I don't know. They seem okay."

"What's your family like?" she asked.

Derek hesitated but decided this was just the sort of conversation he should have with Lucy now, a genuine one, one that would make her think it impossible that he'd just murdered her neighbor.

"I've never met my biological father, but I've always had a sort of stepfather. His name is Tim, and he's a big, flaming fag, but a good guy. He's always looked after me." Derek was quiet for a moment as he thought back at his life with Tim. He was frugal but still good to Derek. His first bike was from the flea market, but it ran well, and Tim had taught him how to oil the chain and tighten the bolts while holding the tires fast, how to patch a tube and fill the tire with air. There was the bat and ball, similarly appropriated the year Derek decided he wanted to play Little League. And money, small amounts here and there that allowed him to rent a tux for the prom and go on the senior class trip to Florida. And always, always, always, there was a roof over his head and food on the table. Derek shared it all with Lucy. It was the first time he'd ever told anyone how he felt about Tim.

"What about your mom?"

Derek swallowed hard, real tears. What could he say? "She's an alcoholic. She tries to be there for me, but it's hard for her. When I was little, she'd get me on the bus to school and then go back to bed. I know this, because in the summer, and on weekends, that's what she did, too. She wakes up around two in the afternoon, does what she has to do. She made me do my homework and made sure I did my chores for Tim. Then she'd play board games with me. Every night, I was in bed by eight, and at five after, I'd hear the door close as she left. Sometimes, I'd hear her come in, but mostly I fell asleep wondering if she'd be home in the morning. On a few occasions, she wasn't, and that's when Tim really took over."

"It sounds like Tim's a good guy. I'd like to meet him."

"I'd like a couple of oxys. You in?"

She smirked. "I'm always in."

He slipped four tablets from his pocket and popped them into his mouth. He kissed her and passed two of them to her. They both swallowed without the benefit of water.

He enjoyed the quiet time with her, and when they grew cold, they walked inside. Lucy made him coffee, and they had seconds of pumpkin pie before Derek made his excuses, telling them he had to get back for dinner with his family. And truthfully, he did. He was taking Tim and his mother out to eat.

At home, he threw all of his clothes into Tim's washer, then changed into a nearly identical outfit. He owned two button-down shirts and two pairs of chinos, so that was easy. He had only one blue tie, so on instinct, he checked Tim's closet for something that looked similar to the one he'd worn earlier. If the police came looking for him, he'd appear as if he hadn't changed.

In Tim's shower, he scrubbed himself clean and then quickly changed his clothes. While the laundry dried, he tidied up Tim's place and helped him dress. On the way to the pancake house, he stopped by a clothing box and threw in the freshly laundered shirt, tie, slacks, and shoes. He had a few million dollars in his trunk to buy more.

Chapter Twenty-one

Cold Turkey

All the relief Jess had felt after finding Hawk's briefcase dissipated on the Sunday after Thanksgiving as she stared at the TV screen, facing a new crisis.

Dr. Ball was dead.

His murder had consumed the local television stations since she'd awakened and turned on the five o'clock news. He'd last been seen alive on Thanksgiving Day, and his wife had found him dead in their home that day after returning from her parents' house. The Ball house was in the woods, and the doors had been left open. Animals had wandered in, devouring his body and contaminating any evidence that might lead to his killer.

It was horrible. Jess hadn't particularly cared for the doctor, but still, he was a human being. And her doctor. Where was she going to get her bup?

After the news sank in, the first thing Jess did was sit down and count her medication. She had a week's supply. If she was lucky enough to move from the waiting list to the active patients, she might get in with one of the doctors in the area. But many other people would be jamming the phone lines in the morning, all with the same sob story. Her odds weren't great.

Jess sat on her comfy queen-sized bed, then collapsed all the way back and stared at the ceiling. It was already dark outside, and only a bedside lamp and the small television screen lit the room. The darkness was closing in on her. She'd come so far, made so much progress in getting her life together. How could she lose it now? But if she couldn't find another doctor to refill her prescription, eventually she'd run out. Then what? Faking injuries so her colleagues would prescribe her oxys or buying them from her patients? Maybe she'd take a ride to Philly and see how the supply on the street was flowing. Philly…yes, Philly. Dr. Gompers! Surely the doctor would take her back. But what if she couldn't? What if she had her hundred patients?

She'd always felt the same panic about her drug use. Because she had the money, she was able to buy large quantities of drugs at a time and showed remarkable restraint in using them judiciously. Yes, sometimes she took way too many, but usually she budgeted them, often for a couple of weeks at a time. Then something would stress her, and she'd pop pills by the handful and find herself scrambling to get more. Now her fix was a strip of medication, but it was just as hard to get as—no, harder than—the drugs she'd used before. Because only a few doctors could prescribe bup, she couldn't get an appointment. And because it was long-acting, and therefore less expensive, it had come into favor with everyone on the street trying to save money or avoid withdrawal.

If only she'd taken the prescription for the three strips a day Dr. Ball had tried to push on her. But she'd wanted to do her sobriety the right way, and she'd told him she wouldn't take any more than the twelve milligrams a day she'd been taking when she walked into his office. He'd acquiesced, reluctantly, and now Jess felt like an idiot. This was why people keep extras, she thought. Your doctor could get murdered any day and leave you stranded.

Rolling onto her side, she stared at the television set, the images no longer registering in her brain: the driveway of Dr. Ball's house flanked by trees and guarded by two police officers; the coroner's car pulling out of that driveway, carrying his body; a photo of Dr. Ball taken from one of the television commercials for the nursing home he owned; interviews with shocked neighbors, employees, and the state-police officer assigned to the case.

Pulling the pillow over her head, she rolled into a fetal position and stared at the wall, too numb for tears. *What if I just quit?* she asked herself. She was stronger now than she'd been when she tried before, and so much smarter. She considered herself an addiction expert at this point. She knew all the signs and symptoms, all the treatment plans, all the statistics about success and failure. She wanted so desperately to be a success!

She was due for her next dose of medication in twelve hours, when she came home from work. In twenty-four hours, she'd be feeling a little sick, and in thirty-six, she'd be in full withdrawal. That would be Tuesday morning. Her next shift in the ER wasn't until Friday, and she could blow off the committee meeting she had on Wednesday. That gave her body three whole days, seventy-two hours to fight through the agony and start to function without narcotics. Was that enough time? Maybe. Maybe not. Either way, she didn't feel like she had much choice. Even if she found another doctor, she suspected something would always come between her and her fix. The only way to control the situation was to get off the stuff.

Her decision made, she showered and got ready for work.

❖

"I didn't realize it was flu season already," Mac said. "I mean, usually they warn you about it on the news."

"Mac, I really can't talk anymore. I'll text you later, okay?"

Jess heard the disappointment in Mac's voice as she said good-bye, but she couldn't worry about it. She had to focus all of her energy inward—on breathing, imagining the lake in summer, a putt rolling into the cup. In an attempt to distract herself from her physical misery, Jess was concentrating on pleasant things. Perhaps it was working, because she'd made it through thirty nearly sleepless hours of withdrawal without reaching for the narcotics in her drawer. It was now Wednesday afternoon, and she figured this was going to be an awful day. If she made it, though, Thursday should be better. By Friday she'd feel somewhat human. At least that's what she hoped. If not, she'd call on one of her colleagues and have them take her shift. What else could she do? The bup in her drawer would end her misery, and in twenty minutes she'd feel like herself again. But she'd be right back where she started.

That wasn't what she wanted. She was not giving in this time. No matter how much pain she had to endure, she would do it. She wanted her life back, the life before narcotics had taken control and changed everything.

Could that life include Mac? Jess had thought about sharing her secret, but she didn't feel like it was the right time. It would be so much easier to say "I'm a recovering addict" than "I'm an addict." If she could make it through this withdrawal and get off the bup, she could tell Mac later, when and if they decided to date or sleep together, or whatever it was they were heading toward. If they reached that point, then Mac deserved to know.

And it sure seemed they were heading that way. Mac spent more and more time with her, sat beside her as they watched movies, helped her with little projects around the house on their mutual days off. They had many common interests to keep them talking and occupied. Both favored action movies and spicy food, neither of them partied much, and both of them were up before the sun. Both liked to experiment in the kitchen and to take what they'd cooked and eat it outside on the patio. They loved the outdoors and had already logged over a hundred miles on the trails at the local parks and the hunting club, and at Mac's lake.

There was a spark of passion there, too, and for Jess, that was amazing. Sex was sex, as far as she was concerned. Her occasional desires had never controlled her, driving her thoughts and distracting her. Yet with Mac, that's where she found herself. As they watched television, she'd look at Mac's hands, so strong, the nails clipped immaculately at the ends of her long fingers, and couldn't help fantasizing. What would they feel like on her, in her? What would Mac's mouth feel like on hers? Just her breath drove Jess wild, and she pulled away from their good-night hugs feeling urges she'd never experienced before. Hmm. Jess suspected Mac would take her to whole new places. Not just because she was Mac, but because of the person Jess had become in her sobriety. Because of the person

Jess was making herself become. New, better, stronger, more fun. More sexual.

In the end, the thoughts of her and Mac might just turn out to be fantasy. They were powerful visions, though, and they were helping fill the hours while she sequestered herself from the world and pulled her body through this cleansing.

Sipping from a straw, she was careful to take only a small amount of the flat Coke in her mug, and she allowed it to warm in her mouth before she swallowed it. She needed the fluid, but for some reason water wasn't sitting well in her stomach. Every sip came back up within seconds. The cola was working better and gave her some sugar, too. If she held it down, she'd try some crackers, and maybe a few aspirin for the headache and body pains.

Her CD of nature sounds had stopped playing, and she slowly raised herself off the couch to restart it. It was all her mind could handle. Television plots demanded too much concentration, and she'd started a few puzzles but wasn't able to concentrate for long enough to finish them.

Hobbling to the bathroom on aching legs, Jess splashed tepid water onto her face. Twirling the toothbrush around her mouth seemed to take away some of the grime there. She didn't even care what she looked like. She couldn't do anything about it. Grabbing some crackers, she headed back to her couch and collapsed into her comforter. It probably stank, but if it did, she couldn't smell it. Her nose was too congested to function.

Jess allowed her mind to drift, this time to a great waterfall. In her kayak, she guided herself toward the edge, and just as the tip floated over the edge, a sail popped out of the frame, and she flew across the great gorge below the falls, drifting slowly down to the calm waters in the distance. The vision was exhilarating, and beautiful and peaceful. The only thing wrong was the ringing sound. The birds and water were soothing, but that buzzing was annoying.

The buzzing changed to pounding, and Jess opened her eyes. The dream was over, and she was amazed that she must have fallen asleep. Now, though, someone was pounding on her door. Her father was too scared of the flu to enter the house, and besides, he had a key. It must be one of her neighbors or someone from the hospital.

The temptation to ignore the noise was great, but the buzzing, knocking person was persistent. She forced herself to her feet, shuffled to the back door, and looked through the curtain. Mac was wearing a black knit cap with a Pennsylvania State Police logo, a matching coat, and a smile.

"Fuck," Jess thought. Mac was the last person she wanted to see at the moment. And also the only one.

"I had my flu shot," she said when Jess opened the door. Then, "Maybe you should give me a key. For emergencies."

"Mac, don't make me talk, okay?"

A brown paper bag emerged from somewhere, and she dangled it in front of her. "Soup. And fresh rolls. Carbs are good for the flu."

"I've never heard that," Jess said as she turned and walked back toward the couch, with Mac at her heels. She eased herself back into her cocoon.

"I figured you could use a little company. Or a little help. You've been under quarantine for forty-eight hours now. You need human contact."

Jess looked up from the couch and frowned. "I hadn't noticed."

"Jess, you need a shower." Kneeling beside her, she pulled the comforter toward her nose and sniffed. "And your blanket needs a bath. You both…stink."

"Please, be honest, Mac. No need to sugarcoat it."

"C'mon. I'll help you."

"A shower would require me to remove my clothing. I thought we were in the platonic phase of this relationship."

"I won't look."

"I'm probably not that tempting at the moment."

Mac gazed at her, and her eyes warmed, her face softened. "You are the biggest temptation I've ever met." She leaned in and placed a tender kiss on Jess's lips.

Jess tilted her head, angling it like a baby bird trying to take the food its mother offered. Mac was offering herself, and Jess wanted her. Their lips met, and lingered, and Jess tingled everywhere for the second they stayed together. For a moment Jess forgot her pain and felt pleasure, and the flash of desire that exploded was more powerful than all the misery she was suffering. Even when Mac pulled back and smiled at her, the pleasant sensations continued.

"C'mon. Let's get you naked."

Jess allowed Mac to help her up the stairs, but she insisted she could shower herself. Holding on to a little bit of dignity was important. While Jess was in the bathroom, Mac laundered the bedding, and Jess emerged twenty minutes later feeling cleaner but no more human than she had before. The kiss had played through her mind as the water fell over her body, and she'd wondered if this was the time.

Mac had come here to help her, to take care of her. She'd kissed her. Mac's intentions were clear. It was time for Jess to be honest. If Mac walked out the door, it would be hard for Jess. But if she didn't tell her, it would be harder to lose her later, after she knew what those soft lips felt like on other parts of her body.

"Why don't you try the chair for a while? And I heated the soup for you."

"What kind?"

"Chicken noodle, of course. You're a doctor. Surely you're aware of the healing powers of chicken-noodle soup."

"I've heard rumors."

As instructed, Jess sat, accepted the mug of soup, and even took a sip. Then she summoned all of her courage and told Mac to have a seat as well.

"I thought I'd straighten up a little."

"Sit down, please," Jess said as she met her gaze. Mac pulled a chair from next to the fireplace and placed it next to Jess's.

"What's wrong?"

"That kiss rocked me, Mac. You rock me. I feel something with you I've never felt before. You challenge me and make me laugh. I want more from you. I want you in my life, in my house, in my bed."

A smile erupted on Mac's face. "That all sounds good to me. So good. I've tried to fight this, but I just can't anymore."

"I have to tell you something. Before we go any further here, you need to know the truth about me. Then you can decide for yourself whether we explore our feelings any further."

Mac studied Jess for a moment. Though she tended to be serious, Jess had been relaxing more, joking, less stressed. Not now, though. She was all business.

Was it because she wanted to talk about their relationship? Because, truthfully, that was all Mac could think about lately. The way Jess's sarcasm matched her own and made her laugh. How they liked the same food and movies. That Jess was the only woman she'd ever known who understood the demands of her job. Mac didn't get close to people, yet she'd opened up to Jess.

"Okay. What is it?"

Silently, Jess looked at the floor. Mac closed the space between them, touched her arm, her pulse pounding at an alarming rate. Suddenly, she was nauseated. Something was wrong. Something was wrong with Jess. "What is it?"

Finally, Jess met her eyes. "I'm an addict, Mac. I don't have the flu. I'm in withdrawal."

Mac felt her mouth fall open, but instead of the flurry of words that typically flew out around Jess, she felt helplessly mute. Jess wasn't sick, as she'd feared. Not really. She was an addict. A drug addict. Before she could force her tongue to move, Jess continued with a drawn-out sigh.

"I was a patient of Dr. Ball. The guy who was murdered on Thanksgiving. He's been treating me with buprenorphine, which I'm sure you know about. Since he's dead, my medication supply will run out soon. I decided to quit cold turkey now instead of later."

"Wow. This is some news, Jess." Mac clasped her hands in front of her and rolled her thumbs. It was a lame reply, but Mac was too stunned to do better. She looked at Jess, though, searching for answers, some way to understand this. How did a doctor become a drug addict? Someone who had it so together and was so amazingly accomplished? How had she fallen in love with someone who'd managed to hide such a big part of herself? Because, honestly, that's what this was. It wasn't a familiar feeling, but you didn't need to see the bullet to realize you'd been shot. And she'd definitely been hit by the full force of Jessica Benson. What the hell did she do now?

Jess looked away from Mac's searching gaze. It made her feel even more uncomfortable than she already was. "I know. We've never really talked about drugs, and I'm sure as a police officer you have strong feelings about them, so I thought I'd better tell you now because you kissed me, and it was wonderful, and I want more. You need to know the truth before you kiss me again."

Mac leaned back and slipped down in her chair. Defeated? Jess wondered.

"So what is the truth?" she asked.

Jess told her the entire story, from her broken arm to her buying drugs, to her stint at Hartley and her experience with Dr. Ball.

"So your goal is to get off narcotics completely, instead of staying on the bup?"

"Yes."

"Why? If you're stable, why mess with it?"

"Because addiction is never stable. I was doing great with Dr. Ball, and now he's dead. First I have to find a new doctor. Maybe I'll be able to locate someone, or I can stretch my strips a little, take one a day instead of one and a half. What's the difference? Eventually I'll run out. And if I find a new doctor, who's to say another crisis won't occur, and I'll be in the same boat. As long as I'm taking these drugs, I'm vulnerable. I want to get off this stuff and regain control of my life."

Mac nodded. "What makes you think you can do it this time?"

Jess smiled. "I don't know exactly what happened, Mac. Near-death experience, maybe? Or the feeling I had on bup, like I was normal. I'd forgotten what that feels like. If I can get off this stuff, I think eventually I'll feel good. I have a lot of reasons to live, and I want to. I want to enjoy my life, and my job, my friends—you—without this hanging over me. And I can see that life now. I can envision it. I have something concrete to aim for."

Mac reached out to Jess, took her hand, squeezed it. Staring at the tangled fingers, Mac knew how tangled her life already was with Jess. Her first thoughts in the morning had always been about cases, and interviews, and evidence. Now, she wondered if Jess was awake, if she could call. And she would, and they would talk about nothing at all, or something on their minds, until Mac absolutely had to get ready for work. During the day, Jess crossed her mind dozens of times, to the point of distraction. Focusing on her job had never been hard; it was what she lived for. Now, she found herself redirecting herself from visions of red hair and blue eyes and long legs. At night, when she couldn't sleep, the Jess of her fantasies kept her warm, kept her company.

Mac had no idea what life with a recovering addict would be like. Odds were, Jess would fail. Even if she were able to maintain her sobriety, it would be measured in days, a count-up, instead of a countdown, until she failed at her Herculean task and started over. Was that the life Mac wanted? Did she want to share the burden of addiction and recovery? Because it was a burden, a huge weight that could pull them down, force them apart, destroy their relationship, perhaps destroy them.

Entering a relationship with Jess would be hard. Friendship was no longer an option. Mac was way past that stage. If she walked away from Jess, how would she feel?

Mac supposed she could return to her former life. Her job had always offered an escape, a vacuum to eat up the hours of her days and the days of her weeks. She still had friends, and she still had her family.

Jess brought something else to her life, though. It was a brighter and happier world with Jess in it. Mac liked it. She wanted it.

"I've never had a relationship with an addict before. And if you're in recovery, I can live with that. I can be with you. But I'm a police officer, Jess, and I can't be with you if you're doing anything illegal. I just can't."

Jess understood that would be a challenge for Mac. "Nothing illegal, I promise. But even by the books, this might be hard."

"What's your plan?"

"I'm going to sweat it out. Be tough. When I'm through the

physical part, in a couple of days, I hope, I intend to keep going to meetings, because they ground me. And I plan to exercise, and meditate, and live a little. Enjoy things and people, take pleasure that way, stress less. I want to have no reason to take drugs, so I'll have no desire. And I need an escape plan, so when I feel stressed, I can do something safe to alleviate it, so I won't use."

Mac nodded, and they were silent for a minute before she spoke again. "Let me check the dryer."

Jess sat in the chair, staring at the vacant fire, wondering about her future. Would she be able to work on Friday as planned? She hoped so, but she couldn't go to work without a clear head. Lives depended on her, literally. She would not put anyone else in danger just to avoid the questions that would inevitably come with a request to change a shift. Would she be able to make it through the next thirty-six hours, or however long it took, fighting the pain and anxiety? She thought she could. She wanted this, badly, and she intended to lock herself in the bathroom and just meditate until she felt better, if that's what it took. What about the future, though? Did she have the resolve to stay clean? She thought so. In rehab, she'd seen so many people who really had it tough—they were in abusive relationships, or wracked by poverty, or had health issues. Some had no one to turn to for support.

Jess faced none of those issues. If anyone could beat this disease, it was her.

She only hoped Mac was willing to join her in the fight.

On cue, she came down the stairs carrying a bundle of bedding and proceeded to fix the couch for Jess.

"I don't suppose there's anything they can do for you in the ER, is there?"

"Fluids, maybe. But I think I'm okay. I haven't thrown up in an hour."

When the couch was ready, Mac suggested a movie.

Suddenly, Jess was overcome with emotion. This was the time to escape. Mac had done her duty as a friend, making sure Jess was alive and had a little soup and clean blankets. Now she could walk out the door and go on with her life. But instead, she'd suggested a movie. Mac wanted to stay, to be with her. She was willing to give this a try.

The last thing Jess wanted to do was watch a movie. Listening to the dialogue was taxing, and the lights and noises were almost painful. "Okay, you can pick," she said, and she moved back to the couch and lay down on her side, her feet tucked up against Mac's thigh.

Emotionally and physically exhausted, she fell asleep that way and awoke hours later, to find Mac asleep beside her.

Chapter Twenty-two

Sponsor

Using his small finger, Derek pushed the pills aimlessly around the kitchen table. His supply was dwindling, and he had no way to replenish it. He always told himself he could quit using when he wanted to, but for the past few years, he'd had no reason to. A steady supply of narcotics was at his command, and he made use of it, regularly taking ten or more pills a day. Since Dr. Ball's death, not only was he out of a job, but he was also out of pills. He had no source, other than the orthopedics office in the strip mall. He'd been cruising it regularly, but it had been hit-and-miss. They had been slow on the day after Thanksgiving, and the Monday after as well, since apparently some of the bone specialists had been out deer hunting that day. He'd made his supply stretch for a week, but he was feeding two mouths, not one, and Lucy was quite hungry. Her narcotic needs were double his, and as a result, he'd started taking less. And he felt it. Aching muscles, anxiety, sniffling. If he didn't replenish his supply, it would only get worse.

It was time to pay Dr. Jessica Benson a visit. He'd been sitting at the table trying to work out the details. He was usually good at such things, but today, he just wasn't able to focus. Maybe it was the withdrawal, or perhaps just stress in general. Dr. Ball's murder was all over the news, it was all everyone in town was talking about, and if that wasn't enough, the police had questioned him. Apparently, he was the last one known to see the doctor alive. Well, no shit.

Browsing the Internet, Derek found the phone number for

Garden Memorial's emergency room and dialed. "Hi," he said. "This is Dr. Roman from Endless Mountains Medical Center. I'm wondering if I can speak to one of your doctors about a patient we have here."

"Sure, just a minute, Doctor. I'll get Dr. Benson for you."

When he heard the elevator music, Derek disconnected the call, hopped into his car, and was in Garden an hour later. He told the registration clerk he had back pain and was placed in a room to await his meeting with Dr. Benson. This might not have been the most carefully crafted plan of attack in history, but he was truly desperate.

She arrived with a smile on her face, but Derek could see the skepticism in her eyes. She'd probably checked his chart and knew he'd been here before for back pain. It was months earlier, but still, it had probably alerted her that he might be abusing drugs. And who would know better than her, right?

Sitting in a bariatric recliner beside the bed, she opened her laptop and began typing. After a moment, she looked up. "So it says you have back pain. What happened to your back?"

Derek sat up in the stretcher and dangled his legs over the side. "Here's the deal, Doc. I was one of Dr. Ball's patients. I've been scrambling for medication for the past week, and I need help. I need you to prescribe me some oxys, enough to get through until I can find another source. I have three friends who also need their medication, and I need you to do the same thing for them."

He saw her take in a deep breath before she spoke. "Sir, I can empathize with you about your situation, but the ER is not the appropriate place to get your medication. Have you considered rehab?"

Derek leaned forward. "Who says I need rehab? Why would you assume I'm an addict?"

The doctor stammered. "I'm sorry, I, I shouldn't have implied that. But still—"

"No need to apologize. You're right. I am an addict. Just like you."

He stared at her for a moment, watched as her cheeks flushed bright red. "You're mistaken," she said, not meeting his gaze as she fumbled with her computer and stood.

Derek laughed. "Listen, Doc. I'm not here to argue. I'm here to help you. I know you need your drugs as much as I need mine. I'll make you a deal. You write me the prescriptions, me and my friends, and I'll get you your supply. Easy enough?"

She looked confused, and shocked, and she sat back in her chair, staring at him, her mouth slightly open, her hands slack at her side.

"Doc, it's okay. I won't tell anyone. I'll treat you right if you treat me right."

Meeting his eyes, Jess found the courage to speak, even though she felt like passing out. Her sweaty hands were shaking and her heart was pounding. "I don't need your drugs. I'm clean. I weaned myself off. Now I think you should leave." She tried to sound firm, but she was frightened. Who was this Derek Knight, and how did he know about her? Did he work in the doctor's office, or had he somehow broken into the electronic medical records?

Studying him a moment, she thought he looked familiar. He was wearing jeans and a North Face sweater, and boots that probably cost more than she made in a day. She pictured him in a uniform, though, and she remembered. He'd waved to her on several occasions outside Dr. Ball's office, and her friend had mentioned someone buying drugs. He was the ambulance driver.

"Good for you, Doc! You're clean. But what are the rest of us supposed to do?"

Jess stood. She needed to get out of this room, away from Derek Knight, and she hoped like hell he didn't follow her into the ER and say something defamatory or become violent.

As he stood, Jess tried to maneuver around him, but he grabbed her arm, pulling her back. "I'll scream," she said.

"Go ahead. You scream, and it'll be the last thing you do. I'll slice your windpipe just like Dr. Ball's. Help me, and I'll leave you alone. I won't say a word. What's everyone going to think about the star witness in the kidnapping trial when they find out you're an addict? That creep Hawk will walk. Will the hospital let you work here? What will you do for a job? What will the state board have to say? You'll probably lose your license. You'll be fucked. Even if you live, you'll wish you were dead."

Jess stopped and met his gaze with one of fire. She hated him. He was no different than Hawk, holding her hostage in a different way. "What the fuck do you want?"

Chapter Twenty-three

You Can Never Leave

The next day's shift dragged as Jess waited for Derek to arrive. Finally, in the late morning, his name appeared on her computer screen.

She leaned against the wall outside the room where her fate awaited her, wondering how this could be happening again. How could she be in the crosshairs of another killer? Because she had no doubt Derek Knight had killed Dr. Michael Ball. By this time she was an expert on the doctor's murder, having watched every television news account and read every written report, and none of them, not a single one, had mentioned his trachea had been lacerated. Only the killer had that piece of information, and she wondered if Derek even realized he'd let it slip. He'd been angry, and anxious, no doubt desperate for his narcotic fix, and she wouldn't have been surprised if he'd forgotten his way home the night before. He'd confessed to murder and probably didn't even know it.

Since his confession, she'd spent countless nauseating, anxious hours trying to figure out what to do. If she cooperated with him, would he kill again? Perhaps her, or someone she loved? If she didn't, would he follow through on his threats to expose her?

It was time to find out.

"Hi, there, Mr. Knight. How are you today?" she asked as she walked in the room.

He studied her for a moment before speaking. "How the fuck do you think I am?"

After a moment of scrutiny, she nodded. "Not very good. You're in withdrawal."

"Well, no shit. I told you I need a prescription, and I need it now. Don't fuck with me, Doc. You do *not* want to make me mad."

"Or what? You'll murder me just like you murdered Dr. Ball?"

"That's fuckin' right, bitch!" He jumped off the stretcher and slashed his hand across his throat. "I'll slit your throat just like his—"

"Hands up!" Jess heard Mac shout as she burst into the room, pushing Derek away from her before he had a chance to react. Another officer on her heels pulled Derek around and handcuffed him, and he turned his head, glaring silently at Jess. Mac spun her around and pulled her from the room, out of the ER. They'd arranged for another doctor to take over after the arrest, and he was already there. Jess hung her lab coat in the staff locker room and, with Mac beside her, walked out into the bitter December day.

Garden's old Victorians were dressed for the holidays, with huge wreaths hanging from doors, plastic sleighs on rooftops, and inflatable snow globes creating miniature blizzards on front lawns. Her own house was modestly decorated. She and Mac had hung lights and a wreath. They planned to find a tree this weekend.

"That was crazy," she said.

"I think it went pretty smoothly, actually."

"I guess our definitions of crazy might be a little different."

"You were very brave," Mac said, stopping on the sidewalk and pulling Jess into her arms. "I think you're one of the bravest people I know."

Cloaked in the cold winter air, Jess found Mac's heat intense. The softness of Mac's face against hers became too much. All of it had been too much, and she could no longer control the desire for Mac she'd been holding at bay. Sliding her lips along the front of Mac's ear, she found Mac's mouth with her own. They wrestled for a moment before both just let go, and they seemed to collapse into each other. They held each other up.

Chapter Twenty-four

Unimpaired

Jess leaned against the wall inside the Wayne County Courthouse and let go of the tears she'd been holding. It seemed inappropriate to cry in the courtroom, so she'd left.

It had taken ten months, but Hawk had finally been brought to trial in her kidnapping case. Her testimony had blown apart Hawk's defense. His lawyers had claimed he'd just snapped, but the DA had been able to show the murders as a motive for the attack on Jess. The death certificates they'd found were additional proof, and the IT geeks at the FBI were able to break into Hawk's cloud and tie him to many additional murders.

Jess had remained calm while she'd faced him, turned it into a game, where every answer was directed toward him, meant to be one more nail through his miserable flesh. They'd allowed her entire testimony, and she'd told them how Hawk had told her he loved murdering people and wanted her help to find his mistakes, so he could continue.

Because he'd been unarmed, and the hostages had been released after only twelve hours, the defense argued to reduce the charges against Hawk. The sux injection got him then, when the DA was able to use that as evidence to convict Hawk of aggravated kidnapping. He was sentenced to two life sentences, for kidnapping her and Wendy, and another fifteen years, for her dad.

It had been a stressful week of trial, but now it was over, and Jess was so happy to have it behind her. She was ready to move on with her life. If she never stepped foot in court again, it would be too soon. Fibers from the reusable grocery bags in Dr. Ball's closet were matched to fibers found in the trunk of Derek's car, so they had a pretty solid case against him. They'd taped his pseudo-confession in the ER as well, and Jess was hoping she could avoid testifying against him. One psychopath was enough.

She'd dwelled on him, and Hawk, for months, until one evening in Mac's self-defense class, when she'd had another moment of clarity. Derek Knight was Hawk all over again. If she hadn't put herself in that position in the first place, their paths never would have crossed. If that wasn't enough to keep her clean, nothing was.

"I thought you'd run away," Mac said softly, touching her arm, breaking her trance.

Speaking of reasons to stay clean, she thought. "And miss the chance to celebrate? Never."

"It's over."

"At last. Good job, Detective."

Mac took her hand and pulled her away from where others leaving the courtroom were gathering to discuss the case.

"I spoke with Sergeant Wallace, my boss. I've been taken off the Hawk murders."

"What does that mean? Why?" Jess asked, searching Mac's face.

Mac reached into the inside pocket of her Brooks Brothers suit. This one was black with pinstripes, with a pale-pink shirt beneath. It brought out the blush in her cheeks, which seemed to be growing by the minute. Pulling out an envelope, she handed it to Jess.

She studied it. It said TRAVEL DOCUMENTS.

"I had a hunch the jury would come back today, so I booked us on a flight tomorrow. How'd you like to go to Jamaica?"

Jess felt something else wash over her. Love. Mac had been beside her through two of the worst experiences of her life, and she hadn't faltered. She'd pushed Jess, and pulled her, and once in a while, she'd even carried her. And now that was behind them, and they were ready to move forward. She couldn't imagine her life without Mac in it, and she couldn't imagine anyone she'd rather travel with. "It's one of my favorite places."

"And you have the next week off?"

Jess had taken it off, to recover. She nodded.

"Do you think it's okay to kiss you right here in the courthouse?"

"It's all legal now."

Mac moved toward her, and Jess opened her arms, pulling Mac into them. Their lips met in a tender kiss, filled with love, and friendship, and the promise of tomorrow. For the first time in ages, she looked forward to her future.

Pulling back from the kiss, Jess took Mac's hand. "Let's get packing," Jess said.

About the Author

Jaime Maddox grew up on the banks of the Susquehanna River in northeastern Pennsylvania. As the baby in a family of many children, she was part adored and part ignored, forcing her to find creative ways to fill her time. Her childhood was idyllic, spent hiking, rafting, biking, climbing, and otherwise skinning knees and knuckles. Reading and writing became passions. Although she left home for a brief stint in the big cities of Philadelphia, PA, and Newark, NJ, as soon as she acquired the required paperwork—a medical degree and residency certificate—she came running back.

She fills her hours with a bustling medical practice, two precocious sons, a disobedient dog, and an extraordinary woman who helps her to keep it all together. In her abundant spare time, she reads, writes, twists her body into punishing yoga poses, and whacks golf balls deep into forests. She detests airplanes, snakes, and people who aren't nice. Her loves are the foods of the world, Broadway musicals, traveling, sandy beaches, massages and pedicures, and the Philadelphia Phillies.

On the bucket list: Publishing a novel, publishing a children's book, recording a song, creating a board game, obtaining a patent, exploring Alaska.

Jaime can be reached at JaimeMaddoxBSB@gmail.com or at her website: http://www.jaimemaddox.com.

Books Available From Bold Strokes Books

Basic Training of the Heart by Jaycie Morrison. In 1944, socialite Elizabeth Carlton joins the Women's Army Corps to escape family expectations and love's disappointments. Can Sergeant Gale Rains get her through Basic Training with their hearts intact? (978-1-62639-818-4)

Believing in Blue by Maggie Morton. Growing up gay in a small town has been hard, but it can't compare to the next challenge Wren—with her new, sky-blue wings—faces: saving two entire worlds. (978-1-62639-691-3)

Coils by Barbara Ann Wright. A modern young woman follows her aunt into the Greek Underworld and makes a pact with Medusa to win her freedom by killing a hero of legend. (978-1-62639-598-5)

Courting the Countess by Jenny Frame. When relationship-phobic Lady Henrietta Knight starts to care about housekeeper Annie Brannigan and her daughter, can she overcome her fears and promise Annie the forever that she demands? (978-1-62639-785-9)

Dapper by Jenny Frame. Amelia Honey meets the mysterious Byron De Brek and is faced with her darkest fantasies, but will her strict moral upbringing stop her from exploring what she truly wants? (978-1-62639-898-6)

Delayed Gratification: The Honeymoon by Meghan O'Brien. A dream European honeymoon turns into a winter storm nightmare involving a delayed flight, a ditched rental car, and eventually, a surprisingly happy ending. (978-1-62639-766-8)

For Money or Love by Heather Blackmore. Jessica Spaulding must choose between ignoring the truth to keep everything she has, and doing the right thing only to lose it all—including the woman she loves. (978-1-62639-756-9)

Hooked by Jaime Maddox. With the help of sexy Detective Mac Calabrese, Dr. Jessica Benson is working hard to overcome her past, but they may not be enough to stop a murderer. (978-1-62639-689-0)

Lands End by Jackie D. Public relations superstar Amy Kline is dealing with a media nightmare, and the last thing she expects is for restaurateur Lena Michaels to change everything, but she will. (978-1-62639-739-2)

Twisted Screams by Sheri Lewis Wohl. Reluctant psychic Lorna Dutton doesn't want to forgive, but if she doesn't do just that, an innocent woman will die. (978-1-62639-647-0)

A Class Act by Tammy Hayes. Buttoned-up college professor Dr. Margaret Parks doesn't know what she's getting herself into when she agrees to one date with her student Rory Morgan, who is fifteen years her junior. (978-1-62639-701-9)

Bitter Root by Laydin Michaels. Small town chef Adi Bergeron is hiding something, and Griffith McNaulty is going to find out what it is even if it gets her killed. (978-1-62639-656-2)

Capturing Forever by Erin Dutton. When family pulls Jacqueline and Casey back together, will the lessons learned in eight years apart be enough to mend the mistakes of the past? (978-1-62639-631-9)

Deception by VK Powell. DEA Agent Colby Vincent and Attorney Adena Weber are embroiled in a drug investigation involving homeless veterans and an attraction that could destroy them both. (978-1-62639-596-1)

Dyre: A Knight of Spirit and Shadows by Rachel E. Bailey. With the abduction of her queen, werewolf-bodyguard Des must follow the kidnappers' trail to Europe, where her queen—and a battle unlike any Des has ever waged—awaits her. (978-1-62639-664-7)

First Position by Melissa Brayden. Love and rivalry take center stage for Anastasia Mikhelson and Natalie Frederico in one of the most prestigious ballet companies in the nation. (978-1-62639-602-9)

Best Laid Plans by Jan Gayle. Nicky and Lauren are meant for each other, but Nicky's haunting past and Lauren's societal fears threaten to derail all possibilities of a relationship. (978-1-62639-658-6)

Exchange by CF Frizzell. When Shay Maguire rode into rural Montana, she never expected to meet the woman of her dreams—or to learn Mel Baker was held hostage by legal agreement to her right-wing father. (978-1-62639-679-1)

Just Enough Light by AJ Quinn. Will a serial killer's return to Colorado destroy Kellen Ryan and Dana Kingston's chance at love, or can the search-and-rescue team save themselves? (978-1-62639-685-2)

Rise of the Rain Queen by Fiona Zedde. Nyandoro is nobody's princess. She fights, curses, fornicates, and gets into as much trouble as her brothers. But the path to a throne is not always the one we expect. (978-1-62639-592-3)

Tales from Sea Glass Inn by Karis Walsh. Over the course of a year at Cannon Beach, tourists and locals alike find solace and passion at the Sea Glass Inn. (978-1-62639-643-2)

The Color of Love by Radclyffe. Black sheep Derian Winfield needs to convince literary agent Emily May to marry her to save the Winfield Agency and solve Emily's green card problem, but Derian didn't count on falling in love. (978-1-62639-716-3)

A Reluctant Enterprise by Gun Brooke. When two women grow up learning nothing but distrust, unworthiness, and abandonment, it's no wonder they are apprehensive and fearful when an overwhelming love just won't be denied. (978-1-62639-500-8)

Above the Law by Carsen Taite. Love is the last thing on Agent Dale Nelson's mind, but reporter Lindsey Ryan's investigation could change the way she sees everything—her career, her past, and her future. (978-1-62639-558-9)

Actual Stop by Kara A. McLeod. When Special Agent Ryan O'Connor's present collides abruptly with her past, shots are fired, and the course of her life is irrevocably altered. (978-1-62639-675-3)

Embracing the Dawn by Jeannie Levig. When ex-con Jinx Tanner and business executive E. J. Bastien awaken after a one-night stand to find their lives inextricably entangled, love has its work cut out for it. (978-1-62639-576-3)

Love's Redemption by Donna K. Ford. For ex-convict Rhea Daniels and ex-priest Morgan Scott, redemption lies in the thin line between right and wrong. (978-1-62639-673-9)

The Shewstone by Jane Fletcher. The prophetic Shewstone is in Eawynn's care, but unfortunately for her, Matt is coming to steal it. (978-1-62639-554-1)

Jane's World by Paige Braddock. Jane's PayBuddy account gets hacked and she inadvertently purchases a mail order bride from the Eastern Bloc. (978-1-62639-494-0)

A Touch of Temptation by Julie Blair. Recent law school graduate Kate Dawson's ordained path to the perfect life gets thrown off course when handsome butch top Chris Brent initiates her to sexual pleasure. (978-1-62639-488-9)

Beneath the Waves by Ali Vali. Kai Merlin and Vivien Palmer love the water and the secrets trapped in the depths, but if Kai gives in to her feelings, it might come at a cost to her entire realm. (978-1-62639-609-8)

Girls on Campus, edited by Sandy Lowe and Stacia Seaman. College: four years when rules are made to be broken. This collection is required reading for anyone looking to earn an A in sex ed. (978-1-62639-733-0)

Miss Match by Fiona Riley. Matchmaker Samantha Monteiro makes the impossible possible for everyone but herself. Is mysterious dancer Lucinda Moss her perfect match? (978-1-62639-574-9)

Paladins of the Storm Lord by Barbara Ann Wright. Lieutenant Cordelia Ross must choose between duty and honor when a man with godlike powers forces her soldiers to provoke an alien threat. (978-1-62639-604-3)